TO BUY A VOW

Chencia C. Higgins

To Buy A Vow

Copyright © 2018 Chencia C. Higgins
Cover design: James, GoOnWrite.com
Edited by: Little Pear Editing

This book is a work of fiction. The names, characters, places and incidents are products of the writers' imagination or have been used in a fictitious manner. Any resemblance to persons, living or dead, actual events, locations or organizations is entirely coincidental. No part of this book may be reproduced in any manner without written permission from the author except in the case of brief quotation embodied in critical articles or reviews. All rights reserved.

ISBN-13: 978-1980431190

Table of Contents

CHAPTER ONE 4
CHAPTER TWO 15
CHAPTER THREE 30
CHAPTER FOUR 51
CHAPTER FIVE 63
CHAPTER SIX 81
CHAPTER SEVEN 101
CHAPTER EIGHT 114
CHAPTER NINE 128
CHAPTER TEN 145
CHAPTER ELEVEN 159
CHAPTER TWELVE 182
CHAPTER THIRTEEN 196
EPILOGUE 210
More From Chencia 214

To Buy A Vow

CHAPTER ONE
Nedra

I knew exactly what I was doing when I emerged from my bedroom, clad only in a thin tank top and a pair of pale pink bikini panties.

My plan: simple. The execution: flawless. The results: undeniable.

Operation *"Get the dick"* was now in full effect.

I crept down the stairs, my socks silencing my descent against the carpeted steps. When I hit the bottom floor, I paused and listened out for any sounds of life. It took a moment for Chris's laughter—a deep, rich baritone that never failed to put a tingle in my spine—to reach from the bowels of the 1,800 square foot home we shared up to my ears where I stood in front of the staircase behind the front door.

I moved quickly and determinedly through the house, stopping first into the kitchen to grab a few props before making my way to my destination. The den was a free space adjacent to the back of the house, with only three walls that we had converted to a television room. That was where I often found Chris as of late. This was his hiding place when he didn't want to deal with the rest of the world. I usually left him alone for a while when he was back there, understanding that he needed to decompress after dealing with a bunch of hotheaded kids every day.

Lately, he'd been disappearing into that room even when he didn't have to work, and although I found it odd, I didn't question him about it.

Today, though?

Today, I had awakened to tender breasts and slick thighs. My sleep had been dreamless, so my hyper-aroused state confused me. Chris had left for work before I'd even stirred in the bed, and I'd done my very best to take my mind off of the constant thrumming of my core all day.

After meeting one of my girl-friends for breakfast, I spent a productive hour at the gun range, blowing off steam and releasing tension. When I returned home, I knocked out a couple of loads of laundry before heading back out to pick up my mama for lunch at my granny's house. Lunch had actually stretched into a four-hour affair and before I knew it, it was almost five o'clock, and I had to rush home to make dinner.

Throughout it all, I was in a constant state of arousal that nothing had been able to distract me from. I needed a cure, and there was no remedy for what ailed me.

No remedy except getting my back blown out by the only man to ever do it.

The anticipation of a well-executed plan made me giddy as I rounded the corner of the den. Instead of walking behind the couch and up the other side of the room, I purposefully crossed in front of it, making sure to place my weight on the heels of my feet which in turn isolated each of my ass cheeks and made them jiggle as I walked. I could feel Chris' amber eyes on me, and the heat from his gaze fueled me. It confirmed what I already knew; I looked good.

My sepia-toned skin was glistening from the lavender, shea and coconut body butter I had slathered on after my shower. The tank clung to my ample breasts and bore my slightly rounded midriff, showcasing my hourglass figure. I sauntered by him casually and turned to my right, maneuvering the items in my arms to hand him a bottle of beer.

He took it silently, eyes dropping from my face down to my ass, which had already begun to swallow the fabric of my underwear. I wanted to smirk but instead kept my expression neutral as I turned my back to him and bent over invitingly. The sight of my wide, round cheeks in his face was one I knew he couldn't ignore. It was my ace in the hole and his reaction didn't disappoint.

Just over the laugh track of the comedy show playing on the television, I heard him mutter a low, "Goddamn, girl".

Pleased with his response, I continued with my plan, setting a large bowl of popcorn on the coffee table along with a bottle of hot sauce and, accidentally on purpose, dropping the bottle opener strategically so that it fell from the table and hit the floor.

I dropped to my knees before "Oops" was even fully out of my mouth, arching my back and hiking my ass exaggeratedly in the air in a fake attempt to retrieve the instrument. The couch groaned as Chris shifted behind me and just as my hands closed over his tool, I felt Chris' hands palm the globes of my ass. It had been nearly three weeks since he had touched me, and I desperately missed the feel of his calloused hands on my naked flesh. All I wanted to do was press back against him, but my mission wasn't over just yet. I still had a few, final lines to deliver.

Leaning forward slightly, I turned my head to the right and peered at him over my shoulder. "What are you doing, babe?"

Chris had moved from the couch to the floor and was now kneeling behind me. One hand squeezed while the other jiggled my ass cheeks.

"Shiiid, I'm just enjoying the view."

This time, I did smirk. "You see with your eyes, not with your hands."

He bit his lip and worked both of his hands up to my waist. "Oh yeah? Well, let me take a look then." His fingers slid under the elastic of my panties and pulled the material down over my ass and halfway down my thighs, digging into my flesh as he spread my cheeks.

"Why you tryna tease me with this pretty ass pussy, Ned?" He punctuated his question with a slap to one of my cheeks.

"I'm not," I whined as the lie caught in my throat. I was so close to my goal.

"The hell you ain't." He slapped my other cheek. "*Goddamn.* Look at this." He swiped a finger along my seam and stuck the soaked digit in his mouth, sucking off the evidence of my arousal. "You so wet for me already, tasting all good and shit."

I dropped my head in between my shoulders and let out a low moan as Chris rubbed the head of his dick along my slick opening.

"Chris…"

"What's up, babygirl?" The murmur was low and husky in his throat. He pressed his hips forward, and I gasped as his smooth, hardened tip slid inside of me briefly before he pulled back.

"Baby, *please*." When he repeated the move, I wanted to cry.

"Please what?"

"Don't tease me."

He chuckled and I clenched at the arousing sound. "Tease you? Never that, babygirl." Once again, he pressed forward, this time until nearly half of his length had disappeared into my folds. Slowly, he pulled back until only the tip was inside.

Desperate to feel all of him, I pushed my hips back and cried out his name in frustration when he backed, just out of my reach, causing him to slip free of me.

"*Christopher*!" I twisted my neck to look back at him. "Stop playing with me! I need you!"

He smirked at me. "You need this dick?"

I shook my head, my face twisting into a pout at being denied what I had craved all day. "I need *you. Please.*"

I watched the smirk fall from his face. His eyes widened in

surprised disbelief, and his expression became so earnest that my heart squeezed as my breath caught in my chest.

"I need you too. Don't ever forget that."

My eyebrows furrowed. There was something in the undercurrent of his voice like he was trying to communicate a hidden message to me. I opened my mouth to ask him what he meant when he *finally* pushed his entire length inside of me. The question on my lips morphed into a moan and my fingers dug into the plush carpet.

"Ah, shiiiiit."

"Mmhmm."

I rotated my hips as Chris rocked into me. He swore and I echoed the sentiment. His fingers dug into my hips, his grip firm as he hovered over me, pressing his chest against my back as he licked a trail up my spine.

"Ooh."

With each thrust, I slid further along the carpet until I was lying prone with my head under the coffee table and Chris on my back. He used his legs to close mine and began to grind slowly into me, his every thrust hitting a spot inside of me that sparked my nerves.

Before long, I could feel my body begin to heat as my orgasm loomed. Sensing my impending explosion, Chris increased his thrusts until the added sensation of his skin slapping against mine had us both barreling toward the edge. I flew off the precipice, releasing a keening cry into the carpet. As my walls tightened around him, Chris pressed his face into the crevice between my shoulder blades and groaned through his release.

When I no longer felt him twitching inside of me, he pulled out and rolled so that he was on his back beside me. I turned my head and observed him quietly as my breathing slowed down. His red-brown skin—that always reminded me of the terra cotta pots in my granny's garden—was beaded with sweat. He had slung an arm over his eyes, although there was no chance of the light bothering him since both of our heads were still under the coffee table. His chest heaved beneath his t-shirt, and that's when I realized that he was still dressed. I hadn't felt his mesh shorts against my skin, so he must have lowered them for this quickie and then pulled them back up as he rolled over.

I frowned.

That he hadn't removed even one article of clothing bothered me, but I couldn't articulate why other than it being unusual. It just felt wrong. I shifted my thighs, and the wetness I felt between them made me bite my lip in sweet victory.

Mission: accomplished!

I pressed my palms against the floor and shimmied backward until I cleared the coffee table. In one smooth movement, I rolled onto my back and quickly lifted my hips to roll my panties up my thighs. I sat up and looked over at my husband who was still halfway under the table and showed no signs of moving. My brows furrowed.

What is up with him?

The question was on the tip of my tongue but would have to wait until I made a trip to the bathroom to clean up. When I returned to the den, I stopped at the entrance and my face twisted in confusion. The air felt heavy and thick. A strong foreboding came over me and something felt wrong.

What the fuck is going on?

I tried to shake the sudden and unwanted feeling off as I continued into the room. As I once again rounded the couch, I saw that Chris had finally gotten off the floor and moved back to the couch. But instead of slouching comfortably with his eyes on the screen like he was when I first entered the room, he was sitting on the edge of the cushions, hunched over, balancing on his knees with his head in his hands.

That foreboding slammed back into me with a force so strong, I backed up a couple of steps. My mouth went dry with fear.

My voice was laced with concern when I spoke. "Chris?"

I didn't just call his name; I'd asked him a question.

What's wrong?

What's going on?
What's happening?

When he lifted his head from his hands and finally looked at me, I gasped and rushed to his side. His eyes were red-rimmed and his jaw was clenched to where I could see the vein running along his temple.

"Baby!" I cried with my hands on either side of his face. "What is it? What's wrong?!"

"Nedra…" He sucked in a breath, his eyes flicking over to the television then back to me. "We need to talk."

♥♥♥♥

I was angry. So damn angry. I felt like I was on the brink of a full-on rage. I'd never wanted to hurt Chris as much as I did right now. My life was falling apart right in front of me, and I was unable to salvage anything. It was like a horror film; every time I tried to pick up a couple of pieces and hold them together, they shattered in my hands, the edges sharp shards that hurt even as I tried to mend them. To make matters worse, the man who was supposed to be my partner in everything—my *life* partner—was the one exacerbating the issue.

How did I end up here?

Oh, right. *The talk.*

As soon as the words left his mouth, I knew that my post-orgasmic euphoria was about to come to an end. I stood up from that couch so fast, I gave myself vertigo. Clutching my head for a minute, I willed the room to stop spinning. Chris grabbed my hand and pulled me back down to the couch. He waited for me to look at him before he spoke.

"Ned?"

"Hm?"

"You know I love you, right?"

My heart squeezed at that preface. The vibes I felt right now weren't very loving, but okay. "Of course, baby. And I love you too."

He squeezed again, this time gathering both of my hands in his and bringing them to his mouth and placing a kiss on my knuckles. I looked at our joined hands and wondered why, even with the tender action, I felt such dread.

Chris nodded. "I don't want to drag this out and make it worse than it—"

"Well, just say it then!" My interruption came out harsh due to my anxiety. I wanted to pull my hands from his and simultaneously burrow myself into his chest and stop him from completing his speech.

"Okay, well," His eyes burned into mine, earnest and determined. "I'm filing for a divorce. Well...actually, I already filed. Two weeks ago."

I sucked in a breath so deep and fast that I started to choke. "Wha—what?" I couldn't even think, let along formulate a response to the bomb he had just dropped on me.

He *what*?

And *when*?

Apparently, he didn't expect me to say anything because he kept right on speaking. "I'm sorry Ned, but I had to do it. Our marriage just isn't what it used to be, and we've both been so miserable for a long time that I just thought it was the best thing to do."

I couldn't believe what I was hearing. My husband of seven years had filed for a divorce *two weeks ago* and had not only failed to tell me, but he'd just fucked me doggy-style on the floor of our television room while Kevin Hart argued with Nick Cannon about who Mariah Carey belonged with in the background. This was surreal. I had to be dreaming. I *had* to be.

A light bulb clicked on in my head. *Oh!* Okay, if this is a dream then I can't feel any pain and no one dies, right? *Right.*

I nodded, twisting and yanking my hands until Chris finally released his hold on them.

"Ned?"

Mind already made up, I ignored him and got up off the couch. I walked to the front of the house and grabbed my keys from the side table before taking the stairs to my bedroom on the second floor. I moved methodically as I placed the stool I kept in my closet into position and stepped onto it. Just as my fingers brushed the corner of the locked box stored on the top shelf, Chris wrapped his arms around my waist and pulled me out of the closet.

"Nedra, what are you doing?!" He kept me wrapped in his arms so his panicked voice was loud in my ear. I jerked my head to the side and gave him a stupid look.

"What does it look like?"

He shook his head adamantly. "No, it can't be what it looks like. You can't be doing what I think you're doing. There is no way you'd walk off while we are in the middle of a conversation to go get your gun. Nope. I refuse to believe that."

I scoffed. "Nigga, please. You fucked me and then asked for a divorce! Between the two of us, walking off is the least of our issues."

"What do you need your gun for?"

I rolled my eyes. Now, he wanted to play stupid? Cool, we can both play, then. "I was going to give it a bath and tuck it in for the night."

He squeezed me tightly and the bite of his nails into my arms started to hurt. "That shit ain't funny, Ned."

Fed up with his bullshit, I began to struggle to get free from his grasp.

"It doesn't fucking matter anyway! This is all a dream! Once I get Precious and shoot your ass—because everyone knows you can't feel pain in dreams—then I'll wake up and this will be a distant memory."

His arms steeled around me and quicker than I could blink he had spun me around until we were facing each other. His eyes bored into mine.

"Are you being serious right now?"

I nodded. "Of course. I know that I'm dreaming because there is no way in hell the man I've known since I was fourteen years old would file for a divorce without *at least* discussing his issues with me first. He wouldn't let me walk around mistakenly thinking that I was in a happy, fulfilling relationship for two motherfucking weeks while he knew he had no intentions of staying married to me."

I saw the guilt as plain as day before he averted his gaze and my heart froze over. Was he—was this for real? Was he really doing this to me? To us?

"Ned…"

That's when I checked out. All of the adrenaline that carried me upstairs drained out of me, and I slumped over in his arms. He moved us over to the bed, and I sat on the edge, staring blankly at the open closet door. He shifted until he was standing in front of me and crouched so he was in my line of sight. I stared at his Adam's apple, watching it bob as he worked his mouth around the bullshit he planned to spit at me.

"Ned, look. We're different people than we were seven years ago. We have different expectations now, different wants, different needs. And," he took a breath, "I'm not the right man for you anymore. I'm not that guy who's going to give you everything that you need and bring out the best in you. The thing is, that guy is out there for you. I know it, and if you really thought about it, you'd know it too. Hell, you've probably already thought about it but tossed the thought away because it made you uncomfortable."

I lifted my eyes to meet his then. He must have taken that as a good sign because he gave me a small smile and continued on. "I did that for the past year and honestly, I'm tired of being comfortable. I'm done with just being satisfied. So, yeah…I'm an asshole because I made the decision without talking to you first. And no, I didn't try to salvage what we have. I just…took the step and now, I have to move out of the way so you can see that we weren't really happy after all. Then you might find the guy who is truly meant for you. And…maybe discover your own happiness without me while you're at it."

Then he searched my eyes looking for...something, I don't know but when he didn't find it, he stood, kissed my forehead and then went into the closet. When he came out, he had my reinforced gun box under his arm.

"I'm just going to take this for now. Just until you are sure you aren't dreaming." He blew out a breath and rubbed the back of his neck with his free hand. "I know you're angry with me right now and probably even hate me. Trust me—I know that I deserve all of that hate. I just want you to think about what I said. Really think about it. You'll realize, in time, that you agree more than you know."

I didn't respond and eventually, he stopped waiting and left the room, closing the door quietly behind him. I don't know how long I sat there in that empty room, still wearing the tank top and soiled bikini panties from my "mission". It felt like a lifetime had passed with how quickly my world was turned upside down.

How in the hell did a quest for sex with my husband turn into a gotdamn divorce?

CHAPTER TWO
Nedra

"Aww boo, why didn't you call me?"

I looked up from the triple-layer chocolate cake that I had just placed on a rotating cake stand and saw one of my best girlfriends standing in the archway of the kitchen. She stood arms akimbo with her hands fisted upon her wide hips. Shanice was a classic coke bottle shape, where I was more of a two-liter. I know I looked good, there was just more of me to admire.

I smiled, wiped my hands on my apron, and walked over to give her a hug. I was immensely happy to see her round, impish face.

The past few weeks had consisted of me dodging all attempts at communication from everyone but my mama and granny, and I had just reached the point where I was sick of hearing my own thoughts. I felt like I was falling into a pit of depression, and I knew that I needed to let my two boos know what was going on with me. Figuring out how to tell the two women who'd known me throughout the entire development of Chris and my relationship had been harder than I expected.

It was easy to avoid telling Ashton since she was in a completely different timezone. Shanice was a different story. We usually spoke to each other every day and saw each other several times a week. Dipping out on her had been a lesson in ninja skills. My reverie came to a halt as one of the women in question took it upon herself to come see me.

"Hey, Niecy, girl! What are you doing up from under Daddy Byron?" I stepped back as I teased her. I was still tickled at how she blushed when I mentioned how her new man—who was significantly younger than her—gave her grown man dick. Today was Sunday, and she usually spent Sundays in bed and quite literally under her young tender, Byron.

Picking up the offset spatula I had abandoned, I pointed at a barstool and motioned for her to have a seat. She passed up the stool and came to stand next to me. Her skin, the color of red clay, was free of makeup and I could clearly see her redden at my quip.

"Don't call him that! And for your information, I received an emergency phone call that was important enough to pull me from the warmth of my bed and my boo."

I gave her a sidelong glance as I mixed the resulting crumbs from trimming the cake with a third of the whipped cream frosting I had made from scratch. As I applied the layer of crumb coat, I asked the obvious question.

"What was the emergency?"

She tilted her head at me. "That my best friend was getting a divorce."

I froze mid-stir as tears instantly pricked my eyes. I dropped my head back and stared at the ceiling in a weak attempt to keep them at bay.

Shit.

Niecy laid her head on my shoulder and rubbed the middle of my back. "Imagine my surprise at having to hear this news from her sister-in-law, a woman we *all* know doesn't like me."

I huffed out a laugh at the thinly veiled shade she threw at me. "Niecy..."

She held up a hand. "Don't try to tell me any different. That girl practically *hates* me."

I chuckled and shook my head. "No, I wasn't going to do that. She really can't stand your ass." I would never lie about that. After Ashton finished school on the east coast, she landed a job and never moved back home. That one year that Shanice and I shared a dorm room as freshmen brought us extremely close, and Ashton got tired of hearing me talk about the girl who she felt encroached on her position as my best friend.

It was what it was. Even after leaving school, Shanice became my *other* best friend, and Ashton never held back her opinion on that whenever we talked on the phone and I mentioned Shanice, *especially* when she made the trip back home. I would often try to get the three of us together so that I wouldn't have to split my free time between the two of them. Although she'd thawed some, more than a decade later, Ashton still felt some way about it. So, to hear that she had actually voluntarily called Shanice was mind-boggling.

"Yeah, well, she called me at the ass-crack of dawn, breaking news that should have come from you. Why'd you tell her and not me?"

I released a deep sigh as I twirled the cake on the turntable, inspecting the completed crumb coat. "I didn't tell her," I murmured. "She must have heard from Chris." I carried the rotating cake stand over to the refrigerator and put it on the shelf I had cleared for the exact purpose.

"Oh, shit."

I nodded at her sentiment. "Yeah." Chris was already informing his family that he was leaving me. He didn't waste any time. It had only been a few weeks, but I guess that's just how secure he was with his decision.

When I turned from the fridge, I jumped at Shanice's proximity. She stood right behind me, her face the picture of sympathy. Her arms wrapped around me tightly and reflexively, my own encircled her in return.

"What happened? I feel like I just saw y'all all loved up on each other at dinner the other week."

I shook my head and stepped out of her embrace. "It definitely wasn't the other week. But honestly, girl? I don't know. He just came out of left field with this one."

"Damn; and you didn't have any inclination that he wasn't happy? That something was brewing?"

"No. That's what fucks me up the most. I thought we were good. I mean, yeah, he was spending more and more time at work, volunteering to work every game for every fucking sport they offered at that damn school but *shit*. I thought he just loved his damn job. Loved working with those kids. It didn't occur to me that he was trying to avoid me."

Shanice looked at me thoughtfully. "What about you?"

I narrowed my eyes at her. *I know she's not asking me what it sounds like she was asking me.* "What *about* me?"

One of her brows lifted at my attitude. "Had you been having any second thoughts before he asked for a divorce?"

My chest lifted as I sucked in an angry breath. *"Hell no!* I had planned to be married to that nigga until I left this fucking earth! I meant my vows when I said them!"

She held up her hands in surrender. "I know you did. I was there, remember?"

"If you knew that then why would you fix your mouth to ask me some shit like that? I love that man! Would do anything for him, including sucking the skin off his dick and scrubbing his shit-stained drawers! I go to the doctor like clockwork for birth control because he said he wasn't ready to be a dad, but I would have given him kids at the drop of a hat if he would have said he wanted them. I love that man with everything that is in me, and to find out that that love ain't enough—that *I* ain't enough—hurts! *It. Hurts. Niecy.* I gave him all of me, and he threw that shit back in my face and said 'Nah, I'm good'. My heart is broken, and you brought your ass over here asking me if I wanted this too when all I'm trying to do is keep my head above water."

My face was covered in snot and tears, and my voice cracked on those last few words, but at that moment, all I wanted to do was to bury my head under the covers and not emerge until everything was back to normal or the world ended. Whichever came first.

Shanice's hands covered her mouth, but I saw that she also had a face full of tears. She shook her head before pulling me back into a tight hug. She squeezed me for a full minute without saying a word, and I hadn't realized how much I needed that hug because a wave of emotions washed over me and the dam broke as I sobbed into her shoulder.

She cried, "I'm sorry."

She whispered, "I'm here."

She affirmed, "I got you."

And when my tears tapered off, I took a deep breath and pulled out of her embrace for a second time that morning. I reached into a drawer for a clean kitchen towel and pressed it against my face. For a moment, I just inhaled and exhaled deeply into the cloth. When I felt like I would be able to look at my friend without shedding more tears, I dropped the cloth on the counter and reclaimed my abandoned position in front of the counter.

Shanice finished dabbing at her cheeks with a napkin and once again hugged my side.

"I know how much you love him, and I'm sorry that he hurt you. You know you're going to be okay, right?"

I shook my head as I bent my neck and touched my temple to the top of her head. I *didn't* know that I would be okay. All I'd known for so long was how to be a part of a couple. To be Chris' other half. Years before we were married, I was his and now, abruptly, I was supposed to figure out how to be something else. I'd live, sure, but whether or not I'd be okay was to be determined.

Shanice leaned back until she could see my face. "You're

coming to stay with me."

I sputtered a laugh and ironically, a couple of errant tears I'd thought were all released spilled down my cheeks. Lifting the corner of my apron, I flipped it over and wiped my face. I shook my head. Again.

"Thank you Niecy, but I'm not leaving. This is my house, and he's not going to run me out of it. My name is on the deed just like his."

She pursed her lips, and I knew she wanted to argue with me. "Nedra, I know you don't want to leave your home, but I really don't think this will be a healthy environment for you."

I rolled my eyes and stepped away from her to go dump the remaining crumb filled frosting in the trash can in the corner. "Girl, what are you talking about? I'll be fine. Just like he acted like nothing was wrong for two weeks before telling me he'd filed for a divorce, Chris'll behave himself until this thing is over."

I heard her suck in a breath, and I mentally cursed. I guess Chris had failed to inform his sister about *that* little tidbit.

"That fool did *what*?"

I shrugged. "It doesn't matter."

"Well, that's sure as hell not true! That's some shady ass shit and something I would never have expected from Chris! What the hell was he thinking?!"

I could almost feel the heat from her, fuming behind me, and surprisingly, it brought a small smile to my face. It felt good to have someone in my corner, to be just as angry on my behalf.

"You know I'm not happy about this, right?" She leaned against the counter with her arms folded as she stared me down.

I shrugged again. "You'll be alright."

She sighed dramatically and straightened, dropping her arms to her side. "Just know that if at any moment, you change your mind, my home is open to you. You don't even have to ask; you have a key; use it."

My throat felt too tight for me to respond verbally, so I nodded my understanding. I had no plans to abandon the house that I had single-handedly made into a home until the ink was dry on the divorce decree, but I would do whatever I could—within reason—to appease my friend who was only trying to look out for me. That singular chin drop must have been enough for her because she hugged my side and kissed my cheek before stepping back and nodding at the bowl of fresh frosting on the counter.

"So, uh…when is this cake going to be done?"

I laughed wetly, grateful for the change of subject. "In a little bit." I tossed my chin in the direction of the fridge. "That crumb coat needs to get firm before I can put the final layer of frosting on it, then we can eat."

She grinned and rubbed her hands together. "Cool, then you can join me for lunch at *The Greenery*. It's this new restaurant in the Heights that everyone on that review app loves, so I've been tasked with giving my professional opinion."

"Ooh yesssss! I'm down for that."

I was glad to have something to look forward to. Shanice was a food critic for a popular magazine and often invited me to tag along on her assignments. Food and I were BFFs, so I was always a more than willing participant. I used that as inspiration to finish the cake quickly, removing it from the refrigerator and throwing an almost sloppy final coat of frosting on it.

With instructions for Shanice to help herself to the cake, I ran upstairs to change clothes and wash my face of all traces of tears and despair. I had no plans to lament on what to wear and without deliberation, I had thrown on an oversized sweater and a pair of dark rinse skinny jeans tucked into calf-high boots. I completed the look with large, wooden earrings, dangling from my ears, and with a quick run of the brush over my tapered fade, I was downstairs in less than fifteen minutes.

I don't know what I was expecting, but The Greenery was not that. We parked on the street and walked along the sidewalk until we reached what looked like an older craftsman style home. The path to the porch seemed to be dropped smack dab in the middle of a garden. On either side were clusters of flowers. It looked like an English garden the way there were no rows and so many different varieties of flowers were cropped together. My eye caught on a large stone fountain in the corner of the yard with water flowing from a cherub's mouth.

As we approached the steps to the porch, I noticed a small group of people standing to the left of the door. In the center of the group was a man who stood more than a foot taller than the two women on either side of him who were tucked under his arms. The three of them were smiling for a fourth person, a man just as tall as the one opposite him but significantly broader, who held a cell phone in his hands as he took a picture. Well, the women were smiling. The man in the middle had the hood of his sweatshirt pulled down over his head and covering more than half of his face. *Hm. Probably a baller.*

They finished their picture and entered the building before we hit the landing but failed to hold the door open for us, even though we were just behind them. I frowned as Shanice grabbed the handle of the door before it closed in her face.

"Damn, they can hold the door for some blond bitches, but they don't see us, huh?"

Shanice whipped her head around and regarded me with wide eyes at my outburst.

"Nedra!"

I bucked my eyes at her. "What? Am I lying?"

She shook her head and continued on through the two sets of doors before stopping at a hostess stand. She angled her head at me and whispered, "I don't think the big guy saw us; he was trying to the catch the second door before he was left behind."

I sucked my teeth. "Okay, Niecy. If you say so."

We were greeted and led to a table in a moderately full section. I looked around the room. It looked like the entire front end of what used to be someone's home had been converted to a dining area. There couldn't have been more than twenty tables in the cozy space with a five-foot frosted glass partition splitting the space down the middle and separating the tables into two sections. What was once an attic was now an impressively high ceiling with exposed beams.

The floors were a wood that was distressed to look like the original flooring of the house. On each table was a jar of succulents and a carafe of ice water, and hanging above each table was a small pendant light that cast a warm yellow glow. The entire space just felt earthy and natural. I relaxed and poured myself a glass of water, sipping the cool beverage before opening up the menu I had yet to touch.

Um...what?

I flipped through the pages of the menu before casting a glare at Shanice. "I think you forgot to mention a significant detail of this restaurant to me, Niecy."

Her eyebrows lifted dramatically in a fake ass attempt to look innocent. "What you mean, boo?"

I didn't even answer; I just narrowed my eyes at her. She giggled and shrugged.

"The Greenery is a vegetarian spot, Ned."

"Okay, why didn't you tell me that?"

"I didn't think I had to. You're always down no matter the cuisine."

"Well *yeah*, but I don't know if I can handle white people's vegetarian. They like to create weird stuff out of vegetables and I'm not trying to eat science experiments today."

Shanice threw her head back and hooted with laughter. "Nedra! For real?"

I gave her dumb look.

Amused, she rolled her eyes. "Well, you don't have to worry about that. The Greenery is black-owned. As a matter of fact, the same restaurant group who owns Capital Grill owns this place."

I heaved a sigh of relief as I processed that information. Then I realized what she said and smirked. "Uh, isn't this a conflict of interest for you?" Her boyfriend's brother was co-owner of Capital Grill

And because she was my bestie, she already knew what I was

talking about. "Nope; Byron has nothing to do with this, and I have never been biased when it comes to his brother. Besides, it is more of his brother's partner who owns this spot. Apparently, his wife is a vegetarian, so he came up with the concept of The Greenery as an anniversary present."

My eyes widened. I was impressed. "Wow, that's actually beautiful as fuck."

Shanice nodded. "I know right. Talk about grand, sweeping gestures of love. And black love at that. I love it."

I bit my lip. It must be nice to have someone love you so much they'd open a restaurant based on your dietary choices. Chris would never have even thought of something like that. Hell, he knew I loved to shoot and wouldn't even buy me a membership to the range. It's amazing that it took him divorcing me to see something like that.

"Nedra?"

I blinked out of my thoughts and looked up at my friend. The sympathy and concern I saw in her eyes made my throat tight. But I had cried enough tears today, so I tried to give her a reassuring smile, but I know that shit looked as weak as it felt.

"I'm good, Niecy."

"Are you sure?" Her tone was as disbelieving as the look she gave me.

I nodded and sipped my water.

"As a matter of fact, I was thinking..." I rubbed at the condensation that collected on my glass as I considered sharing my news. "Since I'm getting a divorce, I think I want to have a baby."

Shanice's mouth dropped open and her eyebrows shot up. She was clearly as shocked as I expected her to be. "Are you serious?"

Her expression made me laugh. "Yeah, I am. I've been thinking about it for a little while now. It was actually the first thought I had after I got over my initial shock. The thought hit me out of nowhere and I was like '*Hm, now I can finally have a baby*'."

She reached across the table and grabbed my hand. "Oh, Ned.

You could have had a baby before now." Her face had twisted into a frown.

I pursed my lips. "No, actually, I couldn't have. Chris told me straight up that he wasn't ready for kids so what the fuck would I look like, letting myself get pregnant? And risk him leaving me to raise our baby by myself? No thank you."

She tilted her head. "Do you really think he would have left? Just abandoned you and his child?"

"I don't know and I didn't want to find out. Hell, my daddy left."

Shanice squinted her eyes at me. "Girl, your dad died. I went to his funeral."

"I know that!" I snapped at her. "He left before that, though."

Exasperated, Shanice spread her arms out. "Left where?! You told me that he was always around when you were growing up."

My lip curled, why did she have to bring up old stuff? "Yeah, he was *around*, but he left me and my mama. The three of us weren't a family."

With an annoyed sigh, Shanice looked me in the eye. "You know what? Right now you are projecting your current emotions on old situations that have nothing to do with anything. You don't have to muddy the memories of your father to justify how you feel about Chris. You can just hate him, and that's okay. I promise I'm not judging you because I sure as hell hate him for what he's doing to you."

I bit my lip and looked away from her piercing brown eyes. I said I wasn't going to cry anymore today and here she was trying to make me out to be a liar. I just wanted to eat some good food and spend a few hours with my mind occupied by something other than my failure as a wife.

"Okay," I said simply. "Let's order."

She eyed me for a moment longer, probably trying to decide if she wanted to push the issue but then, thankfully, she nodded and returned her attention to her menu. Our waiter appeared at my side and we gave him our order. I made sure to request a bottle of hot sauce for my collard greens. I thought it was a simple request, but when he gave me an apologetic smile that I was unfortunately all too familiar with receiving at the fancy-ass restaurants Shanice brought me too, I begin to think differently.

"My apologies, ma'am, but we don't offer condiments to guests before they have tried the food."

My brows lifted in surprise, and I looked at Shanice. I hope she was making a mental note of this for the review she would be writing.

"Oh, wow. Okay then. Well, keep it on standby for me."

He winked at me. "I don't think you'll need it, but I will definitely do so." Then he trudged off to submit our requests to the kitchen.

Immediately, I turned back to Shanice. "What kind of controlling mess is that?"

She shrugged, obviously used to the quirks of niche restaurants. "I don't know about controlling. It *is* highly arrogant, though. But hey, if it's warranted then I'm all for it." She lifted the carafe and poured herself a glass of water before taking a sip.

"*I guess.*" I pushed my chair back from the table and stood. "I'm going to the restroom. I'll be right back." I made my way through to the back of the dining area cautiously. I was unfamiliar with the layout and didn't want to end up in some place I wasn't supposed to be. After turning down a hall and passing a couple of doors, I finally found it.

Getting back to the table turned out to be more difficult than I anticipated, and I ended up turned around and coming out on the other section of the dining room. That side was empty, save for one table. The two men who were taking pictures outside sat at the one occupied table against the wall.

The one who had been in front of the camera had lowered his hood and was hunched over his plate. His back was to me, and I noticed that his head was bald and shiny like he oiled it regularly. I had to pass them to round the partition and get to the side where I was sitting, and I tried to do so quickly. Being over here with just them was awkward as hell. *Hm. Definitely a baller.*

I'd almost passed them up when something on the table caught my eye. On the corner near the jar of succulents was a bottle of hot sauce, and my heart leaped at the sight of the round wooden top. Without thinking, I stopped and turned to them. I faced the bigger guy—the photographer—since he was in my direct line of sight.

"Excuse me—"

The big guy held up a hand, cutting me off. "No pictures or autographs, please. Just let us eat in peace."

My head snapped back at his rudeness. The other man's head popped up. "Aye, Boobie! Chill out with that, man."

My lip curled and I slapped a hand on my hip. "First of all, I don't even know who you are. Second, why would you assume I want anything from you when your inconsiderate ass can't even hold the door open for a woman behind you!"

His eyes widened in surprise. "Hold up—"

I cut him off. "No, you hold up! I came over here to ask for the damn hot sauce, but if the shit means that much to you then keep it with your rude ass!" I turned around and damn near power-walked to the end of the section, hitting the curve on two wheels.

When I dropped down into my seat, chest heaving with anger, I noticed that Shanice was looking at me crazy.

"What?"

"Girl, everyone heard you over there."

"Huh?" I looked around and saw that several patrons were gaping at me. "How?"

Shanice pointed to the partition. "That thing isn't sound-proof. It doesn't even go up to the ceiling. We are in one big room." She leveled me with a knowing look. "*And*, you were yelling."

I huffed. "Well, all I wanted was some damn hot sauce. That fool was rude as fuck and *for what*? He talking about a damn autograph, and I'm just trying to season my food!" I clenched my fists as I got angry all over again. I was also embarrassed. That man had spoken to me like I was a peon, and I know he thought he was allowed that right because his friend was *most definitely* a baller. I don't give a shit how many zeros are in your bank account; no one will talk to me crazy.

Shanice started regaling me with stories of her future stepdaughter and eventually, I let the encounter go. I focused on having a good time being out of the house for a much-needed get-together with Shanice, and when my food came, the waiter backed away but hovered near enough that I knew he, too, had heard the drama about the hot sauce.

I let Shanice take her required pictures of my plate then I forked some of the collards into my mouth and groaned. They were tender with just enough bite to let me know that they had been cooked fresh.

"*Niecy*. These greens are bomb!" She nodded at me as she snapped the last picture of her own meal. The waiter came back, but this time sporting a smug grin.

"Hello, ladies. I still have that hot sauce on standby; do I need to bring it out?"

I narrowed my eyes at him. He was a little smart ass, but I can't deny he was right. "You know that you don't. You were right."

His smirk widened into a full grin, and I returned the gesture. He nodded and disappeared until we finished our meal and it was time for him to clear our plates. We declined dessert since I still had a whole cake at the house and asked for the check.

I sat back in my seat, rubbing my full and sated belly. "Girl," I waited for Shanice to look at me, "I love your job."

She laughed like she did every time I said that. "That makes two of us." She took a picture of the receipt before putting a few bills inside the envelope and throwing her purse over her shoulder.

We stood from the table and headed out to her car. The ride back was silent but comfortable. Shanice hummed along with the radio while I was wrapped in my thoughts.

I had to admit that I was grateful for Chris telling Ashton about our divorce. Dread had consumed me when I had thought about having that conversation, but Chris actually ended up killing two birds with one stone for me as Ash, in turn, told Shanice. I was still surprised about that but would have to hold my questions until I saw her in a couple of weeks when she came home for a visit.

Without a doubt, she would have some of the same questions that Shanice had for me because although he'd broken the news, I knew Chris had failed to go into detail. Hell, if I was really lucky, Shanice might return the favor and fill Ashton in on what she knows.

I dropped my head back against the headrest and sighed.

I was so glad I had my girls to help me get through this bullshit.

CHAPTER THREE
Nedra

"What you over there breathing so hard for? You got something you want to say?"

My jaw was clenched and I could feel my teeth grinding back and forth. I forced myself to relax. Braces had ruined three years of middle school class pictures deemed mandatory by my mama and I had no desire to revisit that experience by fucking up my teeth behind some bullshit. I dropped my eyelids and inhaled a slow, deep breath, willing myself to calm down.

"Huh, Nedra?"

Just that fast, the momentary calm that my relaxation technique had given me evaporated as my granny called my name in a haughty tone. She was intentionally pushing my buttons today and I couldn't figure out why. My eyes popped open and collided with my mama's across the table. Her eyebrows raised dramatically as she averted her gaze and pursed her lips. I narrowed my eyes at her. It was her fault I was in this position in the first place.

I was too damn old to be getting lectured on a regular basis, but my snitching ass mama put me in this position, knowing good and damn well that I couldn't say nothing to my granny except "yes ma'am" and "no ma'am." I twisted in my seat and looked behind me at my granny who stood in the doorway of the kitchen.

"Why you sweatin' me, Delores? I'm just trying to enjoy this meal you graciously prepared."

Her hands fell from their perch across her chest and landed on her wide hips. Hips that had skipped my mama and landed right on me. She pursed her lips.

"Oh, I'm 'sweatin' you, am I? Hmph. Well, maybe you need to be 'sweatin' that husband of yours and beg him not to divorce you."

She hadn't raised her voice from that even tone that was laced with disappointment and an accusation, the tone that she'd taken to using with me lately, but nevertheless, her words sounded deafening in the small room. I sucked in a breath and twisted back to face the table. That wasn't just a button pressed, it was a shot taken and it hurt something fierce. Avoiding my mama's burning stare, I focused on the bowl of red beans and rice in front of me. Mechanically, I shoved a spoonful of the perfectly spiced dish into my mouth but I hardly tasted it.

Just as my spoon hit the bottom of the bowl, my granny dropped a plate on the table at the edge of my placemat and dropped down into the chair on my left. I glanced at the slice of pecan pie then back at my bowl. This was her acknowledging that she may have done wrong—gone too far. Historically, she never apologized with words, but instead gave peace offerings. Edible peace offerings, in my case. Pecan pie was my favorite and I hadn't even seen it in the kitchen when I fixed my bowl of beans and rice. I don't know where she was hiding it but I was happy to see it.

On the other hand...

My feelings were still hurt; pie wouldn't fix that, but I *almost* appreciated the gesture. I'd appreciate it even more if it meant she would leave this conversation on the table forever. That was beyond wishful thinking, however. Granny meant well, I know she did, but *shit*. The situation was more complicated than she could understand.

I crumbled the last of the sweet cornbread that had accompanied the meal into the dregs of my beans and rice and scraped at the mixture until I had consumed every possible morsel of food. Without touching the pie, I pushed my chair back from the table. Granny reached out and grabbed my hand, halting my descent from the table.

"Ned."

I kept my face blank as I looked at her. "Hm?"

"Eat your pie, baby."

It was neither a question nor a request. She was *telling* me to eat the pie. I wanted to laugh even though it wasn't funny. She really thought that if I ate her pie, then I forgave her. Of course, I wanted the damn pie—I loved pecan pie—but I wasn't in the mood to play with her today. I just wanted to go.

"That's okay, I'm pretty full from lunch. Don't really have room for dessert. Thanks though, Granny." I patted my soft belly then quickly stood from my chair and carried my bowl into the kitchen. I dropped it into the soapy, lukewarm water that filled the sink and washed and rinsed it quickly. After setting it on the rack to air dry, I wiped my hands with a paper towel and exited the kitchen through a side door that took me to the living room, instead of back into the dining room.

I had already shrugged on my jacket and was slipping the strap of my cross-body bag over my head when my granny ambled into the room with a scowl on her face, my mama right behind her.

"I know you weren't going to try and sneak your narrow behind out of this house without so much as a word to me!" There was even more attitude in her voice now than before and her tone was definitely elevated.

My mama smirked and dropped down on the suede couch,

seemingly to watch the show. "Ain't nothing narrow about *that* behind."

I cut my eyes at her then took a deep breath before addressing my beloved grandmother.

"Granny, I'm tired—"

"Tired of what, baby? Not from fighting for your marriage."

Fighting for my—Oh hell no. Fuck this shit!

A mirthless chuckle fell from my lips. "You know what…" I stopped myself before I got really disrespectful. What I was NOT going to do was stand here and listen to her continue to berate me for something she didn't even know the half of and was honestly none of her damn business. I spun on my heel and stomped to the front door.

"Nedra!"

I ignored my grandmother's voice calling me back into her house and cleared the steps quickly, walking to my car and throwing open the door. I was in the car and pulling away from the curb in less than two minutes. It wasn't until I reached my destination and put the car in park a half an hour later that I realized that I had left my mama behind. I sucked my teeth. She had ridden with me to my granny's house because she wanted me to take her to the store later.

Aw shit.

I'd never hear the end of her mouth for this shit. I shook my head and pulled out my phone. With just a few swipes of my fingers, I had sent her twenty dollars for the rideshare app she used when neither I nor her boyfriend was around to give her a lift. Hopefully, that would buy me some reprieve.

I stepped out of the car and pulled up Instagram on my phone, switching over from my personal account to my professional account. I took a picture of the building in front of me and typed out a quick caption.

@blackgirlmagicbullet: Impromptu session at my sanctuary. Will be here until 6 at the latest. If

To Buy A Vow

you're free, join me for half-off a half hour lesson. As always, come empty-handed and open-hearted ♥♥.

I clicked the buttons that ensured my photo would be shared across all of my social media pages then submitted the post, shoved my phone into my back pocket, and I made sure my car doors were locked before entering the building. As soon as I stepped over the threshold, I felt much of my tension melt away. Just as I'd said in my post, this place was my sanctuary. I'd been coming to Bullseye since I was thirteen-years-old. That's when my granddaddy decided I was old enough to learn how to shoot.

Inside the small lobby, behind the counter, sat the owner, Mr. Albert. Seeing Mr. Albert brought as much comfort as being in his business did. It was always his smiling ebony face that I saw when my granddaddy brought me and even now he smiled at me although I'm sure he surprised to see me.

"Good afternoon, Mr. Albert."

He grinned at me, his bright white teeth gleaming. "Good afternoon, Ms. Nedra."

I pursed my lips to stifle a giggle. He'd been using the honorific on me since I was a child, and it still amused me.

"Is my lane free?" I was a creature of habit. I used the same lane every time I came. Even when I had lessons, I demonstrate on "my lane" and have my client on an adjacent lane.

Mr. Albert's eye perused the sheet on the counter in front of him. "Well, I wasn't expecting you but let's see…Ah. You're a lucky woman, Ms. Nedra." He reached under the counter and handed me a wooden dowel with a small flag on the end.

"Do you need anything else?"

I started to say no, then I remembered that all of my equipment was at home, including my bullets. "I need some ammo." I rattled off the type of gun I had and gave him my debit card as he slid me a small box of 25 rounds. Once my card was safely back in my purse I said my thanks and headed for the door that led to the range.

Once he pressed a button on the wall, there was a loud buzz and the door unlocked. I yanked the heavy door open and stepped into the next room. There were lockers against the wall and a shelf that held soundproof earmuffs and goggles. I would hang the flag on the outside wall of my lane so that others would know the lane was occupied and that they needed to use caution when approaching because I was more than likely unable to hear them.

This had been an unplanned trip so I didn't bring my .45 with me. I always rode with my .380, though, so I pulled that out of my purse and put the bag into a locker. I put on my protective gear and made my way down the range until I reached the eighth lane. I stuck my flag in the holder and set my gun and ammo on the tall, narrow table in the space. There was a stack of unused paper targets on the table. I clipped one to the hanging mechanism and pressed the button that would pull it to the back wall.

I readied my firearm and steadied my breathing. On my exhale, I started firing.

I never went to Bullseye in the middle of the day like this. I either came in the morning because I preferred to get my time in early, or I came in the evening. The women that I gave handgun handling lessons to usually worked during the day so evening lessons were better for them. I tried to be as flexible as possible by offering several time slots, understanding that free time was hard to come by when you worked for someone else.

The lessons had always been a side thing for me, sort of like a hobby. I loved to shoot and was good at it so when friends learned of my skill, they solicited me to teach them. My granny actually suggested that I turn it into an actual business. After the insurance firm I had worked at since I was fresh out of Franklin let me go six months ago, I had been struggling to find my footing. I didn't know what to do with myself after being an executive assistant for so long.

Granny had brought me here to Bullseye and told me to turn

my hobby, my passion, into my livelihood. From there, *Black Girl, Magic Bullet* was born. I went right to the county clerk's office to register my business name and immediately set up social media accounts. Then I came to see Mr. Albert. He didn't hesitate in allowing me to offer my lessons in his building. I was overjoyed and overwhelmed by the growth of my little hobby-turned-business. Currently, I had four women who came for weekly lessons. My plan was to eventually have my own range so that I could recruit more clients.

At that thought, the red light above me blinked rapidly. It caught my attention, and I stopped shooting immediately. I engaged the safety on my gun and set it on the table before turning around.

"Oh, hey!"

Two of my regular clients and one woman I didn't recognize were standing behind me. They were all dressed in the appropriate safety gear and my clients each held a box that I knew held the firearm and rounds they owned. I gave all three ladies a hug and put my thoughts aside to give them the lessons that they had shown up for.

Two and a half hours later, my clients had left, and I had a bit more money in my bank account. I gathered my targets, tossed the empty box of rounds in the trash can, and headed back to the locker room. My shoulders were a little stiff, but my head was clear and for that, I was happy.

I pushed open the door that led to the front of the shop and stopped in my tracks. Sitting in one of the chairs of the lobby, chatting with Mr. Albert, was my granny. She looked up as I entered the area, and our eyes connected. Mr. Albert followed her gaze over to me then turned back to her. He leaned toward her—closer than necessary—and said something that made her smile; then he walked in my direction, coming to a stop in front of me.

"I'll see you next week, Nedra."

I glanced suspiciously at him and my granny. I started to nod then I thought about Ashton's arrival the next day. "Actually, you might end up seeing me again before the week is up, Mr. Albert."

He nodded like he expected that and I wondered what my granny had been telling him. Hell, I wondered what she was doing here. He patted my arm.

"That's no problem. I'll see you then."

My attention shifted to my granny. She sat in her chair and watched me make my way over to her. The front door tempted me to pass her up and simply exit the building, but I'm sure I'd already garnered enough ire by leaving her house hours earlier.

"What're you doing here, Granny?"

She waved her phone in the air. "I saw on Facebook that you would be here until six."

Mentally, I rolled my eyes. My granny had no business being on Facebook, especially if she was using it to stalk me. I held out my hand and pulled her up from her seat. Getting to the door before her, I held it open and just before she exited, she turned her head and called out, "See you later, Albert!" I frowned at the flirtatious note in her voice, but my eyes widened when I was sure that I heard Mr. Albert reply with, "Yes, you will, Delores!" in an equally flirtatious tone before the door closed fully.

What the fuck was going on here? Certain I didn't want to know, I walked my granny to her car and stood silently, waiting for the fussing I was sure to get. A few minutes went by, and all she did was stare at me expectantly. My brows furrowed in confusion.

"Don't you have something to say to me?"

I shook my head. "No, ma'am. Is there something you're expecting me to say?"

She cocked her head but didn't say anything.

I sighed. "Why don't you give me a hint because I'm lost."

"Does your storming out of my house like a petulant child ring a bell?"

That was an inaccurate account of events, but okay. "The storming does; the petulant child part sounds made up."

Her hands went to her hips. "So, you don't think there's a

problem with you running out anytime you don't want to hear what someone has to say?"

My mouth dropped open, and I gaped at her incredulously. "That's not what happened, Granny!"

"That's exactly what happened."

"No, you were attacking me, and I—"

"Here you go." She rolled her eyes. "No one was attacking you, little girl. I'm just trying to help you avoid making a horrible mistake. But I guess you think you're too grown to accept advice from anyone?"

I threw my hands in the air. "What advice? *Beg* Chris not to divorce me?"

"Yes, if need be! You made vows before God that you need to uphold! The Bible says—"

"I'm sorry, Granny, but that's where I have to stop you. If your biggest argument is to tell me what the Bible says then you might as well save your breath. I need something tangible."

"What about experience? I was married for forty-eight years; you don't think I know a little something about this?"

I pursed my lips. "Well, you were married for forty-eight years so I'm going to say, no. No, I don't think you know anything about how it feels to go through a divorce."

"Your granddaddy and I almost divorced once." She took a deep breath and looked across the parking lot at Bullseye before bringing her steady gaze back to mine. "I'd packed up your mama, and I was prepared to leave him."

This was a story I hadn't heard before. My granddaddy had died ten years ago and to my knowledge, they had been happily married until the day he took his last breath. "Why? What happened?"

"I fell in love with another man."

I gasped and grabbed my chest above my heart. "Granny! What?!"

She nodded. "We'd been married for fifteen years, and I was tired of being ignored by your granddaddy. He was never home, always working and never had time for me during the rare moments he was home."

"So, you cheated?" I couldn't believe what I was hearing. All that shit she talked about vows and the Bible, and she was a old, thotty hypocrite!

"Will you let me finish?"

I nodded hurriedly. This was crazy.

"As I was saying before I was rudely interrupted, your granddaddy was never home, and since I didn't work back then, I filled my time with hobbies while Rose was at school. I became close friends with a man I met through one of those hobbies, and before I knew it, that friendship became a lifeline for me."

"Then what happened?"

She narrowed her eyes at me but I just shrugged. She had me hooked on this story, and although I know how it ended, I needed to know what happened next.

"I told you; I packed up my and Rose's things and told him I was leaving."

A long pause came and when she didn't continue, I prompted her. "And then what, Granny?"

"Well, he cried and begged me to stay. He promised to change his ways and asked if we could renew our vows. And Rose didn't want to leave her daddy anyway. She cried and clung to him and begged right along with him. That was a daddy's girl if there ever was one." She chuckled but it was hollow. Her eyes were red, and mine prickled with empathy as my own feelings resurfaced of being presented with a divorce by someone I love.

"I never told him about my feelings for another man. I simply agreed to give my husband another chance because he was worth that much, and I promised to fight harder to be a better wife."

I wiped at the two tears that trickled down my cheeks. "What happened to the man you fell in love with? Was he waiting for you?"

"What? No. He didn't even know I was planning to leave for him." Her voice was thick with unshed tears, and she cleared her throat. "Nothing happened to him. We remained friends, but I distanced myself from him. He was a danger to my marriage; what I felt for him was…dangerous. And your granddaddy really did make a change. And our family was better for it." She looked at me. "So, now, do you see?"

I stared at her for a few moments without saying anything and she looked away from me, back in the direction of Bullseye and cleared her throat again. When she looked back at me, it was the controlled sauciness of my granny that I knew. I spoke before she could

"I see that you're still broken up about it."

"Nedra—"

"I see that you haven't moved past it if the emotions you feel right now are any indication. I see that you are the one who was mistreated yet you're also the one who had to sacrifice."

"Now, wait a minute—"

"You know what else I see, Granny? I see that even though you were ready to leave Granddaddy, you didn't have both feet out of the door yet. He asked for a second chance, and *you* gave it to him, even though you could see a better life on the horizon. *You* were willing to work it out, so you did. That's not the case with me and Chris. He wants a divorce, and there is nothing I can say that will change that." I shook my head. "I appreciate you sharing your story with me, Granny, but now all I can think of is *what if*? What if you had left? What if you had told that man that you were leaving Grandaddy for him? Or, what if Granddaddy didn't care that you were leaving? If he was on some 'Bye Felicia' type ish? What then? But I guess we'll never know."

Granny grabbed my hands and shook them. "All I want is for you to try everything you can before you throw in the towel."

"Why do you think I haven't? That's what I don't understand about all of this. You don't even know what I've done, but you automatically decided it wasn't enough!"

She gave me a knowing look. "Did you suggest counseling?"

"Yes." The lie slipped out of my mouth so fast, I almost choked on it.

The lights in the parking lot flickered on, and I glanced at my watch. "Granny, it's almost eight o'clock. We need to get out of here." I started to pull my hands back but she gripped them tighter.

"Hear me when I say this, Nedra. If you don't give this marriage all you've got, you will always wonder what if. You're so hellbent on being unphased that you haven't even demanded to know why he's divorcing you. Chris could be laid up with some other woman right now, a *friend* that he's made over the past few months, and you wouldn't even know. Listen to me good, little girl. Stop trying to be so big and bad and go see about your husband."

After those carefully and successfully aimed shots, she released my hands, throwing them back at me like they disgusted her and climbed into her car. She didn't give me a second glance as she drove off.

♥♥♥♥

What my granny didn't know was that I had researched marriage counseling and planned to approach Chris with the suggestion that we consider it. I stand firmly by what I said about the desire to stay making the difference. Before I'd had the opportunity to broach the subject with him, he cut me off at the knees. Apparently, Chris had found the printouts in our room—the one he no longer slept in—and felt the need to question me about them right away instead of waiting for me to come to him.

I was stepping out of the shower when I noticed him standing in the doorway of the bathroom, waving the papers around with a confused look on his face. He asked me why I kept trying to fix something that was beyond repair and he stood there, genuinely curious to hear my answer. Until that moment, I didn't know it was possible to simultaneously feel white-hot rage and bone-shaking despair. What kind of fucked up shit is that to ask the woman who had given you almost half of her life?

Then again…maybe he had a point. I can admit that I was fully expecting him to change his mind at some point. Maybe when I brought up the counseling or maybe if I really started to withhold sex, Chris would come to his senses. For putting me through all of this, I'd planned to make him sweat it out a little bit but ultimately, I was going to forgive him, and we would move on from this.

However, now that I'd heard my granny's story, the thought of trying to go back to what we once were made me sick.

What was I doing?

If you had asked ten-year-old me what I would do if a boy I liked didn't like me back, I probably would have given you all of the attitude I could muster back then and tell you that said boy could do the 1990s equivalent of kicking rocks. Hmph. What happened to all of that confidence? To that self-assured girl with the big afro puff and an even bigger helping of sass?

Oh, that's right!

She became a teenager, met a skinny boy named Christopher Phillips, and all that talk became just that: talk.

I'll never forget the day I met Chris. It was a sunny Friday afternoon and I had just walked home from school with my friend, Ashton. My mama had to work late, and after plenty of begging and tears on my end, followed by a long phone call with Mrs. Phillips, she had finally agreed to let me go over to Ashton's house until she could pick me up. We were sitting on the couch, drinking Fruitopia and watching *106 and Park* when the front door banged open and we heard a huge commotion from the front of the house.

Ashton shot up off the couch and raced to the front room, and my nosy behind followed right after her, stopping near the bottom of the stairs when I saw what was going on. My eyes were as wide as saucers and my mouth gaped open as I took in the sight in the kitchen.

The most gorgeous caramel-skinned boy my fourteen-year-old eyes had ever been blessed to see was standing by the sink, gulping down a glass of water. Ashton hit his elbow, and I watched greedily as rivulets of water trailed down his chin and fell onto the front of his already soaked gray t-shirt.

"Hey punk, come say hi to my company."

Ashton was obviously talking about me, but I found myself looking behind me toward the living room as if another person was there. My heart thumped erratically, but it was all for naught as my eye candy wiped his mouth with the back of his hand and shook his head.

"Dang, Ash, can I take a shower first? I just walked in the door." He had a valid point; I could smell the dirt and sweat on him from across the room. As my mama would say, he smelled like an outside puppy. Ashton just shook her head and grabbed his arm, pulling him backward, toward where I stood quietly observing them.

"Nope, come say hi first." She turned on her heel and almost ran into me at the doorway.

"Dang, girl! I didn't know you were right here."

My cheeks heated with embarrassment but even then, the sass was strong with this one. I cocked my hip to one side and slapped my hand on it.

"Well, with the way you ran out of the living room like the house was on fire, I woulda been crazy not to see what was going on!"

Ashton smacked her lips in response, but her brother chuckled, and I felt a smile lift my lips at the sound of his voice even as I initially refused to look his way.

"Anyway! Chris this is my new friend, Nedra. Nedra this is my older brother, Chris. He plays football at the high school. He's a running back." The pride in her voice was evident, and Chris heard it too because he shyly ducked his head and I could see a soft blush creep onto his tanned cheeks. Apparently, though, the Phillips' were raised right because Chris then offered his hand to me in greeting.

"What up Nedra, nice to meet you."

When I placed my hand in his, the thumping in my heart morphed to butterflies in my belly as my initial crush exploded into something thick and heavy that I would bear for the next four years. It was a sick cliche that I hated to admit, but by the time I was a junior in high school, I was definitely in love with my best friend's older brother. And *because* my life had become a cliche, predictably, Chris never acknowledged me as anything other than Ashton's "little friend".

It wasn't until I graduated high school, one year after him, and made my way to Franklin University—without Ashton—that Chris finally showed any interest in me.

Although Ashton had decided to go to school in sunny California, she assigned Chris with the task of "looking out for me". He definitely did that—and more. After a few months of him dropping by my dorm room randomly just to "check on me", he invited me out for pizza and a movie. My clueless ass had been so used to him treating me as an extension of his younger sister that I had no idea it was an actual a date. We went to see a movie, then to Pie Hi, a local pizza parlor, where I tried to pay for myself at both spots. He smoothly rejected my offer each time.

"Come on, girl. I invited you out; I'm not gon' let you pay."

His deep voice had a teasingly flirtatious lilt to it, and even though I knew what it sounded like—had heard something similar from other boys throughout the semester—I reminded myself that I was still just the "little friend" and that he was only doing this to appease Ashton. It wasn't until the night came to an end that I finally got the message that he was trying to send.

I'd been in the middle of thanking him for getting my head out of my books when he shocked the shit out of me. First, he not only walked me to my building as he usually did, but he took it a step further and followed me on the elevator and walked me to my door. The flap of butterflies in my belly from just being near him was so commonplace by that point that I'd actually named them.

Quiet down Sasha, you loud ass bitch! This ain't about you Lisa; let me have this moment, please!

I got myself together and turned to face him, my back to my door. "Thanks so much for tonight, Chris. I know Ashton has been on you about looking out for me, but you went above and beyond, and I really appreciate this."

The way he just stood there, looking down at me was fraying the fuck out of my nerves, but I didn't know how to end the evening like a person with a healthy dose of sense, so I rambled on, twisting my keys in my hand.

"You have no idea how stressed I've been about these midterms. The other night, I fell asleep in my textbook. I drooled on the pages and everything! It was crazy. So…yeah, I'm just saying that I really, really appreciate you getting me out of my room and helping me to loos—"

Before I could finish my sentence, two of his fingers were on my lips, and I damn near crossed my eyes trying to see what the fuck he thought he was doing. I might have been lovestruck, but I'd be damned if he was trying to shut me up. I opened my mouth to ask him if he'd lost his mind, but apparently, after four years of me and his sister being attached at the hip, he must have known what was going to come out of my mouth.

"Dang, girl, do you ever stop talking?" His lips were twisted into a sly grin but "love of my life" or not, I was going to give him a piece of my mind. My eyes widened in disbelief, and I jerked my head back from his hand, ready to cuss him smooth out when he shushed me. Normally, a simple shushing was not effective on me and only served to run me hot, but his was coupled with his face descending upon mine and his eyes drifting closed as his lips made their way to mine.

My heart was pounding out of my damn chest, and although I'd been kissed quite a few times before then, I was nervous as all get out. I slammed my eyes shut and tried to just keep my lips together to prevent ruining the moment that I'd only been dreaming about for the past 1,435 days.

"You 'bout to kiss me or something?"

My eyes popped open as I surprised my damn self by

whispering that question. I looked up at Chris, but his eyes were crinkled with amused confusion. His lips hovered right above mine, and my butterflies flapped furiously. I placed a hand on my belly and acknowledged that Chris hadn't pulled away from me.

"Well, yeah. Is that a problem?"

I rolled my eyes even as my body heated with joy. "I mean…" I let the word draw out. "Why now?"

Shit.

I hadn't meant to ask that. Of course, I wanted to know what changed for him *and when,* but I first wanted to taste those brown sugar lips that I'd memorized an eternity ago.

"Shiiiid. I got tired of waiting for you to lay one on a brotha first, so I had to gon' handle it."

My eyes snapped up to his. No the hell he didn't? He'd been walking around, fine as hell, *for years,* and never even *looked* at me but had the nerve to say some shit like that? Nah.

"Shut ya lyin' ass up!"

"I'm dead serious, Nedra."

"I don't believe you."

"Aight. I can show you better than I can tell you." And he did just that. His hand slid to my cheek as he nudged my head back. This time, he kept his eyes open, holding my gaze with an intensity that scared the shit out of the nineteen-year-old me. The moment our lips touched, it seemed like our eyes closed at the same time as he worked his mouth over mine and ruined my life.

I wasn't confused after that.

His lips and tongue tasted like marinara and Dr. Pepper from our dinner, but it was an intoxicating flavor all the same. My hands wrapped in his t-shirt and pulled him closer to me while his hand fell from my cheek to wrap around my waist so tightly that I was practically lifted from the ground. We stood there in the hallway of my dorm building, sucking face and holding on to each other for who knows how long until the door to my room swung open behind me.

"Okay, Nedra, get ya fast ass in here. You have a test

tomorrow."

Startled by the intrusion, Chris and I clumsily disentangled, and I turned to glare at my roommate who gave me a knowing smirk.

Ole hating ass hoe.

Chris grabbed my hand and squeezed it before letting go and backing up to the other side of the hallway. He acknowledged Shanice with a nod of his head as he grinned at me.

"What up, Niecy; them books ain't getting you down, huh?"

With one hand on the doorknob and the other on her hip, Shanice shook her head. "Nope. Ya girl, on the other hand, is struggling. That's why she needs to be in here in these books instead of in your face."

Chris shook his head, grin still in place, eyes still on me. "Nah, Niecy. You got it backward. I'm in *her* pretty ass face. But you're right. She needs to get back to them books. I just took her out so she could de-stress a lil bit. It's all good." He pushed off the wall and came back to stand in front of me.

"I hope I wasn't too much of a distraction. Ashton'll kick my ass if I disrupt your studies." He chuckled and leaned down to drop another kiss on my lips before whispering in my ear that'd he'd see me later and heading down the hallway.

I stood there silently, watching him disappear down the hallway, with my heart in my throat until Shanice yanked me back into our room.

"Ow, bitch!" I rubbed my arm where her fingers had dug into my tender, heated flesh.

"What the hell was that?!" Her eyes were wide and excited.

My face split into a shit-eating grin, but I didn't have an answer for her yet because I didn't know myself. It wasn't as simple as a kiss. It was *Chris Phillips* blowing my mind and kissing me like it was something that he'd wanted to do for as long as it had been something *I* wanted to do. But that was crazy. He had never seen me as anything other Ashton's friend. I ran a visual catalog of the previous four years through my head, searching for any lingering touches or secret looks when he thought no one was watching.

No, there was none of that. I know because I had *always* been watching. So, if he never felt anything for me before now then what had just happened? That couldn't just change overnight, right? But...that kiss was definitely not the kiss of a man who saw me as his little sister's "little friend".

That kiss—and the many the followed it—was the sweetest and most meaningful kiss I'd ever had that didn't lead to sex. Kissing Chris that first time felt like the last piece of the puzzle of my life clicking into place. It felt like grabbing the last bag of Oreos off the grocery store shelf. It felt like waking up and discovering that Blockbuster was still in business and that not only was Borders still slinging books, but they were having a buy one-get one free sale.

It was everything I had dreamed of since I was a fourteen-year-old with a crush on my best friends brother and yet everything I had never imagined a kiss could be. It was sweet, alluring, and full of the promise of things yet to come. That one kiss had sealed my lovestruck fate with Chris. I was his from that point on. Unofficially, though, because he said he wanted me to focus on school and not on trying to be his girlfriend. At the time, I thought he was completely right and I didn't fight him on it. I had a GPA to maintain, and I wasn't going to ruin it for a few kisses that didn't even come with a side of dick.

Yep, not only did he not claim me as his girlfriend right away, he also withheld sex. When the semester came to an end, he gave me a ride home and didn't even ask to come inside even though my mama wasn't there to welcome me home. Once again, he walked me to my door and kissed me senseless. I was tired of waiting, though, and grabbed his arm as he started to head back to his car.

"Are you saving it for marriage?"

He almost stumbled trying to turn back to me as he gave me a crazy look.

"What are you talking about?"

I dropped my grip on his arm and shrugged my shoulders. "I'm just wondering why you haven't tried anything yet."

His mouth dropped open at my bold assertion. I stared up at him, gaze unwavering. His kisses were driving me crazy and I know Shanice was tired of pretending she didn't hear me use my vibrator several times a week. Her smart-ass gave me a pack of batteries as a Christmas gift and I ran from mall to mall until I found a bag of coal at a gag gift store to give her in return.

Chris's mouth opened and closed a few times like a flopping fish out of water, and I didn't know whether to laugh or be upset that he was at a loss for words. Had he seriously not even considered the possibility of us having sex? Was his regard for me as his little sister's friend so strong that he couldn't move our relationship to the next level? His silence was all the answer I needed.

I rolled my eyes and turned my back to him, finally opening the front door to my house. I was halfway inside when he called my name. As if I didn't hear a thing, I entered the house and started to close the door behind me when Chris stuck his foot in the doorway. He came in and wrapped his arms around me, kicking the door shut and burying his face in my neck.

"Don't be like that, Ned. Let's at least talk about it."

"There's nothing to talk about, Chris." Especially not while he was nuzzling me and getting me all hot and bothered with no intentions of following through.

"I didn't know if you were ready for all of that, and I didn't want to put any pressure on you."

I turned to face him. "So...it has nothing to do with you still being a virgin?"

His eyes bugged and his mouth dropped open once again.

"How...? Who—?" He stopped and shook his head. "Is there anything Ashton doesn't tell you?"

I shrugged. "I hope not, or I'll have to get in her ass about keeping secrets. Now, answer my question." I folded my arms across my chest and tilted my head. I didn't let him get out of that one easily. Earlier in the semester, Ashton had told me that he had experienced a couple of false starts with a girl he dated his freshmen year and that he never seemed to bounce back after that.

As a teenager in love, I had taken that information and twisted it to mean that I was supposed to be his first. Now that I was an adult, I could see it for what it was: a boy who was tired of being a virgin saw an opportunity to fix his problem. Just as Ashton used to tell me all of Chris's business, I'm sure she told him all of mine, and he probably knew that I'd had sex before and that I was in love with him. He was just being opportunistic. Can't fault him for that.

However, looking back on the situation with a fresh perspective and Granny's words swirling around in my head, I had to wonder if I truly was missing something.

CHAPTER FOUR
Nedra

My drive home from Bullseye was a tense one. Every mile that brought me closer to my destination also brought my anger to a boil. I know that I shouldn't have let my granny's words get to me—that it was probably her intention to spur some action from me—but I couldn't help it. Things were starting to make too much damn sense.

I raced my car down the street and punched at the remote for the garage. Seeing Chris's truck parked in the driveway, as usual, further irritated me. Everything looked normal as fuck even though it was far from it.

My impatience almost caused me to drive into the lifting gate. Once parked inside the garage I repeatedly stabbed at the remote until the metal door began to reverse. The garage door wasn't even down halfway before I was out of the car and into the house.

"CHRISTOPHER PHILLIPS?!"

I yelled his name at the top of my lungs with the slam of the door punctuating my anger-fueled outburst. I tossed my purse and keys on the side table by the door and flew through the bottom floor of the house like a tornado, scanning every room with the eye of a hawk, scouring for any sign of the object of my fury. Unsuccessful in my search, I stomped up the stairs with determination, muttering expletives to myself with every step.

"Where is this nigga? I know he here. His truck outside."

I was once again a woman on a mission. This time, it wasn't giddiness that fueled me but ire. I threw open every door in my path, even the closets. I was tripping, but my anger made me irrational.

When I reached the door to the guest bedroom that Chris had chosen to move into after his life-changing announcement two months earlier, I saw that it wasn't quite closed but instead cracked a few inches. The reminder that he'd abandoned our marital bed and relocated in there boiled my blood, and I bent my knee and kicked the door open with all of the force I could muster. It flew back and slammed against the wall. Chris stood at the foot of the bed, his eyes wide with surprise and annoyance.

"Aye, what the fuck are you doing?" He relaxed his clenched fists and dropped his hands to the towel wrapped around his waist.

Realizing that he must have just stepped out of the shower in the en-suite bathroom, I was momentarily distracted by his naked torso and the droplets of water that beaded on his skin.

"Nedra!"

Chris's brusque tone jolted me out of my reverie, and my anger returned full force.

One hand propped on my hip and the other reached out to point a finger in Chris' face. "Who you fuckin', huh?"

The tension dropped from his shoulders, and he heaved an irritated breath. He pinched the bridge of his nose and shook his head.

"I'm not sleeping with anybody."

That admission wasn't good enough for me. I moved further into the room. "I know you fuckin' lying, Chris! You used to want sex all the time, so if you ain't touching me, you must be fuckin' somebody. Who is it, huh?"

Another shake of his head and his face screwed tight with frustration. "I swear I—"

"Stop lying!" I didn't want to hear him deny it again. Using both hands, I reared back and shove him in the chest. The move hardly moved him, but because he was already standing at the end of the bed, the backs of his knees hit the mattress and buckled. He dropped into a seated position at the edge of the bed and reached up to grab my wrists tightly.

"I'm not lying! I would never fuck somebody else while we're married. I wouldn't do that. You *know* that!"

I shook my head and tried to yank out of his grasp. I was so worked up, so angry, I could spit. My mind raced as I tried to pull away from him. "I *know* that you need it regularly, so who you gettin' it from? It *ain't* me. You won't even look at me anymore. So, who you giving *my* dick to, huh?"

"Ned—" He sounded distressed but I didn't care at that moment. I was heartbroken and desperate, and just the thought of the man I had loved since I was barely a teenager sleeping with someone who wasn't me drove me crazy.

"Who, huh?!" My voice cracked and my eyes clouded with unshed tears and I dropped to my knees in front of him. I pressed my face into his lap, nuzzling his dick through the terry cloth material of his towel. His grip tightened around my wrists briefly before it loosened enough for me to finally pull free of his grasp.

"Come on, Ned. Don't do this." His protest sounded firm but the way he dropped his empty hands to the bed and gripped the cover was a contradiction.

I shot him a warning glare. "Shut up!" I snapped and pulled open the towel, revealing his quickly rising dick. When I wrapped my hand around the base and squeezed, he hissed.

"Who you giving my dick to?" I repeated the question as I continued to glare at him.

Chris stared down at me with hooded eyes and licked his lips.

"Bab—Nedra—I swear I—ooh shit!"

He broke off on a grunt as I sucked his length into my mouth. I swallowed him down until I reached my fist then came back up and used my saliva to start pumping him to full stiffness.

He moaned in surrender. "Ned…"

I swallowed him down again, this time, removing my hand and aiming to put my nose in the curls in his lap. I'd almost made it when he hit the back of my throat, and I had to pull back up. Tears sprung to my eyes, and I gasped for a breath, jacking him aggressively. I wanted to hurt him even as I pleasured him.

"Who you letting choke on your shit, huh?"

At this point, I was talking to myself. Chris' head was bent back, and he was twitching in my hands. I used the corner of my t-shirt to wipe the tears from my eyes and focused on my task, determined to prove a point. If I gave him everything he needed, he wouldn't go looking for it elsewhere. If I kept his balls empty, he couldn't empty them into someone who wasn't me.

I bobbed my head up and down in his lap and used both of my hands to jack his dick simultaneously, employing a twisting motion similar to operating a pepper grinder. When his knees squeezed around me, I dropped one of my hands between his legs and tugged on his balls, knowing that the hint of pain would push his pleasure over the edge.

"Fuuuuuck!"

Almost immediately, his sack tightened in my hand and his dick swelled in my mouth. Then he exploded with a drawn-out moan, shooting into the back of my throat. I gulped down his spend, not letting a drop escape, just how I know he liked. I held him in my mouth, sucking at a slower pace until he began to soften. I released him and used the abandoned towel to wipe my mouth and face.

The corners of my mouth were tight and my jaw was sore, but I sat back on my haunches and opened my mouth to speak.

"Who you letting swallow down our kids, huh?" I watched as he jerked his head forward and caught my gaze, his eyes filled with regret. He licked his lips, and my eyes followed the movement briefly. It hit me at that moment that we hadn't kissed in quite a while, even before he told me that he wanted out of our union. How had that fact escaped my notice?

"Nobody but you baby; I swear."

I narrowed my gaze at him, but he stared back, unblinkingly. His eyes were shiny and somewhat honest, but I was no longer sure if I could trust his word and that only served to piss me off even more. Finally, unable to continue looking in the face of the man who wanted to discard me like yesterday's garbage, I curled my lip and pushed off the floor, exiting the room. I trudged down the hall and entered the master bedroom that I'd shared with Chris up until two months ago, slamming the door behind me. I stood in the middle of the room for a minute, just trying to get my bearings.

Nothing made sense anymore. I usually loved sucking Chris's dick, but right then, I was disgusted with myself for doing it. With a heavy sigh, I went into the bathroom to pee and brush my teeth then I stripped out of my clothes and climbed into the middle of our bed.

I laid there waiting for sleep to come and when it didn't, I thought back to what had just happened. Why did I let my granny get me riled up like that? I should have stopped listening to her after she told me about what was obviously an emotional affair. Because of that woman, I had come home in a rage and attacked my soon-to-be ex-husband and for all of that, I didn't even feel better.

Chris' insistence that he wasn't sleeping with anyone else might have proved my granny wrong but if it was true, it only served to confuse me. If it wasn't sex then that was just one more thing to check off on my list of reasons why he didn't want me anymore. After minutes of racking my brain to think of something and coming up blank, I burst into frustrated tears.

What is it? What could it be?

I felt so lost and out of control. What had I done to make him give up on me?

Over my loud sobbing, I heard the bedroom door creak open and I tried to vainly hold in my cries so that Chris wouldn't hear me from the hallway. That resulted in me jerking violently in the bed and my head started to throb from the suppressed emotions. I just couldn't win.

Suddenly, a pair of strong arms wrapped around me and pulled me back against a strong, solid chest. I immediately turned over and pressed my face into Chris's neck, my sobs breaking free once more. He held me tightly, almost too tightly, but I needed that. Needed him. Needed to feel grounded and secure by the man who had been my anchor for so long. Needed to feel him wrapped around me like he would be if things were normal. I cried against his warm skin that still smelled of his favorite soap until I was exhausted and sleep finally overcame me.

♥♥♥♥

When I opened my eyes the next morning, I was in bed alone, save for the dull throbbing of my head, thanks to all of the crying the night before.

Last night…

Ugh. I rolled over onto my back and stared at the ceiling. Last night was a shit show. The way I came at Chris—I squeezed my eyes shut—I was embarrassed by my actions.

No more.

I had finally reached the point of reckoning. This man didn't want me anymore, and I had to accept it. All of the energy I was spending on trying to hold on to my marriage could be better spent making sure I was going to be fine—mentally, emotionally, and financially—when the dust settled. My chest collapsed as I pushed out a cleansing breath. It was past time to get my shit together.

In the shower, I let the hot water rinse away all of my tension. I was done with all of the bullshit. It was draining, trying to appeal to the Chris I had initially fallen in love with. That man had disappeared a while back—without my knowledge—and so I'd been essentially playing old tricks on a new dog, which equated to banging my head against a brick wall. I sighed; that analogy right there was a perfectly reasonable explanation for my headache. I was so damn ready to not have to try anymore.

Oh.

A curtain of realization lifted over me and my eyes widened as I stared unseeingly at the shower wall. When Chris told me that he was filing for a divorce, he said that it was because we had grown apart and that we were *both* unhappy. I got so angry with him when he said that, I could have breathed fire. There was no way I was going to sit there and let him tell me what the fuck *I* was feeling.

But…now that I was thinking about it, though, maybe he wasn't too far off. Over the past year or maybe even two, the relationship that Chris and I had cultivated throughout our marriage had felt…off. That zeal that I once had about being Christopher Phillip's wife had just, kind of, faded away. There was no instant "aha" moment where he did something egregious that made me look at him differently. I just didn't feel the same way about him as I used to.

Sure, some things had changed. I had begun to feel annoyance at how much time he was putting into the high school sports program. He stopped being as touchy-feely as he used to be. His kisses had stopped lighting my insides on fire. We both started to spend more time outside of the house and away from each other than we did in each other's company.

Huh. I never really sat down and thought about all of the changes that were occurring between us. Apparently, though, Chris had. However, instead of seeing the direction that our relationship was heading and trying to steer the ship in the opposite direction, he shined a light down that path and illuminated the final destination.

Divorce town.

I turned my back to the shower head and let the spray pound soothingly against the back of my neck as I accepted my fate.

What's done was done. Did I want to be single again after spending so long being a part of a twosome? A married twosome, no less? *Hell no!* Was I about to be just that? *Looked like it.* The realization hurt but was also a little relieving, if I were being honest.

Shit. I hated to admit it but, Chris was right.

Clean and dry, I stood in the middle of my closet and stared down at my cell phone. The contacts were pulled up and my thumb hovered over the call button. If I made this call, there was no turning back. There was no undo button. It would be me, raising my white flag and saying "Yes, we're going to do this". I had no other alternative after last night. If I chose otherwise, my sanity was at stake.

I blew out a shaky breath and pressed the button. When the call connected, my throat was tight and I couldn't parrot the greeting that I received.

"Nedra? Are you okay?" I could hear the concern in Shanice's voice. I attempted to clear my throat, but the tears were there and weren't going anywhere.

"Niecy, I know you...you said I didn't have to call but I—" I broke off on a sob that I couldn't hold in if my life had depended on it. Thankfully, my bestie knew what I was trying to say.

"You're ready to move out?"

I nodded, though she couldn't see me, and choked out a mournful, "*Yes.*"

I heard rustling on her end of the phone followed by a short, "I'm on my way."

I wanted to feel bad about her decision to come over. In fact, I even tried to fix my mouth to form the words to tell her she didn't have to come. It was Wednesday; she was at work, and it wasn't even 10 a.m. The words never came out because all I felt was relief that I wouldn't have to do it alone. She gave me her estimated time of arrival and hung up the phone.

I needed to get up and get moving. I wanted to be gone before Chris got home from work. The tears were still flowing but my sobs had subsided for the moment, so I headed back into the bathroom to throw some moisturizer on my skin then pulled on some leggings and a tank top before going downstairs and into the garage. I grabbed the whole roll of commercial-sized trash bags that we kept for yard work and reached into a plastic tote to find masking tape and a marker. We didn't have any boxes since I made it a point to break them down and recycle them as soon as they crossed the threshold. Just as I stepped back into the house, I heard the doorbell chime.

Shanice stood on the other side of the door, holding two bottles of wine and an orange and white striped paper bag. "I brought you a honey butter chicken biscuit and some sweet dessert wine to wash it all down." My face crumbled and she pulled me into a hug, smashing the large roll of trash bags against my chest, almost painfully. "Come on, girl, you know I got you." I nodded and she released me. I held up the roll of trash bags.

"We'll fill up my luggage first then move to these. First up is my closet. I have to make sure I take every stitch of clothing with me."

Shanice nodded and after stopping in the kitchen for napkins and a couple of bottles of water, we headed up to my bedroom. I deposited my wares onto the bed and went to get my luggage out of the closet in the guest room. We hadn't done much traveling over the years, so I only had two carry-ons, but they would have to do.

Back in my room, I saw that Shanice had already begun to pull my clothes out of the closet and lay them across my bed. Both bottles of wine and the sandwich from my favorite fast food spot were sitting on my dresser, and Shanice had music streaming from her phone. I started laughing when I realized what was playing.

"Twerk music? Really, Niecy?"

Shanice came out of my closet with her arms full of clothes on hangers and gave me a matter-of-fact look. "Yes. We needed something upbeat and what's more upbeat than twerk music?"

I shrugged. "You're right. You can't isolate your ass cheeks to a four-part harmony."

She laughed. "If you say so. Go ahead and eat your sandwich while I finish pulling your clothes out of this closet."

I nodded and unwrapped my food then unzipped both suitcases. I laid the suitcases on the floor by the end of the bed and alternated between bites of my sandwich and filling the suitcases with the contents of my drawers. By the time I finished one, I was halfway through with the other.

I zipped up my stuffed luggage and moved them out into the hallway. I then grabbed the roll of trash bags and handed a few to Shanice. "I don't have garment bags so these will have to do for now." I pulled a bag down over a group of clothes and made a hole in the bottom of the bag, pulling the hooks of the hangers through. After tying a knot with the flaps of the bag, I held it up and showed Shanice my handiwork. She nodded and we got to work bagging up the rest of my clothes.

Soon, my side of the closet was empty, save for my shoes, bags, and holsters that were on the floor. I tossed all of that in a bag as well, and we started loading up my car with my clothes. We laid the clothes on hangers in the backseat and put the suitcases and filled bags in the trunk.

Back upstairs, I removed all of my hygiene and makeup products from under the bathroom cabinet and in the drawers. All I really had, in terms of makeup, was about a dozen lipsticks and a handful of lip pencils. I didn't fool with makeup too much, but I had been blessed with "soup coolers" and I liked to accentuate them with a variety of colors.

I fit as much as I could in my toiletry bag and put the rest in the plastic shopping sacks I kept in a drawer for the trash can. Last but not least, I used my step stool to grab the box from the top of the closet that held my three handguns. Chris had returned them after a couple of days when he no longer feared that I would shoot him. Little did he know, I still wanted to shoot his ass, but I was more clear-headed now and wouldn't dare. Unless I could be guaranteed a female judge who had been through an ugly divorce, it just wasn't worth it.

With my bathroom items secured in the front seat of my car, I walked through my house and snatched up all odds and ends that I wanted to take with me—a sweater thrown across the back of the couch, a pair of sandals sitting by the back door, a Franklin ball cap hanging on the back of a doorknob, my wedding rings sitting in a bowl on my nightstand…

I stopped mid-reach. No. Those didn't need to come with me. I scooped them up and carried them into the guest room, placing them on the nightstand. Chris could do whatever he wanted with them, but I had no need for them anymore. I backed out of the room and pulled the door shut. That felt much harder than simply putting rings on a dresser. When I turned around, I saw Shanice coming up the stairs.

"Hey, girly, you ready to jet?" She smiled at me and eyed the door behind me curiously.

I released a breath and nodded. "Without boxes, there isn't too much I can take, so for now, yeah, I'm ready." She hugged me then turned me around and nudged me toward the stairs. At the bottom, she grabbed the bag she'd filled with all of my snack items from the pantry and refrigerator and we left.

As I backed out of the garage and down the driveway, I looked up at what had been my home for the last ten years. I'd always thought that the day I moved out would be the day Chris and I decided to become landlords and rent the place out. This trip that I was taking wasn't even in my worst nightmare.

Once at Shanice's bungalow, we unloaded my car and put all of my things into her second bedroom. By the time we finished, it was almost four in the afternoon, and I was mentally exhausted and starving. I dropped down onto the couch since Shanice was draped across the loveseat.

"Niecy, let me know what you want for rent, okay?"

Shanice lifted her head and glared at me. "First of all, bitch, you don't even have a job. What are you going to pay me with? Cake?"

I frowned and clutched my chest. "That stung, hoe."

She rolled her eyes. "Second of all, what kind of friend would I be if I charged you rent on a home that's paid for?"

I shrugged. "I know Daddy Byron flexed his grown man bank account and squeezed some coins out of his inheritance to pay off your mortgage, but you still have expenses. Property taxes, utilities, and such."

"Girl, shut up."

"Niecy—"

"Shut. Up. You are getting a divorce, Nedra. Don't worry about anything over here and I mean that. Besides, you still have bills at your house that you have to pay, right?"

I dropped against the arm of the couch. "Yes, girl. After I lost my job, Chris took over the mortgage, but I still pay all of the utilities and cover the streaming services."

"Are you kidding me? You pay all of that even after you were laid off? Isn't that like paying a second mortgage?"

"It's a couple of hundred cheaper, but he also covers the taxes and insurance so what he pays makes up at least two-thirds of the expenses."

"Still…"

I shook my head. "I pay the stuff that's in my name. I can't risk leaving it for him to forget about, or even purposely neglect to pay; besides, it's really not that bad. The severance package I got was very generous." Equaling almost two years' worth of my salary, it was beyond generous.

Up until a few months ago, I had worked for the same company since I was a senior in college. I started as a sort of a girl Friday and worked my way up to being an executive assistant to the regional manager. A year ago the CEO filed for bankruptcy, and six months ago, the company was bought out. Only the positions of a few in management were secure, but everyone else was laid off in the restructuring. I'd been blessed to have a direct manager who loved me like I was his own daughter, and he made sure to pad the hell out of my pockets.

"Yeah, but you'll have to give up half of whatever's left in the divorce."

I shook my head and grimaced as the hunger started to make my stomach hurt. "Actually, according to the lawyer I've hired, I might not have to. If Chris agrees, we can each walk away with whatever money we have in our separate bank accounts. Plus," I sat up, "I'd taken half of my severance and put it in an account in my granny's name. So, no matter what, I'll have something to rebuild on."

Shanice raised her eyebrows. "Damn, that was smart."

"My mama always told me to keep some money on the side that my man doesn't know about. I always had a little bit of my check going into a high-yield savings account, but when I got that severance, I could hear my mama's voice telling me to put some of it up."

"I know that will help you. Ms. Rose knew what she was talking about."

"Hell, she oughta with all of the men she ran through."

Shanice laughed loudly. "Ms. Rose is a pimp! Always has been."

I smirked. "Always will be." The one consistent lesson my mama always tried to teach me was *fuck niggas, get money*. She was so disappointed in me when I settled down with Chris that she didn't talk to me for the entire year after we were married.

"Maybe my mama had a point. Maybe I need to stop giving my heart to these niggas and just be a hoe."

"Uh..." Shanice shook her head slowly. "That's not where I was going at all."

"No, I'm serious. I didn't get to have a hoeing stage anyway because I was too wrapped up in Chris. But now, it's my time. I can make my mama proud. From now on, I ain't got no love for these niggas."

CHAPTER FIVE
Jermaine

One of my most favorite things about my adopted city was the weather. It was two weeks into February and a warm seventy degrees outside, and even better, it was supposed to get up to eighty-five by the weekend, right in time for the All-Star festivities. I was hype as hell that they were coming to my second home *again*.

I had a short break due to the game, so I decided to make a quick trip to my hometown. When I boarded the plane, it was that balmy, breezy, seventy degrees, even at eleven at night. An hour and a half later, I stepped off into fifty-degree weather. I might have spent the first twenty-one years of my life in Arkansas, but I had gotten used to the warmth of Houston after living there for the past thirteen years. If it wasn't for my cousin, Trina—whom I hired as my personal assistant a couple of years ago—packing my bag, I'd be freezing right about now. As it were, I was bundled in a coat that was heavier than anything I needed when I was further south but was honestly still not *that* heavy a coat. It was *only* fifty degrees.

As a point guard for the Houston Clutch, I'd had to play in some cities where the temperature frequently dropped well below zero. They didn't know anything about that down in southeast Texas, though. Anything colder than forty degrees and everyone lost their mind. Let the sky sneeze out a few flurries, and businesses and schools would be closed with a quickness. Well, not my business. A call center can close, but a professional basketball game is going to happen rain, sleet, or snow for the most part.

If the coat I wore wasn't reminder enough of how I'd changed since I was drafted to Houston, seeing my eldest brother, Jeremiah, clad in a short-sleeved, cotton t-shirt and a pair of cargo shorts definitely drove the point home. A wide smile spread across his face as we rounded the corner and he pushed off of the column he was leaning against. He spread his arms wide.

"Baby boy!"

I shook my head but returned his smile. It didn't matter that I was thirty years removed from being a baby; Jeremiah would call me that until the day I died. We slapped hands and he pulled me into a hug.

"What's good, old man?" I jumped back and ducked as he bucked, pretending to swing on me.

"Oh, I'm old now, huh?"

I laughed. "Gotta be if I'm a baby, and you're the oldest."

"Whatever, nigga." He shoved me to the side and pulled Boobie in for a hug.

Boobie was the entirety of my entourage. He didn't have an actual title, but if I had to call him something, it'd probably be a bodyguard. I was a very low key individual and felt like I didn't need a bodyguard, but being in the entertainment business all but required having one. However, if I was forced to hire someone, it would always be family. Boobie was also my cousin and Trina's brother. Our mothers were twin sisters.

"What's happening, fam?"

"What's good, bruh?" Boobie pulled back, and I watched as the two of them did the same elaborate handshake they had been doing since we were kids. They were both the same age and the first-born of their parents, so I understood that they had a special bond. That bond deepened further when they added "line brothers" to their titles, as they both pledged when they attended college together. When they snapped their fingers and bumped chests, I knew they were done. I'd seen them do this almost my entire life and was used to it but still, I couldn't resist teasing them as we exited the terminal and headed for the parking lot.

"You didn't show me that much love J, and I'm your brother."

Jeremiah glanced back at me and smirked. "You get enough love from everybody else with your attention-seeking ass."

I cracked up and we all laughed as my brother led us to his big-ass, candy-apple-red truck. Boobie jumped his eager ass in the front seat so I caught the back, but I wasn't tripping about it. I took the opportunity to stretch one of my legs across the seat and lean up against the door, resting my head on the window and closing my eyes. It was only a short drive from the airport in Little Rock to my hometown, Pine Bluff, but I used those forty-five minutes to chill out. It was late and I was tired as fuck. I'd had a home game that night and afterward, only took time for a shower at the arena before Boobie and I hopped a red-eye.

The truck jolted as Jeremiah came to a stop, and with a start, I realized I had fallen asleep. I couldn't complain, though; I'd needed that nap. I glanced around and noticed Boobie's absence. Jeremiah must have dropped him off while I was knocked out. I climbed out of the truck and raised my arms over my head in a deep stretch. The sound of a screen door banging caught my attention, and I looked down just in time to see a red blur cross the lawn, barreling toward me. I braced myself for the impact as if I was on the court and it was a fellow player coming at me instead of a five-foot preteen.

"Hey, Unc!"

I bent at the waist, wrapping my arms around my niece and

straightened, lifting her up and squeezing tightly. "J-Baby!" Ja'mya was Jeremiah's daughter and our parents' only grandchild. Suffice it to say, she was spoiled as hell. With her long legs wrapped around my own, I crab-walked up to the door of the home I had grown up in. Jeremiah held the door open as I stepped over the threshold and laughed but didn't say a word. He knew just like I did how much Ja'mya had us all wrapped around her finger.

Just inside the door was the living room. My father stood from his seat on the couch, and I headed right for him. I tickled Ja'mya under one of her arms, and she released me, dropping to the floor dramatically and rolling away in a fit of giggles. I shook my head at her and looked up at the man whose genes I'd been blessed with.

"Aye, Pops! What's good, baby?" We embraced and I tried not to wince from how hard he slapped my back.

"How's my favorite son?" He'd been calling me his favorite son ever since I grew into my looks and turned out to be his twin, reincarnated. Each of my brothers favored my father, but I was his spitting image.

"Awe, c'mon, Pops. Not that shit again." Jeremiah shut the front door and stepped over his daughter to stand next to me. I slapped his shoulder.

"Stop whining and let the truth be told, old man." I laughed and jerked away before he could hit me. Pops threw his arm around my brother's neck and dropped a kiss on his temple. He never shied away from showing us affection.

"You know I love you, son."

Jeremiah sighed and I stifled a chuckle. We both knew where our father was going with this.

"Yeah, I know. You just love him more."

Pops smiled wide. "That's it!"

Both J-Baby and I burst out laughing. Pops was just bullshitting, but he'd been teasing Jeremiah with that line ever since I was nine and Pops heard him tell me I was adopted. I skirted my brother and dropped down onto the couch, shrugging out of my coat and laying it on the seat behind me. J-Baby hopped up off of the floor and sat next to me, resting her chin on my arm. I pulled off her red skull cap and brushed a hand down her hair, and she beamed up at me. Pops sat on my other side while Jeremiah took the reclining chair.

"How long you staying?"

I yawned. "Just through tomorrow, well, today. I have to get back Friday morning to practice for the game. Y'all coming, right?"

Pops nodded. "We'll be there, right J?"

We all had J names, thanks to Pops, but when he said "J" he was talking to Jeremiah. I was 'Hawk' and our middle brother, Jereth, was Jer.

My brother nodded. "Of course, Pops."

I looked down at my niece, who was content to listen to the adults around her converse. "Are you coming, too, J-Baby?"

She sat up and nodded vigorously. "Yes! Daddy said I can go this time!"

I smiled. My heart warmed at the fact that my family would be in the stands as I played in what would probably be my last All-Star game on Sunday. Not my *whole* family, since Jereth was in another country but it was as close as it could get.

"That's what's up."

I leaned my head back against the couch and yawned so hard, my eyes watered. Jeremiah stood up and handed Ja'mya her hat and jacket.

"Alright, let's head home, babygirl. Your uncle's tired and he needs to get some rest."

"Aww." She pouted but stood and put on the items he'd handed her. I grabbed her hand and squeezed it.

"It's all good, J-Baby. I'll see you later when ya'll come over to kick it."

She gave me a mournful look as she zipped up her jacket. "Yeah, but everybody will be taking your attention, and I won't get to tell you about my basketball game yesterday."

I glanced at my brother. She was right. It was unavoidable; someone was going to want my opinion on their favorite team as if I was an analyst, and it never failed that someone would try to give me their, or their son's, basketball stats as if I controlled the draft. I raised my eyebrows at Jeremiah. I'd make some one-on-one time for my niece.

"We'll come by a little early so you can talk to him."

"Yes!" She jumped into my arms and hugged me tight then squeezed her father. "Thank you, Daddy!" She bounced across the room to hug my Pops' neck. "Bye, PopPop; I'll see you tomorrow."

We said our goodbyes, and they disappeared out the door. Jeremiah's truck revved up loudly in the quiet of the night. Pops looked at me, half-asleep on the couch. He swatted my knee.

"Get some sleep."

I nodded; he didn't have to tell me twice. I was upstairs and in the bed of my old room in less than five minutes. I made sure my phone was muted and buried my head under the pillow. In no time at all, I was out like a light. My first thought when I woke up seven hours later was that my parents needed to invest in blackout curtains. The sunlight was streaming directly into my eyes with only the blinds and a sheer, gauze-like curtain at work to block it. The enticing smells of breakfast hit my nose, and I stretched, laughing when my feet hung a foot over the end of the mattress.

My parents had upgraded me to an extra long mattress when I was in high school, but I was 6'1" when I moved into athletic housing on campus at the University of Arkansas-Pine Bluff at eighteen and continued to grow another three inches until I was twenty and entered the draft. I slid out from under the warm covers and shuffled into the bathroom to empty my bladder and brush my teeth. When I made my way downstairs, I found Pops sitting in his reclining chair reading the paper and drinking a cup of coffee.

"Morning, Pops."

"Good morning. The ladies from the church brought you some breakfast." He nodded toward the kitchen and I took off with a grin.

In the kitchen, I found two square aluminum pans covered in foil. One held a French toast casserole that smelled heavenly and the other held an egg, vegetable, and potato casserole. Those church ladies loved making casseroles, but I wasn't complaining. I scooped a hefty amount out of each pan onto a plate and carried my meal into the living room. Once I'd made a dent in my plate, I addressed my father.

"How is everything?" I didn't elaborate; he knew what I meant. *How was business? My business.*

I owned several rental and retail properties across Arkansas and Texas that were managed by my parents and Jeremiah and two vacation rentals in Mexico that my brother, Jereth, managed. My parents had been in the real estate business for longer than me and my brothers had been alive. The way they saw it, land was wealth and they needed to put themselves in a position to get some. It was just a natural inclination for my brothers and me to follow in their footsteps, although I took a sports detour, of course. Pop's official career was working at the paper mill in town, but he started taking classes to earn his real estate license as soon as my mama obtained hers.

My parents met when they were teenagers. Mama was a student at UAPB, and Pops worked at a barbecue spot down the street from campus. Even while wearing a hair net and a sauce-stained apron, Pops was able to charm Mama out of her phone number, and they soon started dating. Pops said that he knew Mama was going to be his wife the moment she walked into the restaurant, but he didn't tell her that until he could do something about it.

"Sabrina never asked, but she knew I wasn't making much at that restaurant. She never asked for anything from me and never frowned at any of the cheap gifts I gave her. That's why as soon as I was hired at the

paper mill, I took my first check and bought her a ring."

Pops had been telling that story to me and my brothers since we were five years old. He impressed upon us the importance of finding a woman so amazing that you wanted to be a better man so that you could deserve her. That story was why I never got caught up with girls as a youngin'. Yeah, I was focused on basketball—which actually brought more girls my way—but outside of Mama making sure all of our free time was filled with classes at SEARK, Pops' story was always on my mind.

Then, there was DB. DB was my Pops' ace boon from way, *way* back, long before Pops met Mama. He'd been the best man in their wedding and, even though he hadn't been married at the time, was christened as each of our godfathers. DB was the uncle we didn't have since Pops was the only male in a family of five children, and Mama's twin sister was her only sibling.

While Pops was schooling us on how to spot the right woman, DB was telling us to avoid them altogether. It went from *"Leave them girls alone"*, when we were kids, to *"Women ain't shit"*, as we entered high school, to finally *"Fuck bitches, get money"* once we were started working, and I was preparing to enter the league.

My brothers and I laughed about it as kids, but that last one took root in me once I hit college and started showing up on national television. Girls started coming out the woodwork, and I couldn't help but hear DB's voice in my head as they tried to sweet talk me. I could see the dollar signs in their eyes from a mile away as I heard, more times than I could count, how they had a crush on me "since forever" but had *just* built up their courage to say something.

Yeah, okay.

That was a lie if I ever heard one. I don't think I had ever met a shy woman. Not in Pine Bluff and not since joining the league and moving to Houston. I'm sure they existed but not in my world. Even as a youngin', girls—*and* grown women, who shouldn't have even been looking our way—would compliment me and my brothers on our good looks.

Listen, I wasn't a narcissist but I knew that I was a good-lookin' dude. All three of us inherited my mama's smooth mahogany skin and my father's height and slim build. We also inherited male pattern baldness, but it wasn't until five years ago that I finally acknowledged my plight and shaved my head bald, following in the footsteps of my father and older brothers. When the four of us were together, heads turned. If it wasn't for the fact that Pops' beard had started getting a little gray, we'd be mistaken for brothers.

As it were, rarely did we all end up in the same room. I lived in Houston, but outside of work, had no problem getting up to PB to see my family and the same was true for Pops and Jeremiah. Mama traveled back and forth between Arkansas and Texas, acquiring properties and was currently in Dallas. The one who was missing was Jereth. He'd relocated to Mexico a couple of years ago to manage the rental properties I had purchased in Los Cabos. I'd intended to have them maintained by a property management company but some things went down out here in Pine Bluff and my acquisition of the properties created an opportunity for Jereth to get away.

I was deep into the conversation with my father and pleased to hear that everything had been going well when the front door opened.

"Well, if it ain't another bald muthafucka!" I looked up to see a grinning DB standing at the door as the screen door slammed behind him.

"DB!" Instinctively, I stood, placing my now empty plate on the end table, and went to him for a handshake and a hug. He held the embrace for a couple of beats longer than I expected, and I looked at him curiously when he finally let me go. *What was that about?* He must have seen the question on my face because he smiled and shook his head subtly. *Okay then, later.*

"It's good to see you, young man." I stepped back and he moved further into the room, claiming the seat that I had abandoned. I brought my plate into the kitchen and rejoined the two most influential men in my life. "How long we got ya for?"

I dropped to the arm of the couch. "Just today."

"That's it?"

I nodded. "Yeah, I have to get back to work."

"Well, I definitely understand that." He was quiet for a moment and again, I wondered what was going on with him. In all of my thirty-four years, he'd never been quietly contemplative, instead, speaking a mile a minute whatever was on his mind. I looked at my pops who shook his head. That only confused me.

"You good, DB?"

He looked up at me as if surprised that I was still in the room. *Was he that gone in his thoughts?* "Huh? Yeah, Hawk. I'm good." Then he grinned. "So when am I going to get some grandkids out of you?"

I laughed hard at that. He was the last person I expected to ask me that. "Wow, man. Et tu, DB?"

He shook his head. "No backstabbing intended. Just genuine curiosity."

"Nah, ain't no such thing as 'genuine curiosity' when we're talking about kids. Kick it to me straight, old man."

"Aye youngblood, this old man is just concerned about your legacy is all."

My eyebrows furrowed. "My legacy?"

DB looked around the room. "We got an owl in here or something?"

"Ha!" I laughed but I was still confused. I wanted to dig deeper, but DB shook his head with a long sigh and changed the subject. His line of questioning worried me, but I shook it off and allowed him to pull me into a debate about whether or not the changes to the All-Star game were necessary.

Not even an hour went by before J-Baby came barreling into the house. She regaled me with the highlights of her game and had Jeremiah show me a video of it from his cellphone. I was proud of my niece. I could see from the video that she had been working on the techniques I had shown her over her winter break when my brother brought her down for a visit.

Soon, more family started showing up at my parents' home. Extended family from both sides poured into the house, carrying trays of food into the kitchen and lining up bottles on the bar in the corner. I usually kept my drinking to a minimum, but my family had shown up to see me, and I planned to kick it with them all night.

The night wore on, and a few cousins had started up a game of spades while Pops and DB set up an old, faded card table for a boisterous game of dominoes. Everyone was occupied by food or by watching a game, and I managed to slip out into the backyard. There, I found Jeremiah sitting around the fire pit while J-Baby ran around the yard with some of her cousins from her mom's family. I claimed a seat next to my brother and squeezed his shoulder as I sat down.

"Where's Lisa?" I hadn't seen Ja'mya's mother at all today, which was out of the ordinary. Ever since she came on the scene, even before giving birth to my J-Baby, Lisa had attended every family get-together. She and Jeremiah had been so attached at the hip that I had to wonder why they hadn't started to look alike.

Jeremiah snorted and took a mean swig from the bottle of beer in his hands. "She's probably with her fiance."

My eyes bugged. "What the fuck did you say?"

His eyes cut toward me then out at the lawn, presumably to see if J-Baby was within earshot. "You heard what I said."

I shook my head as if it would help clear my ears. There had to be something in them because there was no way he'd said what I think he said.

"I heard you alright, but I think my hearing might be a little fucked up because it sounded like you said Lisa was with her fiance. I know that can't be right since she ain't here with you."

Another snort. Another drink. "Yeah, well…"

He had to be drinking just for something to do because there wasn't a beer on earth that could get a Hawkins drunk. "What did you do?"

"Shit, I didn't do anything."

"Nah, that can't be true. Lisa wouldn't just leave you after sixteen years for nothing." Not after basically building a life with him. They had met in when Jeremiah was a senior at UAPB and Lisa was a sophomore and they had J-Baby two years after Lisa graduated. After Jeremiah bought her a house and they moved in together, I thought everything was good. Hell, they were damn near one person.

He looked at me and the misery in his eyes shook me. How the hell had I missed that earlier?

"Think again, baby boy. Those were her exact words."

I was confused as hell. "Bruh, you lost me."

"Lisa wanted to get married."

And the other shoe dropped. *Oh.* Now I got it. Marriage was something the three of us were very careful about. We had an amazing example in our parents, along with decades of advice from them—and DB—and it wasn't something to be taken lightly. Every woman had the potential to be a wife, but—for me—I didn't want a "potential" mate. I needed *the one*. That perfect woman for me. In thirty-four years, I still hadn't found her, although, for the record, I wasn't looking.

Jeremiah was different. He was like Pops in the way that he met his right woman early on. At least, I had thought so. It didn't occur to me to question why he never married Lisa. I was so busy being "Hawk" that their relationship wasn't on my radar. And honestly, outside of Mama, who was going to ask him about some shit like that? I mean, Pops, maybe, but that's it. I wondered briefly if Jereth had ever questioned him about it.

"I'll be honest with you, man," I stroked my goatee, "I thought Lisa was 'the one' for you. You were so in love with her…"

"Am not were," he corrected swiftly. At my raised eyebrows, he cleared his throat. "I love her but I don't know if that makes her 'the one'." *Ah, so big bro was in denial.*

"Well, if she ain't the one then what is all the drinking and tears for then?"

He shoved me so hard, I almost fell from my seat. I laughed.

"Fuck you, nigga! I'm not crying and shit. You asked where she was, and I told you."

I shrugged. "You sound pretty heartbroken about it."

"Nigga…"

I held my hands up in surrender. "I'm just sharing my observations. But what's the big deal? If you love her and you can't stop crying now that she left you then hurry up and marry her before whoever this other nigga is does it first."

He sighed heavily and ran a hand down his face before tilting the bottom of his bottle up and draining the last of his beer. "Shit's not that simple. She met someone and got close enough to him that she thought it was a good idea to accept his proposal."

Damn. "You know who this dude is?" *Maybe Boobie could run up on him…*

"Nah, and I'm not even going to give Lisa the satisfaction of thinking that I care by asking anything about him."

I nodded. "I get that. Not only lie to yourself but lie to her too. That's a solid plan." He glared at me and I laughed. "Nah, you're right. Just let whatever happens, happen." I sobered. "When did all of this go down? Last I heard, you and Lisa were thinking of having another baby."

"We were. Ja'mya is about to be thirteen, and I want a son. Lisa was on board with it until she came back from a weekend trip with her girls. After that, she said she wasn't going to continue being my 'forever girlfriend' whatever that means. I mean, she was more than my girlfriend and she knew it. She was my…" He stared at the fire pit, seemingly at a loss for words.

"Life partner?" I supplied a word I heard thrown around a time or two recently. It was usually by same-sex couples, but I figured the same principle could be applied to whatever Jeremiah was trying to say.

"Yes! That's it!"

I chuckled at how he sounded exactly like Pops from the day before. "Bruh, you do know that most people who have a life partner do so because they aren't able to get married? Not because they refuse to."

The look he gave me was almost offended. "I'm not refusing to get married. I'm just being cautious."

"Okay bruh, if you say so." I wasn't going to argue him down about it. It was his business if he didn't want to get married. That had nothing to do with me. I stood and slapped his hand. He pulled me into a hug and looked me in the eye.

"I'm not refusing to get married."

I laughed at his insistence and pulled away from him. "Okay, nigga, damn! I believe you." I didn't believe his ass for a second.

I jogged out to the lawn and started chasing my niece and little cousins around, their joyous screams cracking me up. I stayed outside, playing with them for about an hour before retreating back into the house to call it a night. My family could kick it all day and night but I had to throw in the towel. I made my rounds through the kitchen and living room, saying goodnight and goodbye to my people. Neither Pops nor DB was anywhere to be found, but I didn't question it. I climbed the stairs and stripped out of my clothes, falling into the bed without even taking a shower first. I'm sure my mama would say I smelled like a 'puppy dog' after running around outside like one but it was two a.m. and I was exhausted. I'd have to make sure I washed the sheets in the morning before I had to leave.

My flight was at ten a.m. so I was only able to swing four hours of sleep before a wake-up call from Trina got me out of the bed. After taking the shower I should have had the night previous, I stripped the bed and carried the linens down with me. The laundry room was through the kitchen, and as I cleared the living room, I saw a familiar figure standing where I had expected my father to be.

"Mama?"

She turned and grinned at me. "Well, it sure ain't your daddy, huh." Nah, it definitely wasn't Pops. The way he'd been knocking back glasses of Crown assured that he wouldn't surface until nine at the earliest. She set the spatula she held down on the counter. "Good morning."

I was surprised to see her. When I'd left Houston, she'd been in Dallas, checking on a multi-unit building she thought I should purchase. She'd been gone for a week, and I hadn't heard from her to hear how the look-see went. Seeing her this morning was a pleasant surprise.

I shifted the linens under one arm and walked over to embrace her. "Morning, Mama. When'd you get in?"

Planting a kiss on my cheek, she patted my chest and turned back to the stove. "About midnight." Her back was to me, so she didn't see the surprised look on my face. I hadn't seen her last night and I—*oh*. That explained Pops' absence. I shook my head.

I looked over her shoulder to see pancakes, grits, eggs, and a potato hash. The smell of bacon was strong and though I didn't see any, I assumed she had cooked that first and had it in the oven to stay warm. I wouldn't eat any but I knew Pops had to have his bacon. I continued on to the laundry room and tossed the sheets and pillowcases into the high-efficiency washer. When I returned to the kitchen, Mama handed me an over-sized mug filled with tea. I smiled at the man-shaped infuser hanging on the rim of the mug.

"Are you surprised to see me?" She'd turned her attention back to the stove to remove the eggs and spoke to me over her shoulder.

I nodded, though she couldn't see me. "Of course. I thought I wouldn't see you until I got home." I'd been in Houston so long, it was home now.

"Oh, you'll see me there, too. I'm flying back with you."

My eyes widened. "Damn, Mama. You just got here, and you're going to turn right around a board another plane within twelve hours? Talk about jet-setting."

She clicked her tongue. "You're one to talk."

"Yeah, but I do that for work, not just for the hell of it."

My mama spun on me so fast, I took a step back. It didn't

matter that she was a foot shorter than me or one hundred pounds lighter. The woman could be terrifying when she wanted to be.

"I didn't do this turn-around trip *just for the hell of it*, Hawk. I missed my husband and the desire to be with him was strong enough that I didn't have to think twice." She observed me with shrewd eyes. "I'm praying that you will find someone you care so much about that you wouldn't hesitate to do the same thing. I'm praying that for all you boys." Her eyes flew to the ceiling, and I knew she was thinking of Jeremiah, whose childhood bedroom was just above the kitchen. "Well, I'm praying for you and Jereth. Jeremiah already found that someone, but he's so caught up in that…that *bullshit* that DB fed y'all as babies that he let her get away!"

I laughed nervously, glad that she changed the subject. "I was talking to him about that last night."

The look she gave me was full of disbelief. "What did *you* say to him?"

I leaned back. *Damn, was I not supposed to talk to my brother?* "Nothing much. I thought Lisa was 'it' for him, and I asked if he knew who her new dude was."

"Hm." She turned back to the stove, this time taking the pot of grits off the burner. "Grab you a plate."

There was a stack of plates on the counter behind the dishes of food. I didn't even realize it, but, as Mama finished the food, she arranged it on the counter buffet-style. I set my mug on the breakfast table and grabbed a plate, loading it up with everything but the bacon. I hadn't had bacon since I was a sophomore in high school. Jeremiah, who was a freshman at UAPB, worked part-time at the Tyson chicken plant. One day, while he was at work, a group of locals who were vehemently against the unethical treatment of animals papered the parking lot with pamphlets of what happened inside the plant.

My brother, along with most of the workers, didn't give a damn and simply trashed the pamphlets. Unfortunately, at least one had missed his sweep, and I saw it when he picked me up from basketball practice. I was up all night researching what I saw in between those pages. After throwing up the fried chicken I'd had for dinner, I declared myself a vegan. A week later, when I realized vegan meant I couldn't eat cheese, I switched to being a vegetarian. That was sixteen years ago.

Now that I was older and understood my gastrointestinal system, I avoided eating cheese for a different reason, but only occasionally ate animal by-products like eggs and honey when I was in Pine Bluff. Since I was waiting until I retired from basketball to buy a home here, I wasn't going to tell my parents what they could and could not serve in their own home. Absently, I ate my food as I thought about the day before. I'd had more surprising conversations with my people in the last twenty-four hours than I had in the last six months.

Suddenly, everyone wanted to talk about relationships, building a family, and having kids. Shit, I needed to stay out of the water. At that thought, I eyed my mug of tea. I know Jereth relocated to escape a situation but maybe that was a two-fold blessing. Living on a different continent automatically came with a reprieve from conversations like the one I'd just had with my mama. The only one who hadn't brought up anything weird was Pops. He was a real G. He knew how to appreciate what he had. One grandchild was better than none.

I watched as Mama turned off every burner on the stove once she was finished cooking and headed around the corner to where her and Pops' bedroom was. Our flight left in three hours. I wonder if she was going to try to get a nap in or would she thug it out by staying up. We had less than an hour before we had to get on the road. Sacrifice for love. That was what she was doing.

I shook my head. I could understand what she was saying without experiencing it for myself. I looked down at my plate and quickly devoured the rest of my breakfast. There was a reason I kept my trips back home short. My head was always spinning soon after arriving, and I was eager to get back home.

Being secluded had spoiled me.

CHAPTER SIX

Nedra

"Let me ask you something."

I looked up from my e-reader and bowl of popcorn to see Ashton perched on the arm of the couch. I'd been staying in Shanice's partially abandoned bungalow for a couple of weeks now. It still took some getting used to, but I appreciated my friend for allowing me this space more than she could know.

Ashton had come into town on Wednesday and was staying for a week. Today was Friday, and she had been reminding me since she landed that we were going to some new club tonight. I looked at her expectantly. So far, she hadn't bombarded me with questions about the divorce, but I knew it was only a matter of time. Maybe this was that time.

"Is there any chance of you reconciling?"

I sighed. And there it was. There was no way Chris was getting this question as much as I was. Or any variation of it. I wish I could record my answers to the frequently asked questions I'd been receiving, and play them back every time I needed to.

Not only was I tired of having to repeat myself, I was also tired of having to give my answers with kid gloves. I was tired of having to gently let people know the few things I was willing to share with them. I was so tempted to start giving out Chris's number to every person who asked me questions about the divorce. *"Here ya go; he's the organizer of the event, and he should be able to answer all of your questions. Have a nice day."* But see, if I did some shit like that, everyone would call me bitter or unnecessarily rude. It wasn't Ashton's fault that she was asking me shit I'd had to answer too many times already, but that didn't stop me from being annoyed all the same.

I gave her a short and sweet answer. "No."

She slid from the arm of the chair down onto the seat. "Oh. Well, have you—"

"Ashton." She stopped talking. "Please don't insult me by suggesting that I haven't tried to save my marriage."

She blinked rapidly. "No! I wasn't going to do that. I was just going to ask if you've already scheduled your 'new to you' dick appointment."

I stared at her. Okay, that is definitely not on my list of faqs. "Seriously, Ashton?"

"Uh, yeah. Seriously. Have you?"

"First of all, I didn't even know that was a thing. Second of all, no."

She tsked as if my answer aggrieved her. *"Oh, Nedra."* She pulled out her cell phone and swiped at the screen.

"What?"

She shook her head and continued swiping at her screen. Finally, she peered up at me. "Have you had any sex at all since…?"

Since that last night with Chris? She didn't have to say it; I knew that's what she meant. I shook my head. "Sex has been the second to last thing on my mind. Plus, I'm still married."

"You're going through a divorce," she pointed that out like it was the answer to the questions of the universe. "You're stressed.

If anything, your pussy needs a massage."

I sputtered. A pussy massage didn't sound too bad now that I thought about it. It *had* been a while. Still…"But I'm not divorced yet. My vows meant something to me. *Forsaking all others* meant something to me. *Means* something to me."

She nodded, an unconvinced look on her face. "I get it. Well, I don't *get it,* but I get what you're saying. No new dick until the old dick has cleared the premises. Got you."

This whole conversation was weird. "I can't believe you're talking about this so nonchalantly like your brother isn't the old dick."

"Man, fuck Chris."

I chuckled. "I did. Quite a few times."

Ashton grunted. "Yes, you did. The only one to do it." She chewed her lip thoughtfully before returning her attention to her phone. "You know, Chris resented the fact that you weren't a virgin when y'all got together."

I tilted my head. Chris had made enough comments over the years for me to know it bothered him that he was a virgin when we started having sex. It wasn't hard to deduce that it was a problem for him. That he resented the fact I hadn't been, however, was news to me, but it confirmed the thoughts I'd had a couple of weeks ago.

"No, I didn't know that."

"Yep, he didn't think it was fair that you'd been with someone before him, but you were his only one."

I frowned. "How wasn't it fair? Why was fairness even a part of that conversation?"

Ashton shrugged, her face still in her phone. *Uh uhn.* Something wasn't right. That ain't no random thing to say.

"Ashton."

Her eyebrows lifted but her face stayed tilted down. "Hm?"

"What aren't you saying?" My question was met with silence and I shifted in the chair. "Don't make me knock that phone out of your hand. Answer my damn question."

She sighed and looked up at me. Her eyes were worried and couldn't hold my gaze. I don't understand; there was nothing she could say that would change the outcome. Chris was divorcing me. The end. Unless she was about to tell me that he had been fucking around on me, it couldn't be too bad.

I sat up straighter, dropping my e-reader and placing the bowl of popcorn on the floor. If she was about to tell me that Chris had cheated on me and *she knew about it*, I was going to beat her ass and then, I was going to go find Chris and shoot his bitch ass like I should have done a couple of months ago. That best friend bullshit would go right out the window because if Ashton put loyalty to her brother over loyalty to me in *this situation*, then they could meet the same fate. At this point, anyone could get an ass whooping and some hot shit in their ass.

Ashton must have seen the fury building on my face. She stood slowly, raising her hands in front of her, palms out in a sign of surrender. "Hold up, Nedra. Let me explain before you jump to conclusions."

My hands clenched into fists. "I already jumped, so you better talk fast."

"Chris never confirmed it, but I'm pretty sure that his lack of sexual partners factored into him filing for a divorce. I think he started wanting some variety or something. I asked him, but like I said, he never confirmed it."

Oh.

The fight drained out of me instantly. "That's it?" Leaning over, I grabbed my bowl of popcorn and pulled my e-reader from where it slid between the cushions, sagging back against the chair. "Girl, I could have guessed that."

Ashton exhaled and clutched at her chest. "I thought you were going to kill me!"

I looked at her like she was crazy, even though I had been prepared to do just that. "Not over some mess like that."

She sat back down heavily and resumed scrolling on her phone. After a moment, she glanced up at me. "You already know we're going out tonight, right?"

"Yes, Ashton. You've told me a half dozen times already."

She swung her head around and arched an eyebrow at me. "Do I detect an attitude, missy?"

"Indeed you do, bitch."

She hissed. "Ooh, so feisty today."

I had to laugh at that as I tapped the edge of the screen to flip to a new page of the book I was reading. Ashton's bubbly ass had been calling me feisty since forever. It was her go-to word when I was ready to square up with somebody. I guess it was her way of lightening the mood or calming me down so I didn't trip over it because I knew that fighting made her uncomfortable. It didn't matter who was fighting; she just didn't like it. I honestly don't know how we became best friends because I was always ready to fight someone. The popular quote, "*If you stay ready, you don't have to get ready*" was a mantra for my life.

We settled into a comfortable silence as I read my book and Ashton resumed doing whatever the fuck she was doing on her phone. It couldn't have been more than twenty minutes before Ashton's phone rang, startling us both. A wide grin spread across her face and she jumped up, running out of the room with the device plastered to her ear. I could hear the murmur of her voice but not the words she spoke as she held her conversation somewhere in the back of the house.

A few minutes later, she ran back into the living room and launched herself into my lap, causing me to almost fall to the floor to avoid being crushed.

I glared at her. "Seriously, Ash?"

"Shh!"

She shook her head and pointed to the phone in her hand. I quieted down and that's when I noticed that it was ringing. She was calling someone and waiting for them to pick up. I lifted a questioning eyebrow at her, but she just winked and pursed her lips at me. I rolled my eyes but couldn't help but smirk at my silly friend.

When the person on the other end finally answered and whoever Ashton had dialed spoke a greeting, my smile dropped off of my face.

"What up, baby sis!" Chris's voice sounded clear and even *normal* as if nothing was wrong in his world. I turned my head to the side and looked away from Ashton, wondering why she even brought her phone call with him to my lap like this.

"Hey, boo, I'm just calling to remind you that I'll be MIA this weekend and you're my emergency contact, so keep your phone on at all times."

I whipped my head back in her direction. Why was she going to be MIA? It was my understanding that we would be attending almost all of the All-Star festivities together. Did that change without her telling me? And since when was Chris her emergency contact? That honor had belonged to her and Chris's mama since we were kids. What the hell was she talking about?

"Where the hell will you be this weekend?" Chris's confusion echoed my own.

Ashton rolled her eyes toward me and shook her head. "Duh, *Christopher*. It's All-Star weekend. I will be…*occupied*."

I covered my mouth to stifle my giggle as the sound of Chris dry heaving floated up through the phone's speaker.

"Why did you have to say the word 'occupied' like that?" He sounded disgusted and even though he was the last person whose voice I wanted to hear, I found it funny how Ashton was teasing him.

My dramatic friend huffed. "Because you're acting dense as if you don't know what people do during this fantastical annual celebration."

I could just picture Chris shaking his head at his younger sister before he replied with, "I know what people do during All-Star weekend, Ash. They watch the games. That doesn't sound like what you're talking about, though, and to be honest, I'm sickened by what you're implying. If you don't mind, I'd like to change the subject."

I rolled my eyes. Did Chris always used to sound this…condescending? I guess it was safe to say that my rose-colored glasses had been removed.

"Fine," Ashton huffed in my lap and I gave her a side-eye. I didn't want to make my presence known to Chris, but I wanted to know why she thought having this conversation *right here* was a good idea.

"Don't forget about the emergency contact thing, okay?"

Oh yeah, and that was questionable as well. I had no idea what the hell this girl was doing. What could it be? I was tempted to whisper it to her, but Chris interrupted my thoughts.

"Yeah, yeah. I got it. You know traffic is about to be a beast. Why would you even risk going downtown?" He sounded so dismissive of her that I became annoyed. Ashton grew up in Houston; she could navigate the traffic without it being made into a big deal. *Damn, was Chris always such an asshole?*

Ashton sucked her teeth and held the phone closer to her mouth. "It's a risk worth taking, Chris. This is All-Star weekend! Everyone who is anyone is going to be in Houston, and I'm trying to secure the bag!"

I chuckled silently at her exuberance, and Chris laughed before speaking. "Ash, I know you were a thot for Halloween, but I didn't know you were making it a lifestyle change."

There were muffled noises coming through the phone that sounded like Chris was trying to hold in his laughter, but that corny shit wasn't even funny. My eyebrows rose and Ashton sucked in a breath. *Ooh, she didn't like that one.*

Her top lip curled, and her eyes narrowed as she stared off into the distance. "*Oh yeah*, there is another reason why I'm risking the crowds this weekend."

Her voice had taken on a sinister edge that made me curiously excited.

"Word?" Chris's questioned response sounded like he was as curious to hear her comeback as I was.

In all of the years that I had known Chris and Ashton, they were always clapping on each other. Although Chris could be corny, rarely was Ashton able to best him. I didn't expect this time to be any different until she said, "My sister is going through a divorce and I've taken it upon myself to find her a big, rich dick to sit on until she feels better."

"Oh shit," I breathed in a low whisper, not even thinking about being heard. I definitely had not expected that, but I was proud as fuck. Ashton was fighting dirty because that was sure as shit a low blow.

This time, Chris didn't echo my sentiment as he yelped out an angry, "What the fuck, Ash?! You know I don't want to hear that shit!"

Ashton stood up from the couch quickly and yelled into the phone as if her brother was standing right in front of her. "DON'T CALL ME A MUTHAFUCKIN HOE THEN, NIGGA!" Her screeching had my eyebrows in my hairline. *Damn, she was really mad about that thot comment.*

"Chill the fuck out, Ashton! It ain't that damn serious, and I didn't call you a hoe." His voice had calmed considerably as he attempted to placate Ashton, and I imagined that he was surprised by the level of ire that his normally easygoing sister possessed at that moment.

"Yes, the hell you did! What do you think a thot is?"

He was quiet for a moment, and I couldn't decide if it was because he was thinking of a lie or because he genuinely didn't know. "I don't know; a gold digger or something."

I heard the honesty in his voice, and I rolled my eyes at his idiocy.

Ashton was unamused. "Thot is an acronym for That Hoe Over There."

"Seriously?"

I almost laughed aloud at his incredulity. What a fucking idiot.

Ashton huffed into the phone. "How about your old ass do some research the next time you want to pick up some slang from your students."

I nodded in agreement with that statement. Chris was so busy trying to be the "cool teacher" that he was making a fool of himself with little shit like this. And how the hell *didn't* he know what it meant? If you hear your students use a word that you know isn't in the dictionary, have them give you the definition and use it in a sentence. Call it a teaching moment *or something*, but educate yourself.

When he spoke again, he sounded remorseful, and I couldn't help but notice that that particular tone had been missing on the night he asked for a divorce. How can a man be sorry about accidentally calling his sister a hoe but not be sorry that he secretly filed for a divorce from his wife?

Yeah...sitting and listening to this conversation had been a bad idea. I knew it would be, but I was just so damn nosy. But just like I felt like shit right now, I had to remember that curiosity killed the cat. I don't know what Ashton's intentions were when she made that phone call, but I should have shut it down as soon as I heard Chris's voice come on the line.

I got off the couch and left Ashton in the living room to continue her phone call with her brother.

A short time later, Ashton appeared in the doorway of the bathroom and stood there watching me as I looked through my makeup bag for colors I wanted to wear that evening.

"You're mad at me." It wasn't a question because she knew the answer already. I didn't say anything, just continued to rifle through my lipstick tubes.

"I'm sorry." She scooted into the room and hugged me from the side. I stopped pretending to ignore her and gave her a hard stare in the mirror.

"What was the point of all of that, Ash?"

Her thin shoulders lifted and fell. "I was just trying to help." At my disbelieving look, she hurried to clarify her statement. "I figured that if Chris thought you were going to meet someone new that he would be jealous and want to stay married."

I guess I could see the logic in her thought process. Maybe

something like that would work for another couple, but Ashton failed to take into consideration that her brother had never been a jealous person when it came to me. From the moment I met him, I'd been a sure thing. He knew I didn't have eyes for anyone else, so he never had anything to be insecure about. I didn't want to think about why I was sad to know that my husband had never been jealous over me.

I sighed. "I appreciate what you're trying to do, Ashton. I really do, but I think it's time for you to accept that nothing is going to keep me and Chris together. He doesn't care enough about me for something like that to work."

She didn't respond to that. What could she have said? There was nothing to say. After a moment of silence, I resumed going through my bag and Ashton disappeared. Unable to concentrate, I set the bag down and went to put away the things that I'd left in the living room. Once the room was clear and I'd straightened the cushions, I went to pull out my outfit for that night. There were about two hours until the time we'd decided to leave, and I was restless.

I thought about the whole conversation between Ashton and Chris. Not once did he ask about me. He knew that she was staying with me, and with me moving out, he had no idea what the status of my living situation was, and yet...nothing. No concern for how I was holding up, no instructions for Ashton to look out for me. Just...radio silence.

He really didn't give a fuck about me.

Even if he didn't love me romantically anymore if he cared about me at all, he would at least try to make sure that I was okay. He might have had time to mentally disconnect himself from me, but this had been sudden for me. It hadn't been easy to completely shut off the faucet of my love, but with every day that went by and I saw just how much of a piece of shit Chris was, the flow got thinner and thinner.

I looked at my clothes laying on the bed and finally figured out what makeup I wanted to wear. I went back into the bathroom and started to pull out the items I had in mind. I always did my makeup before getting dressed. I washed my face and started beating my face.

"I don't remember if I told you this, but I love that short haircut on you."

I stopped applying my lipstick and met Ashton's eyes in the mirror. "Thanks, boo." There was a contemplative expression on her face so I waited to see if she would say something else.

She still hadn't given me "the talk" I had been expecting, and there had been no tears, which was a surprise. That one question earlier couldn't have been it for her. Ashton had wanted me and Chris to get together almost as much as I did and because she and I were as close as sisters, she probably had a lot invested in our marriage and the success of our relationship. Her chest rose with a deep inhalation and I braced myself for the onslaught of whatever she was holding in.

"I'm sorry."

Nothing else followed those two words and I blinked. "Bish, whet?"

She shook her head, and her eyes became glassy. *Noooo!* I didn't need her to start crying right now! If she started crying then I would surely follow right behind her, and I was sick to death of crying over my failed relationship.

"I'm serious, Ned. I feel like this is my fault too."

I spun around and faced her. She stood in the doorway of the singular shoebox of a bathroom, dressed to the gawds in an azure strapless dress that left none of her slender curves to the imagination. The sides of the dress were made of strings crisscrossing all the way down, exposing thick swaths of the same light, red-brown skin she shared with her brother. Her relaxed honey-brown hair was shiny and glossy, brushing her shoulders in a straight bob. Her face was beat; lipstick and eyeshadow matching the striking blue of her dress. *When had she done her makeup? How long had I been lost in my thoughts?*

But my friend's pretty face was crinkled into a pout, and I had to frown at her words.

"Are you really going to make this shit about you, Ash? Really?"

"No! That's not what I'm doing."

I sucked my teeth. "That's what it sounds like. *Your brother* is divorcing *me,* and here *you* go saying it's *your* fault. Do you hear what I'm saying? That's what I hear."

"*Nedra!*" She cried my name desperately. "I said that because I feel like I pushed y'all to get together, so in a roundabout way, this is my fault."

I stared at her. Her face was twisted in agony. *This damn girl was serious.* Being in California had turned her into the stereotypical, airhead valley girl. I couldn't believe it and had to laugh. She gaped at me and her mouth hung open.

"If you don't shut your ass up. This mess is between me and Chris; it has nothing to do with you *at all*. Seriously, Ashton, unless you dragged Chris to a lawyer and physically forced him to file those papers then this is in no way your fault."

The dramatic way that her shoulders collapsed in obvious relief concerned me. "Did you think I would blame you?"

She hesitated and wrung her fingers together. "I...wasn't sure."

I cocked my head and stared at her hard. "What kind of idiot do you think I am? Why would I place any responsibility for my marriage on your shoulders? What sense does that make? Especially when I haven't done that once in the entire time that Chris and I have been together. Not even in college." There had to be something else. Her statements felt deeper than some misplaced sense of responsibility.

"Welllll..." The word dragged for at least fifteen ls,further annoying me. Her eyes flitted about the room, and I wondered if I was going to have to smack her to make her spit it out. "Chris told me how you were going to shoot him and..."

My eyes widened. So his bitch ass went and tattled on me to Ashton? Wow.

"When did he tell you that?" More than two months had passed since that night, and Ashton hadn't brought this up before. Did he tell her on the phone earlier after I had stepped out of the room?

Ashton winced and I knew instantly that she knew before tonight.

"He, uh...he called me that night and told me."

Surprised, I jerked back, my butt hitting the counter. "That night? The night he told me he wanted a divorce?" I was in disbelief. She knew about it this whole time and never asked me about it? I wasn't mad that she'd never brought it up, but that didn't seem like something she would be able to keep to herself.

She nodded. "Yeah. He called me, crying because he thought he'd driven you crazy. He really thought you were going to shoot him. I had to calm him down and convince him that you weren't going to shoot him for real."

I quirked an eyebrow. "Uh, no bitch. I was definitely going to shoot his ass."

Ashton sputtered and grabbed the door frame. "No, you weren't!"

I propped a hand on my hip. "Yes, the fuck I was. He was gon' get some street cred *that night* with his punk ass."

"You were going to shoot my brother?!"

"Bitch, your brother fucked me doggy style then asked for a divorce! I was going to shoot his kneecaps off so he could never doggy style another bitch in his life!"

"Nedra!" She looked like she didn't know whether to laugh or cry.

"That's my name, bitch" I snapped at her. I was irritated. What Chris had said to her was closer to the truth than I wanted to admit to myself. I was undeniably a little crazy that night. My heart was hurting and had convinced my brain that I was dreaming, in an attempt to deal with the pain.

"I want to be mad at you but..."

I sighed. Ashton was my friend, had been my best friend since I was fourteen. But she was also Chris's sister. "For the record, I didn't really think I would hurt him. I thought I was dreaming, and you know how they say that you can't feel pain or die in a dream? Well, I figured if I shot him then I would wake up and everything would go back to normal."

The sympathy in her eyes made me look away from her. I hadn't even told Shanice that part.

"Aww, sissy!" She squeezed into the bathroom and wrapped her arms around me, burying her face in my neck.

I felt the tears rise in the back of my throat and tried to stave them off. I needed to get her off of me. "Ashton, your makeup!"

"Duh, I used a setting spray! This shit ain't going anywhere." Then she sniffled. "I'm so sorry, Ned. You don't deserve to go through this."

I nodded, afraid that saying anything would release the dam of my tears. She rubbed my back and rocked us back and forth for a few minutes and I let her, knowing that she needed this. Ashton was the more emotional of the two of us and the dissolution of my marriage would be hard on her. She'd been calling me her sister since we were kids, and when I legally became her sister you couldn't tell her shit. Now that bond was disappearing, at least legally, and I had no idea how she would react.

Suddenly, her hands froze on my back, and she leaned back to look me in the eye. I met her suspicious gaze with my curious one.

"What?"

She stepped back and propped both of her hands on her slender hips. "Wait a damn minute. If the belief is that *you* can't feel pain or die in a dream then why were you going to shoot Chris?"

I processed her words and cracked up laughing. *"Oh shit."* I bent over at the waist and laughed until my ribs hurt. "Ashton, I really am crazy."

She didn't know why I was laughing, but she started chuckling along with me.

I stood upright and tried to speak through my giggles. "Girl, you know how they say, when you get married, two become one?" I waited for her to nod before I continued. "Okay, so like, I figured that because we were *one*, shooting him *would* hurt me." I shook my head at the logic my heartbroken self had conjured up. "Ooh shit, I am a damn psycho." My laughter petered off and out of nowhere, I burst into tears. "*I'm so fucking crazy!*"

I dropped down to the closed toilet and covered my face with my hands. Ashton rushed over and kneeled next to me, wrapping her arms around me and resuming her rocking motion from before.

"You're not crazy; you're heartbroken. I'm so sorry, sissy."

I don't know how long we stayed like that, but my butt started to hurt from sitting on the hard toilet seat, and my back started to ache from being in a hunched position. Ashton released me as soon as I started to lift up, but she didn't back away. She leaned back and studied my face, presumably to see if I was okay. Grabbing tissues from a box on the back of the toilet, she wiped the tears from my face and shoved some in my hand so I could blow my nose. When I was done, I nodded and she stood up and backed toward the door.

Following suit, I stopped in front of the mirror to look at my face. The waterproof mascara I had applied and nude lipstick that matched my skin tone were still intact, but my eyeliner had run a little bit. An easy fix. I looked at Ashton and was surprised to see her face still looked flawless.

"Damn, Ash, I need to try that setting spray."

She smiled at me and posed for a second, blinking her eyes coquettishly. She dropped the pose and raised her eyebrows at me. "Do you want to stay in tonight?"

I shook my head. After that cry, I definitely needed to get out. I wanted to go to this club and dance. Chris and I never used to go to clubs, but I loved to dance and rarely got to do it. Not only that, I knew how badly Ashton wanted to go out. Her whole trip home was because of this weekend, and I would not hold her back from being the thot she claimed she wasn't.

"Absolutely not. There is twerking to be done tonight. I need copious amounts of alcoholic beverages and random niggas tryna grope my ass as I walk by."

Ashton gave me a knowing look. "All of that is doable. I'll take care of everything, and the groping is guaranteed."

"Good." So I turned and redid my eye makeup then went into my room to get dressed. The dress I'd planned for tonight was something that had caught my eye online more than a year ago. It was a long-sleeved, bodycon scoop-neck dress that I'd purchased, even though I had nowhere to wear it. The soft pink color looked amazing against my dark brown hue, and the smooth fabric felt amazing against my skin.

I paired the dress with strappy sandals in the same pink shade that I had bought from the same boutique months after the dress but also not had a chance to wear. I kept my jewelry understated, going with a simple pair of large wooden earrings in the shape of a black woman's head and afro and a thin gold chain, with an *N* pendant in the center, around my neck. With the fresh haircut I'd gotten that morning plus the mani and pedi that Ashton had treated me to, I looked—and felt—good as fuck. When I walked into the living room, Ashton put two fingers in her mouth and let out a loud wolf whistle.

"Gotdamn, Nedra!"

I grinned and posed as she whipped out her phone and took a picture. I'd taken a couple of selfies in my room but hadn't posted them anywhere on social media.

"Are you ready?" I had a small clutch that held my phone and card case along with gum and a mini switchblade hidden inside of a lipstick tube. I had done my research on this club we were going to, and there were no guns allowed, but I wasn't going anywhere without some type of protection. Plus, I kept a gun in my car at all times. Folks were crazy out there these days.

We were in my car and on the road in no time, and Ashton proceeded to tell me about her foolproof plan to secure a sexual partner.

"Girl, I'm telling you, this app has been the best thing to ever happen to me."

I shook my head at how earnest she sounded, but I didn't

respond. The quickly growing website designed for safe and verified one night stands, JustOneNight.com, had finally created a mobile app and apparently, Ashton was pleased with the outcome.

"All I do is turn on the location, and it shows me if I have any matches within a one-mile radius. I can adjust the range down or up to five miles." She grinned. "Technology is amazing."

I had to agree with that one, especially since it was allowing me to build a successful business from the ground up. "That it is."

When we arrived downtown, I was unsurprised at the amount of traffic. This was a big weekend, and the surge of people to the city had already been planned for weeks. I had purchased a parking permit for the weekend the moment Ashton told me she was making the trip. I preferred having my own transportation than having to depend on a rideshare app or having to hoof it back and forth to the train. The garage that I purchased my permit from was central to all of the event venues.

To my surprise, Ashton had purchased tickets to the game on Sunday as well as the rookie game and the multiple challenges taking place. I know that had cost a grip, but she said she had it, so I didn't ask her any more questions. Cali had apparently been good to my friend.

The line to get into the VR Club & Lounge was literally wrapped around the building. I had started to slow down because as eager as I was to drop it like it was hot, I was not down to wait in a long-ass line.

Ashton noticed that I had fallen behind, and she grabbed my hand and pulled me forward. "Come on, sissy. That line isn't for us." To my surprise, she walked right up to the door and gave her name to the heavily muscled man at the door. He flicked his finger across the screen of the tablet in his hand and two seconds later, turned to nod at the similarly shaped man behind him who was blocking the door. The second man stood aside, and Ashton pulled me into the building.

"What the hell just happened? You were on a list? How?"

Ashton flipped the end of her bob back. "You ain't know, girl? I know people."

If I hadn't witnessed what I'd just witnessed, I would have laughed in her face, but I was walking into a brand new night-club that was owned by a professional basketball player, and it was all because of her. So, maybe she really did know people. *What the hell was Ashton doing out in Cali?*

We rounded a corner and came into a wide open space of the club. It was a huge room that looked to be divided up into zones. There was a bar on either side of the room, each almost as long as the building and already swarmed with people. To our right, on a raised platform, was the DJ, who was speaking into a mic over some random rap song. Across the room, opposite the DJ, was another raised platform that had several sections of couches. At the foot of the short flight of steps that led to that platform stood another large man. That must be the VIP section.

After looking around and taking in her surroundings, Ashton looked back at me and asked in a loud voice, "Drinks or dancing first?"

I didn't even hesitate to call back, "Drinks!"

She nodded and led me over to the bar closest to us. We waited for a couple of minutes for one of the many bartenders to get a moment and acknowledge us. When a woman with a braided mohawk came over, Ashton gave her order then looked back at me.

"Whiskey sour, Jameson, extra sour, please."

She nodded and started on our drinks. While we waited, I looked around the room. There were so many people here. From my limited memory of clubbing back in college, people didn't usually come out until well after eleven. It was just after ten, but the dance floor looked like it was already midnight.

I chose to come early because I anticipated there being heavy traffic and had hoped to avoid the long line that would surely be at the door come midnight. Had I known that Ashton was on the list, I would have waited at least another hour. Looking at the crush of people all around, it looked like we made the right decision anyway.

Ashton nudged me, and I turned to see my drink sitting in front of me. I grabbed it and took a sip. It was perfect. I started to unzip my clutch, but Ashton grabbed my hand, stopping me. I looked up and she leaned in close to my ear.

"Drinks on me tonight."

I smirked. "Say no more." I looked at the bartender who was placing Ashton's dirty martini on a bar napkin and pointed to my glass. "Let me get another one of these." Ashton laughed and pulled a card out of the top of her dress. She handed it to the bartender.

"Start me a tab, hun." The woman grinned and took the card. By the time she placed my second drink on the bar, my first was gone. I sucked down the fresh one quickly and pulled Ashton to the dance floor. She laughed at my antics and shifted her drink to her other hand so she wouldn't spill it.

The DJ was playing Crew by Goldlink, and I loved that song. I started rocking my hips and swaying to the music. Ashton started rapping, and I laughed as she stumbled over the words. The DJ asked if all the ladies were ready and then the song switched to Rake It Up by Yo Gotti. Ashton screamed and bent at the waist, shaking her hips left and right. I put my hands in the air and danced along with her. She stood upright and got behind me, pushing at my back to bend me over. I laughed at her silliness but did as she instructed. I put my hands on my knees and twerked my ass on her. She rubbed her unoccupied hand on my ass but when she slapped my butt, I jerked forward. Her bony-ass fingers hurt.

"Bitch, watch those sticks you call fingers!"

She laughed at me. "My bad, sissy." She'd finished her drink, and the empty glass was dangling from her fingers. "Let's go back to the bar." I followed her back across the dancefloor and requested a bottle of water as she set her empty glass on the bartop. She pulled out her phone and started moving her thumbs across the screen.

"Lemme see if there's some dick in here with my name on it."

I chuckled and accepted my water, downing half the bottle in seconds. Dancing had heated me up, and the iciness of the drink was hydrating and cooling. Ashton gripped my arm and I looked at her.

"You found someone?"

The smirk she gave me answered the question. She told me to follow her as she, in turn, followed the app in the direction it led her. We pushed through the crowd until we were in the back of the room where the VIP platform was. I glanced at her, wondering if she was going to go in another direction or if the bouncer was her new dick. I was surprised when, once again, she gave her name and the man moved to the side.

My eyes widened, and I couldn't stop myself from saying, "*Biiiitch*! Who the fuck are you?" Ashton was on *lists* and shit now, and I didn't know what to do with this new development.

Ashton looked back at me, and that ever-present smirk was on her face. "You ain't know, bitch? I'm Ashton fucking Phillips."

I threw my head back and laughed hard at that. "You right."

CHAPTER SEVEN
Jermaine

I sipped from my tumbler and swept my gaze across the club. It was almost eleven, but the room was packed with women and niggas galore. It was the All-Star effect. It brought out so many people considering it wasn't even midnight yet. It also didn't hurt that this was a celebrity spot.

The owner and my teammate, Fred Pierce, made sure that it was well advertised that VR Club & Lounge—short for Velvet Rope because Fred was a Janet stan—was *his* club and that it would be poppin' this weekend. He wasn't lying. Everybody had come out to have a good time and support Fred. It was good to see; he was a good dude and deserved to have his endeavor take off like it did.

The bass thumped through the speakers, and throngs of bodies pulsed on the dance floor below me. VR was designed with the dance floor as the focal point. At the back of the club, deep into the space, was a raised, two-level platform, which served as the VIP area. On each level were three sections of crescent-shaped, leather sectional couches and low sitting, glass-topped tables. Opposite the VIP, smooth on the other side of the club, was the DJ booth. On every wall were large screens that displayed abstract art that moved in time with the beat of whatever song was playing at the moment.

I sat on the highest platform in VIP in the furthest section. Going out wasn't something I did often. My reputation was almost that of a hermit. If I wasn't on the court, you rarely saw me. But Fred had invited me to his grand opening personally, and since this was All-Star weekend, I decided to show up and support. It was a compromise because he was only getting three hours out of me tonight, and hour two had just begun.

As I bobbed my head to the music and took another sip of my drink, something, or rather, someone to the right caught my eye. I turned to the set of stairs that separated where I sat from the rest of the club and froze. In fact, everything around me froze. The loud music faded away and at the moment, I couldn't even tell you who the people around me were.

The first thing I noticed was her cheekbones. They were so pronounced, sticking out high on her round face. Her smile was wide—all teeth—and genuine. How I could tell that from across the twenty-five feet that separated us, I have no idea. I just knew that it was true. She stood a step under and behind another woman, but whoever that other woman was, she might as well have been a ghost because I saw right through her.

Maybe it was the spotlights dotted around the room and the woman who had my attention just so happened to be standing under one, but she had a glow around her, a golden light illuminating her celestial beauty. She was a goddess. When she threw her head back and laughed at something the woman with her said, my stomach tightened. I wanted to know what her laugh sounded like. Shit, I wanted to make her laugh again. She followed the ghost woman up the stairs, and they started heading in my direction. The closer she got, the more enthralled I became.

Her hair was short, like really short, and faded on the sides with about an inch of shiny black curls left on top. There was a severe part cut into the left side of her hair and while I generally preferred long hair on women, the short style was sexy as hell on her. She wore a long-sleeved, form-fitting dress the color of cotton candy that fell past her knees and wrapped around her wide curves that made my heart beat fast and my dick try to stand up inside my slacks.

She was thick and stacked, and I had every intention of becoming acquainted with her. With a silent prayer of thanks to God for blessing me with this vision, I stood, ready to make my mark. The two women came to a stop in front of me; the goddess had her eyes on the ghost whose face was glued to the screen of the cell phone in her hand.

I opened my mouth to speak but was interrupted by a hand clapping me on the shoulder. I turned to see Fred standing next to me with his cell phone in his hand. Shit, I had been so enthralled with thickums, I had forgotten he had come by to check on me. He looked at me and smirked as he caught my eye before turning his attention to the two women in front of me.

"Which one of you beauties is Ashton?"

Both women snapped their heads up, and I held my breath. Please don't let *my* goddess be Fred's next conquest. Ever since his favorite matchmaking service, JustOneNight.com, had debuted their mobile app, Fred had been fucking a different woman at every turn. He was pretty tame when we were out on the road, but after every home game, he was guaranteed to bring a woman home. I had no interest in using the service, but he swore by it, attributing his lack of drama in the bedroom to the company. If it turned out that this yet nameless woman who had captured my attention was also on that damn site, I might give it a shot.

The vision in pink elbowed her friend, and I exhaled a sigh of relief. She glanced at me briefly before looking back at her friend. Then slowly, as if she couldn't believe her eyes the first time, did a double, then triple take before fixing her gaze back on Fred. I smiled at that but said nothing, choosing instead to observe the interaction between our two friends. Her friend smirked at Fred and tilted her head, causing her long hair to fall over one shoulder in a silky, straight curtain.

"I know you saw my picture on your phone."

Fred threw his head back and laughed. "Damn, you got me." He held his hand out. "Come chill with me for a bit before we get out of here."

She stepped forward and grabbed his hand but was yanked back by her friend's death grip on her arm. She looked back as if surprised that the woman was still there. Then her gaze roved around the area. Her eyes took in Boobie, who was still sitting on the other end of the long couch with his face illuminated by the screen of his phone, then traveled to me and held for a couple of seconds before finally returning to Fred. She nodded at me.

"Is this your friend? He cool? I don't want to leave my sister alone."

Fred was nodding before she even finished her sentence. Without looking at me, he said, "Oh yeah, Hawk is the best dude I know. Plus, he's celibate, so you don't even have to worry about him trying anything."

Ashton frowned; the goddess's eyes went wide, and my jaw clenched. "What the fuck, bruh?"

Ashton shook her head. "Celibate? No, that won't work. I promised to find her some wood to grind on."

My jaw loosened and dropped open.

"Oh shit."

"Well, damn."

Both Fred and I were caught off guard with that one. The goddess rolled her eyes and dropped a hand to her hip.

"Keep playing with me, Ashton. Ole boy gon' be tending to wounds instead of beating that box."

Ashton sucked her teeth. "Fine! Whatever!" She slipped out of the goddess' grip, dropped Fred's hand, and walked over to me. I caught Fred's eye and he nodded. She was cool. I bent my head my knees slightly, bringing my ear close to her mouth.

Pointing behind her, she said, "That's Nedra. She has a fat ass, and she's newly single." My eyes widened. She stepped back, wiggled her fingers at the goddess, and took off toward the stairs, pulling Fred behind her. He shot me a two-finger salute,a shit-eating grin stretched across his face as he pointed at the goddess with his chin before he disappeared down the stairs and into the crowd.

Well damn. That was interesting.

I gestured to the couches behind me. "Do you want to sit down?" She eyed the area before running her hands down the backs of her thighs and having a seat. As she looked out over the dance floor, I took the opportunity to get a better look at her. Her skin looked as smooth as the dark caramel it resembled. The pale pink of her dress complimented her well. On her feet were matching pink sandals with thin heels and laces that snacked up her thick calves.

I was so focused on checking her out that I hadn't realized she had turned her attention to me. Only because my eyes were on her plump lips, shiny and brown, did I even know she was speaking to me.

"Why are you looking at me like that?"

One eyebrow lifted at the incredulous tone in her voice, and my lips split into a grin. "I was simply admiring the work of art before me. I apologize if I made you uncomfortable." I sat back on the couch and watched as her lips fell open into an "o". Her eyes cut away from me, and she rubbed her thighs back and forth. I tilted my head as her ministrations became clear. She was embarrassed by my attention. Hmm…

She stood abruptly and I followed suit.

"Um…I'm going to the bar." She glanced at me briefly and turned toward the stairs.

I raised an eyebrow. "Someone can bring you a drink." I pointed to a server who hovered nearby. There were at least four of them on each platform.

She started to shake her head, it seemed, without even

considering the option, but then she stopped herself. "Okay."

Glad that she wasn't leaving yet, I signaled one of the servers who was hovering nearby. Immediately, a slim woman in booty shorts appeared at my side. I leaned toward the goddess known as Nedra and spoke directly into her ear. She wasn't sitting far from me, and I know I didn't have to get as close to her as I did, but I couldn't help myself. She smelled good as fuck and I wanted to put my tongue on her neck to see if she tasted the same.

"What are you drinking?" I didn't recognize my voice. It was low and husky like I was trying to sound sexy. *What the fuck?*

If my eyes hadn't been glued to her skin, I would have missed the way she shivered when I spoke into her ear. That shit was sexy as fuck. She turned her head slightly, and my lips brushed her high ass cheekbone. Her skin was as soft as I imagined.

"Jameson sour with extra sour." Her voice was as smooth as the whiskey she'd asked for. How could I be hard just from hearing this woman order a drink?

I gave her order to the server, who nodded and disappeared quickly. I scooted back against the seat, trying to give Nedra room. It was as much for my benefit as it was for hers. I'd never been so intensely attracted to a woman before. This wasn't a normal sort of attraction. I wanted to pull her into my lap and run my hands down her thighs, similar to how she had done before she sat down. I wanted to put my face in her neck and listen to her smooth ass voice talk to me.

The server reappeared with Nedra's drink, and I slipped enough cash for a 100% tip. Nedra offered her thanks as she accepted the glass from me, and I swear when her fingers grazed mine, I felt an electric current shoot through me. I know she felt it too because she shifted her drink to her other hand and shook the now empty one.

"You shocked me." She'd said it humorously, but I wasn't laughing. I considered myself an intelligent man. I'd managed to graduate from college the year after I joined the league, and I not only received my bachelor's degree, but I had *earned* it. I read as

To Buy A Vow

often as my schedule allowed, and I listened to and absorbed the wisdom of my elders.

I knew a sign when I saw one. The way everything had slowed down when I first laid eyes on her, the intensity of my attraction to her, and now, this electric shock. My mama always said good things came in groups of threes and all signs were pointing to Nedra.

I watched her intently as she sipped on her drink and looked around the club rolling her shoulders to the beat of the music. As if magnetized, her gaze kept coming back to me, and I relished that. She was affected by me as well. The fourth time she glanced my way, I stood up and held my hand down to her.

Her head fell back as she looked up at me. She didn't ask me any questions, just set her glass down on the table and took my hand. I led her to the stairs and to the dance floor. I held her arm up and spun her until she was facing away from me. I scratched my chin and tugged on my goatee. If I thought she was heavenly from the front, she was straight sinful from the back. Those full hips of hers rounded to an ass so fat, I had to clutch my chest. Ashton had warned me, but damn. How in the hell did I miss that thing from the front? *Whew, shit!*

I stepped up behind her and pulled her back against my chest and wrapped my arms around her. When I bent my neck, my nose fell right behind her ear. Whatever scent she wore was strongest there and when I inhaled, I was instantly hard. *Fuck.* I wasn't trying to make her uncomfortable by putting my hard dick on her lower back, but with the slacks I wore, there would be no way she wouldn't feel all of me. I stepped back and turned her again, but I added an extra twirl to it.

She threw her head back and laughed at my antics, and my chest swelled with pride that I was able to make her face light up like that. We grooved through two songs while dancing face-to-face, not touching except for the one hand that I refused to let go of. That she didn't seem to mind didn't go unnoticed by me.

Although I liked to dance and was pretty good at it, I rarely got the chance to because I never went out. I'd been committed to that hermit life. I crossed my feet at my ankles and twisted my body, ducking under her arm as I spun and she laughed again. I'd keep doing silly shit all night if I had to just to keep hearing her laugh.

The music changed and Pop That by French Montana came on. Nedra squeezed my hand and turned and pressed her back against me again. She put my hand on her hip and bent forward slightly and started popping her ass on me. Shit. I wasn't ready. The song transitioned to Booty Wurk by T-Pain, and Nedra started gyrating like she had been waiting for this song. I gripped her hips with both hands and bent my knees, moving with her. The DJ cycled through about five more hype songs, and Nedra kept her ass on my zipper the whole time.

The music finally started to slow down but it was with some freaky shit that made me wonder if that nigga was tryna get people pregnant tonight. When We by Tank came on, and there was no question about the DJ's intentions. Nedra straightened up and leaned back against me. My arms wrapped around her waist almost reflexively. She felt so good in my arms, her soft body rubbing against me. I dragged my nose against the soft skin behind her ear.

I looked down at the way her ass was grinding on my pelvis, and I know she had to feel how hard I was. I don't know if she was intentionally trying to start something but that's exactly how it felt, and that's exactly what she was doing. She slowed the motion of her hips, rolling against me slowly while she pushed back on me. An involuntary groan slipped out of my mouth.

She tilted her head and looked back at me. I met her gaze and saw the lust I felt reflected in her eyes. I licked my lips and watched as she tracked the motion. My dick pulsed, and I knew she felt that shit because her chest rose as she sucked in a breath. She opened her mouth to say…something, and whatever it was, I was ready to agree to the shit, but she stopped suddenly and looked down.

The smartwatch on my wrist that was currently wrapped tightly around her waist was lit up and vibrating. I lifted it to my face to see the display and cursed. My alarm was going off, and I had a half of an hour until it was the time I told Boobie to get me so I could leave.

To my dismay, Nedra stepped away from me and started to walk off. I grabbed her hand to keep her from getting too far away.

"Whoa, where are you going?"

"To the bar; I need a drink."

I didn't want to let her out of my sight. "Come back up top with me, and we can get your drink there."

Shook her head. "Nah, it's all good. These are new shoes; I wanna put 'em to use." She pointed to her feet and then turned to leave again. Instead of letting her hand go, I walked with her to the bar. I shook my head at how I'd done a complete 360 in less than an hour. It was as if the instant I laid eyes on her, the old me disappeared and all I wanted to do was be around her, hermit lifestyle be damned.

When we reached the bar, I got the attention of one of the bartenders and they came over instantly. I looked at Nedra expectantly, and her face was surprised as flicked her eyes from me to the bartender but she asked for a bottle of water. The bartender made a circle and handed Nedra the frosty bottle. I handed him a bill, and he left to finish the order of whoever he was working with when we walked up.

Nedra cracked open the bottle and downed half of it immediately. She took a breath, and I stared down at her.

"Where to now?"

She looked at me curiously. "Don't you have to leave?"

I blinked at her. "How do you know that?" My watch didn't display any words for my alarm; instead, it was just an animation of a clock vibrating.

She arched an eyebrow. "Maybe because your alarm went off, and it's All-Star weekend. You probably have another appearance or something to go to."

My lips curled into a smile. I appreciated that she didn't try to pretend that she didn't know who I was. There had been no indication on her face at any point since I had met her, so I hadn't been sure. Now that I thought about it, I didn't even introduce myself because I was so used to people knowing who I was as soon as they saw me. It would have been hard to believe that she didn't at least recognize my face, though. I was the franchise player for the Clutch. My face was on billboards all across the city, and I was in a half dozen commercials that were only played locally.

I shook my head. "This wasn't an appearance. My boy Fred asked me to come out and support him, and that's what I did."

She smiled. "Aww, that was sweet of you."

I laughed. "I don't know about all of that. I was just being a friend. Showing up was the least I could do." She nodded and looked back at the dance floor, twirling the water bottle in her hands.

I was about to ask her what she was going to say when we were dancing, before my watch interrupted her when my fucking watch started vibrating again. I looked at it and saw that Boobie was calling me. *Fuck, man!* I gave her an apologetic look as I pulled my phone from my pocket, but she just smiled at me.

"It's fine. I should probably go anyway." She started to back away but I wasn't having that.

I reached out and wrapped the fingers that weren't swiping at my phone around her wrist. I gently pulled her closer to me until there were only a couple of inches between us. I stared at her and watched as she bit one of her luscious lips.

"What's good?"

"The car's here, man. Let's roll."

I pulled the phone away from my face and turned my watch to my face again. *Damn, it was midnight already?* Where in the hell did the time go? I put the phone back on my ear.

"Give me five minutes and meet me at the front." I ended the call and looked at the woman who had unknowingly caused me to change my whole M.O. "What were you going to say back there? Before my watch went off and we were rudely interrupted."

Her tongue slipped out of her mouth and swiped across her top lip. She shook her head and pulled my hand from around her wrist. "You have to go...and what I was going to say is...not important. Thanks for the drinks and the dances."

It sounded like she was trying to say goodbye to me, and I wasn't trying to hear that. "No, don't try to—"

"Aye, Hawk! What's up bro?"

A ballplayer from the San Antonio Sunbursts came up to me, clapping me on my shoulder and diverting my attention from Nedra. I could see her in my peripheral, immediately back away and scurry off and I tried to go after her, but dude was holding onto my arm and holding his hand out for a shake.

Shit!

I hurriedly slapped his hand. "What's good, Mike? Man, listen. That woman that you just stepped in front of? That's my future, and I need to go find her. I'll get at you later." The words just fell out of my mouth and they shocked the shit out of me, but I didn't have time to analyze it. I needed to find Nedra.

He backed up and raised his hands in the air. "My bad, homie! I fucks with that. Go get your Cinderella; the future Mrs. Hawk! Invite me to the wedding, bruh; I love black love."

I nodded, already moving away from him. "Sure thing, Mike." I turned around and tried to figure out which way Nedra might have gone. We had been standing right off of the end of the first bar closest to the DJ's platform. From here, the only place to go was outside because there was no way she would have been able to go back onto the dance floor without me seeing her. *Did she leave? She did say she was going to go. Maybe she meant go home.*

I quickly exited the club and looked both ways down the street, eyes sweeping for dark caramel wrapped in cotton candy. The only thing I saw was Boobie leaning up against an SUV that was idling about twenty feet away from the entrance to the club.

I'd lost her.

Nedra had disappeared at midnight, but it wasn't on some Cinderella shit like Mike had said. She didn't leave me anything to find her with. I didn't get her number, her name, or her social media handles. I had nothing, and I was pissed. When I climbed into the car, I slammed the door behind me.

Boobie looked at me from the driver's seat. "The fuck you slamming doors for, nigga? Something go down in there?"

I ran both hands down my face and leaned back against the seat. How could I explain what my problem was without sounding like a little bitch? I shook my head and buckled my seatbelt. "My bad, bruh. I'm trippin'."

He pulled away from the curb and maneuvered the one-way streets of downtown until we were on Highway 59, heading south.

"So, this don't have anything to do with the lil thickness in pink?"

My head snapped up, and I looked at my cousin. His eyes were on the road but I could see the smirk on his face each time we passed under a light.

"Yo…"

He chuckled. "You ain't gotta say shit, Hawk."

Boobie had basically been my shadow for so long that I often forgot that he was there. Of course, he saw everything. That was his job. I sighed. "She ran off like she was out after curfew and the street lights came on."

"Damn."

"And I didn't even get her number before she dipped."

"*Damn!*"

"That's what the fuck I'm saying, bruh."

It was quiet and I slipped into my thoughts. I had to figure out who this woman was and where she was from. I hoped she was a local. If she was from out of town like so many others who came down just for this weekend, then I'd likely never see her again. And the thought of not seeing her again wasn't an option.

CHAPTER EIGHT
Jermaine

Unsurprisingly, sleep eluded me. I kept replaying the night before and imagining several different scenarios where the goddess had been able to say what was on her mind after that last dance. Each scenario ended with us coming back to my place and both of my heads buried between her thighs. None of it made a difference since I still woke up hours later without any way to get in touch with her. Restlessness had me wide awake an hour before my alarm was set to go off, so I got on my phone. I tried searching for her first name online, but nothing came up except for a local women's gun group. To say I was frustrated would be an understatement.

When my alarm finally sounded, I got out of bed and shuffled into the bathroom. I emerged with an empty bladder, minty breath, and a slightly damp body. It was early, not even seven, and since my parents and my brother weren't coming into town until later that evening, the house was quiet. I grabbed my keys and drove across the city to the gated neighborhood that Fred lived in. We'd made plans to get breakfast from the best spot in town, Chicken or The Egg. It was a tiny spot located in a poorly maintained area near Franklin University. They only opened for eight hours a day, from six in the morning until two in the afternoon, but the food was so bomb that they consistently had a line out the door at all times.

I got to Fred's and rang the bell idly. My mind kept bouncing between the search for my goddess and anticipating for the grub I was about to ingest. The door swung open, and Fred stood there with a huge ass smile on his face. I followed him into the house, closing the door behind me.

"You're smiling like you got a seat filler to hold our place in line."

He laughed. "I should have did that; but nah. This is the look of a man who had pussy for breakfast."

I joined him with a laugh. "Word? Well, since your ass already ate, then I guess I can ride out by myself."

"Bruh, don't even play like that. I had a dream about that fish and grits last night." I laughed. "I'm serious. Just let me cut shorty loose then we can make moves."

We walked through the front room into a wide open great room that comprised the kitchen and living room. I was surprised to see the woman Fred had met up with last night standing in the kitchen, eating a bowl of cereal. I couldn't remember her name, but I knew that she was friends with the goddess.

"Yo!"

Both Fred and the woman looked at me, startled. "What's good Hawk?"

I ignored Fred and addressed the woman. "You were with the baddie in pink—Nedra—last night."

She cocked her head and squinted at me as if she was trying to place my face. All three of us knew that she knew who I was, so this little show was annoying but I said nothing while she contemplated. She nodded and spooned more cereal into her mouth. She made me wait for her to chew and swallow before giving me confirmation.

"I was. My sis was bad as fuck last night."

No disagreement from me. "She left before I had a chance to get her number. You think you could hook me up?"

She lifted an eyebrow. "You got a big dick?"

My jaw hit the floor. "Whoa, what the fuck?!"

Fred laughed hard and came to slap me on the shoulder. "My man's dick is bigger than mine." I shoved his hand off of me and pushed him away, choking on my laughter. This dude was always clowning.

"Fred, shut the fuck up!" He was laughing so hard that tears were coming down his face. His girl stood in front of me, her face the picture of impatience.

"So…"

I shook my head and shoved my hands in the pockets of my sweats. I'd thrown them on this morning without thinking, but with this line of questioning, I felt the need to stretch the fabric so that it pulled away from my body instead of resting against me and giving away private information.

"I ain't answering that shit. Can I get the number or not?"

She pouted and seemed really put out by my refusal, but she pulled her phone out of the top of her dress—a different dress than she was wearing the night before—and swiped at the screen. Soon, she was rattling off ten digits that I promptly saved in my phone under the name of 'Goddess' with her real name in the notes.

I smiled my thanks, and Fred's silly ass elbowed me. "Make sure we get invitations to the wedding, bruh."

I squinted. This was the second time I'd heard that in regards to this woman who I had met not even twenty-four hours ago. It was wild to me how something as simple as showing interest got blown out of proportion. I shook my head.

"Chill out, Fred. I'm about to leave you right the fuck here if your ass don't come on."

"Okay, okay calm down." He moved behind the chick and

wrapped his arms around her waist and whispered something in her ear that made her laugh and slap his chest playfully.

I rolled my eyes. I stood there starving and this nigga was cakin'. They left out of the kitchen and returned five minutes later with Fred pulling on a crewneck sweater and the chick carrying an overnight bag. He grabbed her hand and called out to me.

"Let's roll, Hawk!"

We all went outside, and I climbed into my car. They stood by a town car that I failed to notice was idling in the driveway. He'd called a car service?

Man, Fred really went all out for these women.

When he *finally* gave her one last kiss and damn near picked her up and put her in the backseat of the car, I breathed a sigh of relief. Soon after, he slid into the passenger seat of my SUV. I waited for the town car to back out of the driveway before doing the same and heading in the opposite direction. I glanced at Fred. He was sitting there, looking out the window with a cheesy smile on his face.

"My dude, if you're going to go through all of that with these women, you might as well be in a damn relationship."

He threw his head back and laughed hard. "Nah, man. I only do all of that with Ashton."

Confused, I glanced at him again. "Didn't you just meet her last night?"

He shook his head. "Not at all."

I waited for him to elaborate but he didn't. I could take a hint, so I nodded and chuckled.

"A town car, though?"

"Man," his grin stretched wide, "she's lucky I didn't put her ass in a damn limo."

"It was good like that, bruh?"

He leaned back against the seat. "Shit, it was better."

With one hand on the wheel, I used the other to stroke my goatee. "Damn. I might be jealous."

Fred smirked at me. "What? *No!* Not my dude, the *Celibacy*

King. Not you!"

I laughed. "When are you gon' stop calling me that?"

"When you stop turning your nose up at these women and finally stand up in something wet and hot."

"*Bruh.*"

I had no other words for Fred; all I could do was laugh. Chicken and The Egg wasn't far from where Fred lived, and less than fifteen minutes later, I was pulling into the tiny parking lot. I lucked up and snagged a spot from someone who was leaving right when we arrived. We walked up to the building and sure enough, there was a line down the sidewalk. I glanced over a Fred.

"You definitely should have used the seat filler."

He waved me off. "If you think I'm about to wait in this line, you're crazy as hell."

The parking lot was opposite the line, so as we walked up the sidewalk, Fred stopped to talk to the attendant at the door. He dropped a hand on the young guy's shoulder and gave him a friendly smile.

"What's up, man? About how long is the wait this morning?"

The guy's eyes widened, and his mouth dropped open.

"Fr-Fred Pierce?" His eyes skated over me without a hint of recognition. The beanie, hoodie, and sunglasses I wore were hopefully working well to conceal my identity. If I were lucky, everyone would think I was just a part of Fred's entourage.

"Go right on in, man. No wait for you."

Fred looked back at me, a smug ass grin on his face, and tilted his head toward the door. I followed him inside where we were immediately ushered to a table in the back corner of the room. A waiter met us as soon as we slid into our seats and twenty minutes later, our food was placed in front of us.

Fred bit into his fried catfish and closed his eyes in delight. "This is so good, bruh. And it came fast as hell, too. I swear I'm *never* giving up this celebrity shit!"

I was face down in my raspberry-stuffed French toast but I

lifted my head and glanced at him when he said that; the last part catching my attention.

"This celebrity shit ain't gon' last forever, man. One day you're going to have to be a regular ass dude who waits in line just like everybody else."

His face twisted with incredulity. "Regular ain't even in my life plan! Huh, and if I turn eighty and someone doesn't recognize me and let me slide my old ass in the front of the line for the senior citizen breakfast special, I'll give you one million dollars!"

I snorted. "Okay, Fred."

"I'm serious, dude."

"I believe you, bruh. I just wonder when it's time to hang it up and walk away. When do I get to live my life without the celebrity shit? Or start a family without worrying about them being hounded by cameras?"

Fred sat back in his chair and eyed me shrewdly. "What are you saying?"

I shook my head, forking another piece of the French toast into my mouth. As I chewed, I thought of how to answer his question. Fred wasn't dumb; he knew what I was getting at; he just wanted to hear me confirm it. I gulped down my glass of sweet tea and wiped my mouth with a paper napkin, leveling Fred with an open gaze.

"I'm saying, thirteen years is a long time and fourteen is even longer."

He dropped his fork and ran both of his hands down his face. "Why would you say this here, of all places?"

I didn't even have to look around the room to know that no less than five people in the cozy restaurant had their eyes on us. "I swear I didn't plan this out. I wasn't going to say anything until it was official."

He looked down at his plate; his expression pained. "So, you're serious?"

"As a mortician, my dude."

With a resolute nod, he retrieved his fork and continued eating his meal. Neither of us said another word throughout the meal. I had nothing to say, and Fred was probably still processing the bomb I'd accidentally dropped on him. Although I stayed to myself more often than not, if I would have labeled anyone my friend or even best friend, it would be Fred. He was only a year older than me and had taken me under his wing when I first joined the Clutch's roster.

Fred had been instrumental in establishing the ease with which I gelled with the rest of the team, as a rookie coming from a school whose basketball program wasn't on D1 levels. The two of us had been dubbed the "Terrible Twosome" during that first year by the media, because of how we dominated the court. Our ability to anticipate what the other was thinking had helped us take the team to the championship five times, only losing once. I knew that my retirement would be hard for him; I just hope that he didn't let it affect our friendship. Fred really was like my third brother.

We didn't linger at the restaurant long after we finished eating. Fred was stopped by a few more fans at the door, but after a couple of photos, we were able to get to the car and head toward the area. There was only one team practice before Sunday's game, and that was simply for the players from different teams to get comfortable with each other. Today was the slam dunk contest and the rookie game. I didn't know which event I was more excited to see. The dudes who participated in the slam dunk contest always came with some straight nasty moves, but those young dudes straight out of college balled hard.

As we sat on the sidelines, waiting for the props to be set up, all I could think about was the phone number burning a hole in my phone. I'd been so frustrated that I didn't have a way to contact the woman who had caused me to lose sleep, that now that I had her number, I realized that I wasn't sure how I wanted to move forward. My first thought was to call her up right now and set something up for tonight after the rookie game. The look in her eyes when we were on that dance floor gave me some unforgettably vivid images of what might take place between us.

Then again, the way she scurried off left me with the impression that whatever I had seen in her eyes was something she hadn't intended. She'd almost looked spooked, in how she backed away slowly like I had been rabid dog liable to lunge at her throat at any sudden movement. Nah, I wouldn't call her. She needed something passive from me, something that wouldn't alarm her too much.

I pulled out my phone and navigated to my text messages. It was time for me to reach out to my goddess.

♥♥♥♥

Nedra

In all of my thirty-four years, I had never second-guessed myself as much as I had in the past in the past twelve hours. Not even throughout this situation with Chris. If he was to be believed, there was nothing I could have done differently that would have saved my marriage. I guess I had to agree with him because when I thought back over the years, there was no one "ah ha" moment that I felt contributed to our demise.

This new thing, however, was something completely foreign. I kept replaying the night before in my head, trying to pinpoint the exact moment when I made the wrong move. My morning could have consisted of that pussy massage that Ashton had mentioned if it weren't for me thinking before I spoke. The opportunity had been right there in front of me and I ran from it like a lil bitch. My mama would be so disappointed in me. When I climbed into bed at one-thirty in the morning, I was horny and disgusted with myself.

"Okay! I'm back!"

I was pulled out of my thoughts by Ashton's perky voice. She had instructed me to stay put while she left to get snacks almost an hour ago, and if I hadn't been thinking about my fuck up then I would have called, looking for her ass. There was no way the line was so long that it took her forty-five minutes to get back.

"Where have you been?"

She lifted the two trays of nachos and the drink carrier that she held into the air. "Getting the snacks, duh." She handed me one of the trays and gently shook the cardboard carrier at me.

Once I selected an amber-colored beverage from the carrier, I dropped it into the holder mounted on the back of the seat in front of me and eyed her. "That seemed longer than it usually takes to get chips and beer."

She shrugged. "I have no control over the lines." She sat her nachos in her lap and sipped from her own drink before giving me an excited look. "Ooh! Taste your drink, sissy! It's so good!"

I narrowed my eyes at her for a moment, but she didn't look to be spilling information, so I shook my head and took a sip of my drink. Ooh. It *was* good. I nodded at Ashton.

"This *is* bomb, girl. Where'd you find this?" It tasted like an artisanal craft beer, which was not something that I'd ever seen sold at any of the arena food kiosks.

Suddenly, something on the court became very interesting to her because her eyes darted all over the floor where this season's rookies were warming up for their game.

"Igotitfromaprivateloungedownstairs."

She'd mumbled the words so quickly that they all ran together. I sat there, trying to break up the sentence when she bounced in her seat, nearly spilling the contents of her plastic cup.

"Oh! Tell me about last night. What happened after I left?"

Just that fast, my curiosity morphed into frustration. "Girl, *nothing* happened last night." Nothing but my own self-sabotage, that is.

She cocked her head and observed me. "Well, that can't be true because you didn't text me that you'd made it home until after one. So, what did you do between the time that I left and the time you made it home?"

"I had some more drinks and danced with that guy from VIP."

"Hawk?"

I shrugged. "Shit, I don't know. Is that his name?" It sure as was hell fitting if so. Those first few moments after Ashton abandoned me in VIP had felt like I was being watched by a bird of prey.

"He didn't tell you?"

I shook my head and sipped my drink. "No. He just ordered me a drink, stared at me like I was the second coming of Christ, and pulled me out to the dance floor." It sounded so simple when I described it to Ashton, though, it was anything but. That man had devoured me with his eyes. I felt naked and revered, and it was the most nerve-wracking yet thrilling thing I had ever experienced.

Ashton's eyes lit up. "Ooh! Did you put your booty on his Gucci belt?"

I laughed at her song reference. "I don't know if it was Gucci, but I definitely sat my ass on that damn thing."

"I know that's right!" She held her hand up and I gave her a high-five. "So, then what happened?"

A heavy sigh escaped my lips as my momentary amusement fizzled. I sank back into my seat and recapped the ending of the previous night. The more I said, the deeper Ashton's frown grew until I barely recognized her face.

"Come on, Ash. Don't look at me like that."

I watched as she forced her face to relax. "What were you going to say to him?"

I already knew she meant on the dance floor. I sighed again. "I was going to ask him if he could put his celibacy on pause for one night."

Ashton gasped. "Ooh! You were feeling real bold, huh!?"

I giggled. "Not bold enough. I didn't say it."

She shook her head. "Not because you aren't bold. I think you were just scared."

Somehow, Ashton had hit the nail on the nose. "Damn, how did you guess that?" I dug into my now lukewarm nachos as I watched her contemplate her answer. Finally, she shrugged.

"I know you, sissy. This whole 'fuck niggas, get money' stance isn't you. You're not a one-night-stand type of chick."

I frowned, already regretting telling her about my new outlook on men. Maybe I wasn't in the past, but I could definitely be a one-night-stand type of chick now. It was possible; hell, stranger things had happened. Like Ashton's name being on *lists* and shit. Now *that* was strange!

"Correction: I *wasn't* a one-night-stand type of chick. It's a new year; I'm trying new things. Just consider it my new year resolution."

She gaped at me. "Did you really just try to compare hoeing to starting a new diet or working out? Really, sissy?"

I shrugged. "It's the same thing when you think about it. I'll be consuming more meat and getting plenty of vigorous exercise."

Ashton shrieked with laughter. "Nedra! I'm mad at how much sense that makes!"

I chuckled and sipped my beer. "Don't hate the player, hate the game."

She just shook her head and dug into her nachos. I followed suit and once again wondered what kiosk she'd gone to. The steak on these nachos was so tender that I could cut it with a tortilla chip. I started to repeat my question from earlier when my phone chimed, notifying me that I'd received a text message.

My fingers were covered in cheese sauce, so I decided to answer it later. Ashton must have heard the noise because she glanced at my purse, and her gaze lingered for a moment longer than necessary in my opinion.

She looked up at me. "Hey, so, I guess it's safe to say that you were feeling Hawk last night, right?"

I nodded. "I feel like that's an understatement. I was ready to solicit him for sex like some strung-out hooker." I laughed but Ashton didn't join in; she just looked thoughtful.

"Okay, hypothetically speaking: if you were to see him again, would you still want to take it there?"

I didn't even hesitate. "Hell yes. That man was grown-man fine, and I know he is working something serious because I felt that shit when we were dancing. He was actually being a gentleman last night because he kept trying to back up—I guess so I wouldn't feel him—but he ain't know that all I wanted to do was feel it. And it felt like it could put me to sleep." I pursed my lips. "Mm, mm, mm."

Ashton giggled. "So, you wish you could see him again?"

"I mean, everything happens for a reason. Maybe I wasn't meant to go there with him, and that's why it didn't happen."

Her eyes widened and I quirked a brow at the alarmed look on her face.

"Wha—"

"So, you *don't* want to see him again? You don't want to hear from him?"

I gave her a shrewd look. This heffa was up to something. Lucky for me, she couldn't hold water if I gave her a bucket.

"What did you do, Ashton?"

She gave me a furtive look. "I'm sorry!"

Her whining only annoyed me.

"I asked, *what did you do?*"

She wiped her fingers on a napkin and twisted the paper in her hands. "I gave Hawk your phone number."

I glared at her. I love Ashton—I swear I do—but this bitch was bad for my health. She constantly had my blood pressure all high because her paranoid behind had me thinking she did something horrible, only to find out that she was freaking out about meaningless ass shit. I took a deep breath in an attempt to calm my frazzled nerves.

"Ashton. My love. My boo. My sister from another mister—"

"Please don't be mad at me!"

I grabbed my beer and took a long sip from the plastic cup before dropping it back into the cup holder with a sigh.

"I'm not mad at you, Ashton. I'm annoyed with your dramatic ass, but I'm not mad at you."

She ducked her head, shamefaced. "Are you sure?"

"I said it, didn't I? When did you even have the opportunity to do that, though? You left before both of us."

No longer in fear of being yelled at, Ashton was back to her perky self, bouncing her slender shoulders and munching on a nacho. "Oh, I saw him this morning."

I tilted my head. "You saw him? Where?"

"At Fred's house. I was getting ready to leave when he showed up. He recognized me, though, and asked for your number."

There were so many things that I needed to get a handle on. "Wait, who is Fred?"

Ashton froze and her face got that panicked look again for a brief moment before she chuckled to herself and shook her head.

"Fred is the guy I left with last night."

I eyed her for a second, concerned about the bevy of emotions I'd just seen flit across her face. *What did she have going on?*

"Anyway! You got a text message and that reminded me of this morning. You should look at it; it might be from Hawk."

Oh, right. After Ashton's shenanigans, I'd forgotten all about the notification on my phone. I stuck the last chip from my tray into my mouth and wiped my fingers before digging into my purse to find my phone. The text had come from a number that wasn't saved in my phone. I squinted. The area code said 870, and I knew damn well that wasn't a Texas number.

"Sorry, Ash. I think this was some kind of spam. It's an 800 number." I started to swipe left to delete the message when Ashton grabbed my wrist.

"Wait, let me see."

I held up my phone, so she could see the number. After a glance, she pursed her lips and narrowed her eyes at me.

"This ain't no damn spam, Nedra!"

I snatched my phone back. "The hell it ain't! The only 800 numbers I know come with bill collectors on the other end." I didn't have time for them games today. All of my student loans were paid off years ago, and my credit cards weren't even close to being maxed out. They had no reason to be reaching out to me.

Ashton whipped out her phone and tapped the screen quickly. She shoved her phone under my nose, and my eyes damn near crossed. I leaned back and read the information on the search engine. I bucked my eyes at her.

"And? I don't know anyone from Arkansas, so this is definitely spam."

Ashton's sigh was full of frustration. "Why are you being so dense, sissy? That's Hawk who texted you. He's from Arkansas."

My eyes widened. *Oh.* Okay, that made sense.

I shrugged. "Well, how was I supposed to know that? Hell, how do you know that? Did y'all discuss that at breakfast as well?"

She picked up her beer and brought it to her mouth, mumbling under her breath, "Maybe if you'd read the message you'd know."

Was she giving me sarcasm?

"Okay, okay. I'll read it now." I tapped the notification and read the message.

UNKNOWN: I can't stop thinking about what you were going to say.

I guess Ashton was right. This had to be from him because this message, if read out of context, would be random as hell. I bit my lip. The knowledge that he was thinking about me like I was thinking about him was…heady. What I wanted to say was a tad too intimate to say through a text, though. I needed time to figure out a way to express what I wanted from him, now that we were no longer at the club and in a cloud of lust. I darkened my screen and put my phone back into my purse.

Ashton looked at me expectantly. "Was that him?"

I nodded and focused my attention on the court where the rookie game was beginning.

"Yeah, that was him."

CHAPTER NINE
Jermaine

"Aye, Hawk, look at this."

I peeled my eyes from the screen where I was watching an episode of *30 for 30* and looked up at Trina. She stood over me with my cell phone in her hand. I took the phone and squinted at the picture of me on the screen.

"What's this, Trina?"

"It's an Instagram post."

I cut my eyes at her. "I know that, smart ass. Why are you showing me this?" It looked like one of those man crush Monday posts, but it was from the day before on Sunday.

Trina ran my social media accounts and was instructed to like any post I was tagged in, as long as it was positive, and keep it moving. Unless I was tagged by someone I personally knew, she never even had cause to show me the post.

"Because this shit is funny as hell. Did you read the caption? She posted you for her Side-Nigga Sunday."

"Side-Nigga Sunday? What the hell is that? I've never heard of that shit before."

I now read the post with fresh eyes. It was a picture of me wearing a slim, pale blue suit and no tie. The first couple of buttons of my dress shirt were undone, and I sported a pair of fly, dark sunglasses. The picture was captured as I stepped out of a limousine and buttoned my jacket. I remembered the outfit as one I wore to the NBA Awards the previous year.

When I finished analyzing the picture, I read the caption.

> *@nedgotthatheat: My MCM position is closed until further notice but this man is just too fine to ignore so I had to create a new position just for him. #SideNiggaSunday #GrownManFine*

I smirked at that last hashtag and touched my thumb to the picture, frowning when my handle didn't appear anywhere on the screen. "What the...?"

Trina peered over my shoulder. "Oh, she didn't tag you."

"Then how did you find this?" There were only twenty likes on the picture and even fewer comments. I clicked the comments button and my question was answered for me as I saw where I had been tagged. Of the three comments, one was someone else agreeing that I was, indeed fine. The second comment, though, was the one that caught my eye.

> *@sunnyincaliashton: Heauxs get real bold on the innanets I swear. You know you want @jermainehawkins to be your #mancrusheveryday! Witcho lyin' azz!*

I chuckled at that one. The original poster didn't think it was too funny though and posted a responding comment.

> *@nedgotthatheat: @sunnyincaliashton I knew I should have blocked your creepin' ass a long time*

> *ago. I WILL hit that button if you tag another muthafucka in my comments though. Creepin' ass creep.*

Huh? Whoever this was, she posted about me but didn't want me to see it. It was unusual but not so odd that Trina would need to show it to me. I clicked the original poster's avatar picture to take me to her profile where I hoped to get better insight into what I was supposed to be seeing.

There was no description and almost all of the pictures were of food. I'd had to scroll through three weeks of pictures before I hit pay dirt. I sat up straight on the chair I'd been reclining in while I watched T.V.

There she was.

I vaguely heard Trina mumble a smug "Mmhmm" before she walked off and left the room.

The goddess—my goddess—smiled up at me through the five-inch screen of my cell phone. There was that sexy ass tapered fade that she wore. Those almond-shaped, rust-brown eyes that had regarded me warily at first while at VR were now open and inviting. The tantalizing bow-shaped lips that had been a sensual painted brown that night were a striking red in the picture on my screen.

Damn, I needed to see her again.

She had never responded to the text message I sent her on Saturday, and the way she practically ran away from me Friday made me hesitant to call her, for fear of her hanging up in my face. I might be tough, but getting hung up on was too much for even me. I even acted out of character and revisited VR after Sunday's game, hoping that she might show up.

My thumb hovered over the message button and, unbidden, I thought of what DB would say. I already knew. Just like my mama said, he'd been spinning that same line to us since we were youngins. He'd tell me that the women could wait.

"Pussy will always be there. Focus on ya hustle!"

I shook my head and hit the button. Nedra—my goddess—wasn't *just* pussy. It wasn't about pussy with her. Yeah, I'd like to know how hers felt on the inside but other than that, I felt something when I first saw her. I don't know what it was, but I couldn't ignore that it was there.

So, I slid into her DMs.

> **@jermainehawkins: Ignoring the fact that you never responded to my text message, I'm hurt that you've relegated me to side-nigga status. I'm definitely over-qualified for that position.**

Immediately, I locked the phone and set it on the armrest of the reclining chair. I didn't expect her to respond right away, and I'd be damned if I sat there staring at my message, over-analyzing that shit. I returned my attention to the screen and attempted to lose myself in the program. Five minutes later, my phone chimed, and I snatched it up quickly to see that I had a notification from Instagram. She'd replied to my message.

> **@nedgotthatheat: Nope. Side-niggas stay texting because they know better than to call. Looks like you're in the right position after all.**

She ended it with a winking emoji, and I guess it was supposed to be cute, but I felt like she'd just chumped me off. I'd sent her a text message because of how leery she had seemed to be of me at VR. Now, after reading her message, I wish I had followed my first thought and called her. That could be corrected, though. I scrolled through my contacts until I found her name. Pressing the video camera, I waited while the phone dialed.

Seconds later, the face I had just been admiring filled my screen. I raised my eyebrow at the scowl she wore.

"Hold up. Why that face?"

"I'm trying to see why you video called me instead of voice

called me."

I chuckled. "Because I wanted to hear your voice AND see your face."

Her mouth dropped into an "o" just like it had that night but this time, she recovered quickly, biting her lip for a second before speaking.

"Oh."

I cleared my throat. "So, uh. How do I get promoted from side-nigga status? Do I have to kill the first nigga?" I knew without a doubt that there had to be a dude lurking somewhere. A woman as fine as she was, as dynamic as she was, couldn't possibly be single. It defied physics.

She laughed and it was a throaty sound that shot a zing of desire to my dick. "Nah, he killed himself." She said it so nonchalantly, I had to wonder what ole boy had done.

I whistled. "Damn. How did he do that?"

I watched as she pulled her bottom lip into her mouth and chewed on it for a second before she answered me. I wonder if she knew how expressive her face was. She was contemplating telling me, and I could clearly see that she was both nervous and sad about it. Eventually, she rolled her eyes and huffed.

"He divorced me."

I felt my eyebrows shoot towards the ceiling. Damn. I wasn't expecting that. "Oh, shit. I'm sorry."

"Me too." She muttered that so low that she probably thought I didn't hear it. Her eyes fell to something in her lap, and I could see the melancholy instantly overcome her.

"Well, since there's a vacancy, put ya boy on."

She rewarded my teasing with a smirk.

"Sorry, Hawk, that position has been dissolved."

Instantly, I corrected her. "Jermaine."

"What?" Her brows met with confusion. I didn't blame her; I had been a bit abrupt. As soon as my nickname fell out of her mouth, I knew that it wasn't right. I didn't want her to address me the way that everyone, outside of my family, did.

"Call me Jermaine."

"Why?"

The question surprised me. I mean, I didn't expect her to get giddy over my request for her to be on a first-name basis, but I *did* expect her to just do it. Also, I didn't really know what to tell her. I couldn't say that it didn't "sound right". That shit didn't make sense.

"Because I asked you to."

She tilted her head. "Excuse me? You know what I'm asking you. Everyone calls you Hawk. Why do you want me to call you something different?"

I shrugged and my eyes flitted over to the television. "I mean...it's my name, so..."

She sucked her teeth. Annoyance was written all over her face. "You know what? I'm gonna go. I don't have time for bullshit, and I see that's what you're on, so I'll leave you to that."

Then my phone beeped twice, and I found myself staring at the call log. She hung up on me. Actually hung the fuck up on me. I couldn't believe that shit.

"What the fuck?"

I wanted to say more, but the cryo-sleeve wrapped around my knee buzzed, signaling the end of my session. Trina walked in just as I was bending over to unzip the sleeve. She perched on the arm of the chair and watched as I maneuvered the sleeve off and slowly bent my knee.

"So, did you pull a creep move and slide into her DMs?"

I frowned. "That ain't creep shit."

She laughed. "It definitely is and that must be a yes. Did she respond?"

I nodded, reveling in how loose my knee felt. I'd been blessed thus far not to have any major injuries during my career, but I still beat my body up several times a week so, I made it a point to get in some physical therapy on a regular basis.

"What'd she say?"

I handed Trina my phone to get her to stop asking questions.

Her slender fingers moved deftly across the screen, and her eyes moved fast as she read our short exchange.

"Okay," she trailed off, the word dragging out for seconds. "What happened after this?"

I transferred the sleeve to my other leg and started the session. Then I recalled the even shorter video chat for Trina. When I was done, Trina gave me a dumb look.

"Okay, what's *that* look for?"

"Why didn't you just tell her why?"

I knew she meant why I asked the goddess to call me by my first name instead of the nickname everyone addressed me as. I sighed.

"Shit, I didn't know it would be that big of a deal."

Trina leaned away from me and tossed her long braids over her shoulder. *"You ain't got to lie, Craig."*

I laughed at the *Friday* quote. "I'm not lying, Trina. That 'Hawk' shit didn't even sound good coming out of her mouth. It ain't feel right. I want her to call me Jermaine because that's my name. That's me."

Trina squinted her eyes at me for a moment then a smile appeared on her face. "Call her back."

"What?" My neck jerked back and I frowned. "She hung up on me; she doesn't want to talk to me right now." Plus I hated to be hung up on. I was contemplating not calling her again for a while.

Trina rolled her eyes and stood up. Her fingers started moving over the screen of my phone, which she still held in her hands. When she handed it back to me, it was ringing and I noticed she had initiated a second video call to the goddess. "I guarantee she wants to talk to you. Just give her the details behind your answer, and you'll be fine."

I nodded. She checked the cryo-sleeve on my leg before turning to exit the room just as an irritated face filled my screen. I know it was cliched as hell, but she really was cute when she was mad. I laughed at the expression on her face.

"Are you always going to answer the phone looking like you'd rather be picking up dog shit than talking to me?"

If her widening eyes were any indication, my question had surprised her. She scowled even harder. "If that time ever comes, I'll be sure to let you know."

"*Man,* stop fronting. If you didn't want to talk to me, you wouldn't have answered the phone." I was right and it was written all over her face that she hated to admit it. She shrugged.

"It's not every day that *Hawk* calls a regular ass woman such as myself."

I narrowed my eyes at her image on my screen. "I told you to call me Jermaine."

She cocked her head to the side. "And when you failed to give a reasonable excuse for that, I decided to continue calling you what all the other regular ass people in the world do."

"First of all, you're far from a regular ass person. You don't even carry yourself like you think that's true, so chill out with that mess. Second of all, Jermaine is my name, so that's what I want you to call me. Unless you're from The House, *Hawk* is the celebrity shit that I'm not trying to be on with you. I just want to talk to you and get to know you. I'm just a ugly nigga trying to holla at a beautiful woman like all the other regular ass niggas do." I gave her a taste of her own medicine and threw her words back at her.

Her lips were pursed as she tried to keep from laughing. I widened my eyes comically, and she bust out laughing, throwing her head back and exposing that smooth neck that I wanted to put my lips back on.

"Don't be calling my phone, lying and shit. We both know you are not ugly."

I shrugged and feigned modesty. "I don't know if we *both* know that."

She smacked her lips. "I'm not about to stroke what I'm sure is an already highly inflated ego."

I bit my tongue to keep from saying the nasty shit her words brought to mind. She gave me a knowing look and licked her lips.

I reached down to adjust my hardened erection in my shorts, and although she couldn't see my action, her eyes tracked me anyway. *Shit.* Hunger burned in her eyes, and I wondered how long it had been since she'd gotten some.

I needed to change the subject.

"How long have you been divorced?"

Her eyes rolled around the room. "I'm actually expecting a call from my lawyer any day now. We had to go back and adjust some agreements but my divorce should be finalized like yesterday. Just in time for him to get a celebratory trip in during spring break before he has to go back to work."

I hated the bitterness in her voice and hated myself even more for bringing up her ex and putting it there. Second change of topic coming right up.

"Shoot me your address. You're going to come kick it with me tonight."

Those rust-brown eyes squinted at me. She tried to give me a look of distrust, but that expressive ass face of hers let me know she was thrilled by my declaration.

"How you just gon' tell me what I'm going to do?"

I smirked. "Like I just did. Stop fronting like you don't want to rub on this milk dud and stroke my…ego…some more. So, come over, eat a good meal, bowl some strikes, and kick it wit ya boy."

She looked contemplative as she mulled over my suggestion. Then she met my gaze. "What if I just want dick and not dinner?"

I blinked. Well damn. The matter-of-fact way she said that was sexy as fuck. The idea had merit but… I pressed my hand to my chest in mock outrage. "I am a gentleman! You will not gain access to my body before, at least, showing me a good time first."

Her lips twitched, and I knew she wanted to laugh, but she successfully held it in this time. She sighed and rolled her eyes. "Fine. I'll do dinner, but your ugly ass better put out."

Surprised, I sputtered before throwing my head back and laughing. "Damn, girl, you're vicious."

She giggled. "And don't ever forget it."

I shook my head. "Trust me, I won't. Listen, I have to head down to the gym so, I'm going to go, but I'll see you tonight. And don't forget to *send me your address*." I emphasized my directive.

"Okay, okay. I'll do it as soon as we're disconnected."

I grinned. "That's what's up. Talk to you later, goddess."

"Uh, bye?" Her face was the picture of confusion, and I realized that my nickname for her had slipped out.

Ah, shit. I hadn't meant for her to hear that, but sooner or later it would've been inevitable. I pressed the red button and waited until the call log came up before I locked my phone and set it on the arm of the chair. I reached to unzip the cryo-sleeve, which had buzzed before I ended my call. Lifting my leg, I slowly bent it a couple of times. It felt amazing. I snatched up my phone and headed down to the first floor of my home where the gym was located.

As I hit the top of the stairs, my phone chimed. I touched the screen and smiled. She'd sent me her address. I unlocked the phone and pulled up my contacts. After a couple of rings, the call was connected.

"Hello?"

The smooth voice on the other end widened my smile.

"Hey, Mama, what are you up to?"

"Hey baby, I'm out with Sandra. We just had lunch and are headed back to the house."

"Okay, cool. Can you cook a lil something tonight? I'm having someone over, and I promised to feed them." I tried to keep the details vague, but my mama was like a bloodhound with how she sniffed me out.

"You want me to cook dinner? For you and some woman?"

I groaned as I landed on the bottom step. "That's not what I said."

"Hmph. It ain't what you didn't say either."

I rounded the corner of the living room and headed to the back of the house where the gym was located off of the garage. "What does that even mean, Mama?"

"That means that if you were expecting some of the boys from the team, then you would have said that. If this was an impromptu business meeting, you would have said that. You're always forthcoming."

Until now. She didn't say it, but I heard it loud and clear, regardless. I stopped outside of the gym and sighed heavily. The barrage of questions she was sure to launch at me was already stressing me out.

"Aight, Mama, I get it. Yes, I'd like you to cook dinner tonight for me and the woman who is coming over to join me."

I pulled the phone away from my ear as she squealed, "I can't believe you've kept this from me! How long have you been seeing this mystery woman?"

"Whoa, whoa. Calm down, woman! I haven't been 'seeing' anyone. I just met her a couple of days ago and extended the invite about ten minutes before I called you. It's not that serious, Mama. Just dinner."

She didn't even hesitate. "I'm on my way to the house to cook a romantic meal for a woman you met two days ago. This is the first woman you've invited to the house since you built it, ten years ago, but you're telling me it's not that serious? Hmm?" I heard rustling and then my aunt's voice in the background. She sounded far away, and I couldn't make out what she was saying but I heard my mama's responses clearly.

"I know that's right, Sandra!"

"He's just delusional, girl!"

"Huh? Girl I know. I guess denial ain't just a river in Egypt." She let out a hearty laugh, apparently tickled with her own joke, before returning to our conversation.

"You still there, baby?"

I gritted my teeth. "Yes, ma'am."

"Uh-uh. Don't give me that tone. You're the one lying. The question is, who are you lying to; me or yourself?"

I wanted to bang my head against the wall. All I asked for was dinner. If I didn't think Mama would have been offended, I would have commissioned a private chef and called it a night. Whenever she came down, she did all of the cooking at my house and wouldn't let anyone but her twin sister, my aunt Sandra, even touch a pot or pan.

"C'mon, Mama."

"Alright, fine. I'll leave you alone—for now. To answer your question, yes, I will cook a 'lil something' for you and your guest tonight. Just know, I *will* talk to you about this later, and you'd better leave the lies somewhere else when speaking to me."

I grinned. "Yes, ma'am. Thanks, Mama. Talk to you later."

With a swipe of my thumb, I disconnected the call and shook my head. I pushed open the door of the gym and nodded at Boobie as our eyes met through the mirror. He was sitting on a bench, doing bicep curls and taking pictures on his phone. I rolled my eyes at the sight. Boobie stayed on social media more than Trina, and she managed all of my accounts.

I plucked a pair of headphones off a shelf near the door and dropped down onto the leg press. For the next hour and a half, I cycled through a few different machines and weights, with Boobie spotting me, before ending my session with a series of stretches to help me stay flexible and loose and to prevent any muscle cramps. I was drenched in sweat, so I know I had done something right. Upon exiting the gym, I saw my Pops and Ja'mya in the kitchen, pulling ingredients out of the refrigerator.

"What y'all got going on in here?"

My niece ran over to me with her arms stretched wide but stopped quick just before reaching me. Her nose wrinkled up, and she took a step back.

"Ew, you're super sweaty Unc. And stinky."

I chuckled at the disgust on her face. "I just finished working out, J-Baby. Sweat happens."

"I know that. I'll just wait to hug you until after you take a shower."

Both Pops and Boobie bust out laughing, and I gave her mock pout.

"That's cold, J-Baby."

She shook her head and backed up a few more steps. "I'm sorry Unc, but it has to be this way."

I crept toward her and her eyes widened in sheer horror.

"If you loved me, you would hug me no matter what I smell like."

"Uh uhn. I had a sex-ed class this week, and they told me I don't have to prove my love to nobody."

My jaw dropped, and I froze mid-step. I knew she was getting older, but hearing the word "sex" come out of my baby niece's mouth jarred me. On the other hand, I was glad to hear the message they were teaching her at the private elementary school that she attended. I leaped toward her, and she let out a high-pitched scream before diving behind my Pops who puffed out his chest and stood arms akimbo.

"If you want my grandbaby, you're going to have to go through me first."

I squinted at him then pointed two of my fingers toward my eyes before swinging them in Ja'mya's direction, letting her know that I was watching her.

I held my hands up and backed away slowly.

"You got this, Pops. I'll see you later for my hug, J-Baby."

I left the kitchen and headed up to my room to shower. I dressed simply in a pair of dark-rinse jeans, an orange t-shirt, and all-black sneakers. As soon as I left my room, the smell of garlic and tomatoes carried me into the kitchen. There I found my mama, standing at the stove, stirring something in a pot. I hugged my aunt Sandra who sat at the island, slicing vegetables then kissed my mama on the cheek.

"Smells good mama."

She smirked at me, and I braced myself when I saw the calculating look in her eyes.

"Thanks, baby. I hope your *company* likes it."

I backed away from her, leaning against the countertop of the island. "Aww, Mama, come on with all of that."

She turned her back to me and continued stirring. "What?"

"Shit, you making me wish I hadn't invited her over."

Her back still to me she quipped, "Why? 'Cause I called you on your bullshit?"

"Man, that wasn't bullshit. It really can't be anything serious with her." I hated it but I had to be realistic. As soon as she said the words, I knew that I had to ease down on the brakes. I wasn't going to take advantage of a vulnerable woman by trying to insert myself into her life romantically, but I still wanted to be around her.

Mama spun back around and eyed me. "And why is that?"

I pushed out a breath. "She is going through a divorce. It's almost final, but it's still fresh for her. It's probably too soon for something serious."

She exchanged a look with my aunt that I couldn't decipher and waved her hand at me as if she was dismissing my explanation.

"It can't be too fresh if she's coming over here tonight."

My shoulders lifted and dropped. "I didn't really ask her all of that. I just told her she was coming over."

Aunt Sandra laughed. "You can't make a woman do anything, boy! You oughta know that by now, old as you is."

"I know that's right, Sandra!" Mama chimed in, agreeing with her sister. To me, she said, "If she didn't want to come here, trust me, she wouldn't. Hell, you wouldn't have even gotten close enough to extend the invitation. Best believe, however she feels about her divorce, she is open to something with you. Whether it's that thing between your legs or something else. Whether she know it or not. She open."

I tugged on the hair at my chin while I contemplated what these wise women in my life had to say. I hadn't had a thorough enough conversation with the goddess to really know where her head was at, and so their advice could go either way. Either extremely right or very, very wrong. She didn't shut me down when I said I wanted to get to know her, but in the same conversation she admitted she wanted sex only.

Trying to keep up with all the thoughts swimming around in my head was making me cross-eyed. I sighed and pushed off from the counter.

"Aight, I'm leaving to go pick her up. I'll be back in about an hour or so."

My mama's head snapped up from the shallow dishes she was lining up on the island. "You're going to pick her up?"

The disbelief in her voice made me frown. "Uh, is that a problem?"

Once again, she shared a look with her sister. This time, she gave me a blinding smile afterward. "No problem at all, baby. Tell Boobie to drive safe."

The way she said that seemed…weird. She was being weird. "Boobie ain't driving, Mama, I am."

Her eyes widened and she brought her hand to her chest. "Sandra, get the smelling salts. This boy is trying to make me pass out!"

I burst out into laughter. Why was this woman so damn crazy? "Bye, Mama." I opened the cabinet that held hooks filled with keys and grabbed a set before kissing her on the cheek and leaving the room. Boobie was reclining on the couch, playing on his phone. "Aye, Boobie, let's roll." He lifted his big body from the couch and followed me down the hallway and into the garage.

I hit a button on the key fob and the lights on the Panamera flashed. We climbed inside, and I backed out of the garage.

After the way my mama had reacted to this little dinner date I had orchestrated, I was uncharacteristically nervous. In truth, I'd not brought a woman to my house since I signed with the Clutch, and we moved to Houston. Even before building my house, I knew better than that shit, especially when I first entered the league. If I didn't know anything about professional ball, DB made sure that I knew about the groupies and gold diggers that came along with it. To my knowledge, he had never stepped foot on a court or field, but somehow, he seemed to know something about everything.

It was hard work as a young dude dealing with sudden—and seemingly instant—fame, but thanks to my parents sticking to my side diligently and placing family around me at all times, I was able to skate through those first couple of years without issue. I started dating once I hit my third year in the league. I met some nice women and had a good time, but my focus was always on my career, so I steered clear of anything too heavy.

The fact that I preferred to stay out of the limelight was beneficial in that realm as well. Most women I met wanted to be seen. They wanted to be in the lifestyle pages of magazines and tapped for interviews that would air on entertainment shows. The only place I traveled without being incognito was to Pine Bluff, and that was too far from the camera's lens for them. I never tripped about it, though. So many of my colleagues were in and out of the media behind some bullshit related to a woman, and I was cool on all of that.

Lost in my thoughts, before I knew it, I was pulling into a driveway and the GPS was announcing that I had arrived at my destination. I glanced over at my cousin.

"Gon' hit that backseat, playboy."

Boobie chuckled. "Damn, it's like that?"

"Hell yeah, I'm not going to make her ride in the backseat like a little kid or some shit."

"Oh, but I gotta ride like that?"

"Bruh—"

He laughed. "I'm just fucking with you, Hawk. It ain't no thang." Then he climbed out of the front and settled into the back. "Damn, bro, how she got you wide open already, and you ain't even hit yet?"

I ran my hands down my face. There was no use in denying it. Boobie was with me that night at VR; he saw how affected I was.

"I don't even know, man."

He reached forward and clapped me on the shoulder. "Well, good luck."

I lifted my chin in acknowledgment and slid out of the car,

heading up a short flight of steps that led to a small wooden porch. I knocked and stepped back to wait for the door to be answered. When it swung open, she stood on the other side with a smile on her face. Tonight, her lips were painted black, and at that moment, I was sure that every color looked good against her warm-brown skin.

I watched her eyes quickly do a head-to-toe evaluation of me before she met my gaze. "Hey."

My lips curved up. "What's up; you ready to come kick it?"

She nodded. "Yeah, let me grab my purse."

When she turned away from the door, I admired the curve of her ass in the long-sleeved babydoll dress she wore. The top was fitted against her ample breasts and flared out once it hit her waist. The sheer fabric stopped mid-thigh and although it was loose around her body, it displayed her shape in a way I had no choice but to appreciate.

She returned, shrugging into a lightweight denim jacket and pulling the long, thin strap of her purse over her head. After shutting the door behind her and locking it, she raised her eyebrows at me. "Lead the way."

I nodded, jogging down the steps and opening the door on the passenger side.

"Thanks," she murmured as she slid inside the car.

I shut the door firmly and crossed in front of the car, climbing inside and buckling my seatbelt.

"Nedra, that's my cousin, Boobie, back there. Boobie, this is Nedra."

She tilted her head and looked at me. "I didn't think you knew my name."

I chuckled. "What?"

"Well, with that 'goddess' business you tried to sneak on me earlier, I figured you—" She stopped talking abruptly and her eyes widened, then she gasped.

CHAPTER TEN

Nedra

"Did you say Boobie?" Jermaine nodded slowly as he eyed me curiously, no doubt confused by my sudden reaction. "Yeah..."

I didn't care how crazy I might have seemed at that moment; I screeched, "Turn the lights on!"

To his credit, he didn't even question me; he simply reached for the control panel on his left. Immediately, light flooded the car, and I swiveled around to see the man in the backseat. The name 'Boobie' wasn't a common name, and I needed to know if he was the same guy from that day at the vegetarian restaurant. When my eyes adjusted to the soft light, I saw that he was, indeed, the man I was thinking of. From the look on his face, he recognized me as well.

"It's *you*!" I accused.

He held his hands up in surrender. "I'm just an innocent bystander."

"The fuck you are! You's a rude ass muthafucka is what you

are! Now, I can bust your ass like I should have done that day!" I was almost screaming but I didn't give a fuck. I was *hot*. All of the anger I'd felt that day came rushing back, along with all of the clapbacks I'd thought of long after me and Shanice had left.

Boobie's gaze slid over to the driver seat where Jermaine was looking back and forth between the two of us.

"Hawk, man. That's hot sauce. Get ya girl, man."

Jermaine frowned, apparently unconcerned with my outburst or elevated tone, and put a hand on my exposed knee. "Aye, what's going on?"

I shivered at the warmth his touch sent through me then huffed out an annoyed breath. Now was not the time to be getting distracted; shit needed to be handled.

"I've met Boobie before. A few weeks ago I had a…run in with him at this vegetarian restaurant in the Heights." Even though some time had passed, seeing him again had brought all of my anger back to the surface. I wish I could put his big ass in a full nelson or a fucking sleeper hold. I wanted to kick his ass for how he'd made me feel that day. I glanced at Jermaine, and my eyebrows raised in confusion at the look he was giving me. His jaw had dropped open, and it was almost like he was seeing me for the first time.

"That was you?"

"What do you—" I stopped when I realized what he was asking me. I sat back in my seat heavily. *Oh my god*. Jermaine was the baller with Boobie that day. Taking pictures, hunched over his plate, bald. *Oh. My. God!* He'd seen me in "go mode". Damn, was he going to renege on his invitation and ask me to get out of his car? I glanced at him, and to my surprise, he started laughing.

"Uh…" I didn't really know what to say. I looked back at Boobie, but he just shrugged and cut his eyes away from me to look out the window.

Jermaine clutched his stomach as he laughed harder. "Bruh, are you telling me that the woman who went the fuck off on Boobie at The Greenery is sitting in my front seat right now? No bull? Man,

I swear I can't make this shit up."

"So...you aren't mad that I cursed him out?"

Jermaine shook his head as he wiped tears from his eyes. He was still chuckling and even though I was slightly worried, the sight of him laughing brought a smile to my face. His chestnut eyes crinkled as his cheeks lifted in merriment at the situation.

"Not at all. He deserved it. I stay telling that nigga not to talk to people like that. I even called him out on it that day." He took a deep breath as the last of his laughter died off and looked over at me. He shot a look back at Boobie then winked at me and squeezed my knee. "You're good, I promise." Then, just like nothing had happened, he backed out of the driveway and pulled onto the road.

I twisted in my seat to face Boobie. His face was in his cell phone, and the glow from the phone lit up his face.

"Boobie."

He looked up at me. "What's up?"

"We good?" I extended my fist toward him.

A moment passed where he eyed my fist, and I thought he was going to object but then a smile graced his handsome face, revealing straight white teeth, and he bumped my fist with his own.

"Yeah, we good. Also, lemme apologize for that shit at the restaurant, though. I was just looking out for my boy. He won't say anything, but I can tell when he is tired of having to be 'on'. I thought you were another fan, but even still, I handled you wrong and for that, I apologize."

I nodded, apology instantly accepted. I had no grudge to hold for a man who was mature enough to admit his faults. "I appreciate that." I licked my lips and asked the question that had been on my mind since that day at The Greenery. "So why do they call you Boobie?"

Jermaine laughed loudly. "*Man*, we call him Boobie because he was breastfed until he was five-years-old."

"Five-years-old?" I looked between the two of them.

Boobie shifted in the back seat. "That shit is perfectly normal, bruh."

Jermaine shook his head, still laughing. "Nah, nigga. That shit is odd as fuck."

Boobie looked at me. "Extended breastfeeding is normal and even expected in a lot of cultures. Americans are just caught up in the image of the hypersexualized woman, and that's why they can't stomach the sight of her body being used for its intended purpose."

I blinked. I sure as hell wasn't expecting *that* argument from the giant in the backseat. I racked my brain for what I learned about breastfeeding in my recent research.

"I bet you are rarely sick, huh."

Boobie grinned. "I *never* get sick. No bull."

Jermaine snorted. "That's 'cause your ass was vaccinated."

"Nigga, your bitch ass was vaccinated too and yet you were laid up with the flu last year. Missed four games. Explain that shit!"

I expected a quick retort but instead, Jermaine laughed. "I can't explain that one, bruh."

A chuckle sounded from the backseat. "That's what the fuck I thought. Breast is best, motherfucker."

I joined in on the laughter at that point. These dudes were wild, but I loved how chill they were and how comfortable they were with each other. It made it easy for me to relax. I leaned back in my seat and rode in silence.

As I stared out the window, I noticed that the lights illuminating the highway started to get fewer and fewer, and there were no street lights whatsoever after leaving the exit ramp.

"It's really dark out here."

Jermaine glanced at me then back at the road. He switched on his high beams. "Yeah, they don't care about street lights out in the country."

I looked at him. "The country?"

Boobie's voice chimed in from the backseat. "Hell yeah; it's like back at The House out here. Once they roll the streets up, it's pitch black until sunrise."

The House. Jermaine had mentioned that during our video call earlier.

"What's The House?"

Jermaine shot a quick grin at me before turning his attention back to the road.

"The House is back home."

"That's Pine Bluff, baby!"

That's right; Ashton said he was from Arkansas. I nodded. "Oh, okay."

I glanced at Boobie then back at Jermaine before pressing my face to the window just in time to catch a sign informing us that we'd reached Needville city limits. The population was less than the total enrollment at my high school when I was a senior. I guess this is what he meant by 'out in the country'. We couldn't have been but forty minutes outside of downtown, and it took less time than that to get here from Shanice's house.

Jermaine steered the car down a dirt road and drove about a mile down before turning onto a paved driveway. He stopped the car, waiting for a large wrought-iron gate, with an H emblem in the center, to roll open. As soon as he drove through, the gate pushed closed and I gasped.

There were lights in the paved driveway leading up the house. Like actually inside the ground. "Oh my god," I muttered, amazed by what I was seeing. "How in the world are there lights *inside* the asphalt?"

Jermaine chuckled. "They're solar lights. It's a concept that a local company, Power Up, has been working on. I've known the owner since I first moved to Houston and was all over the idea when he first told me about it. I think I was the first residential client to get these, so I guess you could say I volunteered to be a guinea pig."

I was highly impressed. I'd heard of solar power and all of its benefits and was thinking of having it at my future gun range; if I ever got the idea off the ground.

"*That* is awesome."

"Thanks. The whole house runs off of solar, actually. I'm not even connected to the power grid." He laughed again as he drove the car into an empty spot in the brightly lit, open garage and parked. "The city isn't too happy with me about that, though. I got a lot going on out here, and they hate to miss those coins."

Boobie climbed out of the car, and I reached for the door handle, but Jermaine's hand on my arm stopped me from pushing it open. I looked at him.

"Don't get out." He jogged around to my side of the car and pulled my door open, offering me his hand. I took it and let him pull me out of the car then push the door closed behind me. Still holding my hand, he led me across a garage so large, it resembled a showroom at a dealership. We went through a door and entered what must have been a mudroom. He removed and hung up his jacket on one of the several hooks on the wall beside the door before turning to help me do the same. Then he grabbed my hand again and headed through a second door. The smell of Italian food hit me and I moaned in appreciation.

"Oh my god, it smells so good in here."

Jermaine smirked down at me but said nothing. I followed him down a hallway, which spilled out into the kitchen where the aroma intensified. I opened my mouth to comment on it again but stopped abruptly when I saw who all occupied the kitchen.

Boobie was there, leaning over the island, along with two older women who looked just alike, and a younger woman. They all stopped talking when we entered and I tensed. Jermaine, who still held my hand, looked back at me and squeezed my hand. I guess he meant it to be reassuring, but all I felt was anxiety. This was a whole hell of a lot of people for what I thought was supposed to be a dine and dick situation. He pulled me to stand next to him and placed a hand on my back.

"Everyone, this is Nedra. Nedra, that's my mama, Sabrina." He pointed to one of the older women who stood closest to us. She wore black and white checkered pedal pushers and a white button down with the sleeves rolled up which was covered with an apron. Her hair was away from her face in a curled ponytail at the base of her neck, exposing her smooth mahogany skin and youthful face. She gave me a kind, if not calculating, smile.

Jermaine pointed to the second older woman, who was no doubt his mother's twin sister. "That's my aunt Sandra." She was on the opposite side of the large island from where we stood. She wore a similar outfit to Jermaine's mother, but her hair was in a curly bob. I returned the nod she aimed at me.

The last unfamiliar person in the room was the younger woman. "This is my lil cousin, Trina, and you already know Boobie." Trina moved from where she stood next to Sandra and rounded the island. She surprised me by wrapping her arms around me in a tight hug.

"Hey, girl." She pulled back and gave me the big smile. "You look like a deer caught in headlights. I promise we ain't that bad."

Jermaine pushed his arm in between us and playfully pushed Trina back. "Back, back, Trina. You gon' scare her off."

"Nah, you will, springing the whole family on her like this." Trina stuck her tongue out at him and propped a hand on her hip. "Did you even tell her we'd all be here?"

I shook my head and laughed. "He definitely did not, but it's all good."

"Katrina! Get on out that girl's face!"

Trina spun around at looked at Jermaine's aunt Sandra. "I was just saying hi, Mommy. Dang!"

The older woman clicked her tongue. "How about you 'dang' yourself on over here and help us get the rest of this food on the table so we can get out of their hair."

Everyone but Sandra laughed. Jermaine cleared his throat. "Where's Pops?"

Sabrina looked up from the dish she was filling with cooked spaghetti noodles.

"He and Jeremiah took Ja'mya skating."

Jermaine grinned as he eyed Trina. "Whaaat? And you didn't

go with them, Ms. Roll Bounce? As much as you love to skate, I'm surprised you passed up an opportunity."

Trina rolled her eyes, and Sandra slapped her arm.

"She was too busy trying to be nosy."

Everyone chuckled, but my eyes widened at that. Was my presence that interesting? I glanced up at Jermaine and was startled to find his gaze already on me, observing me with that bird-of-prey intensity of his. I took a deep breath and stepped further into the kitchen, eyeing the pots on the stove. "Is there anything I can do to help?"

Jermaine tugged on my hand. "Nah, you—"

"*Yes*, there is," Sabrina spoke over her son. "How about you finish filling the breadbasket and bring it into the dining room?"

"Mama—" He started.

"*No problem.*" This time, I was the one to speak over him. I pulled free of his grasp and moved over to the island, picking up the set of tongs that lay on the sheet tray and moving the thick slices of what had to be homemade garlic bread into the basket on the countertop next to the tray. When it was near overflowing, I picked it up at looked at Sabrina for further instructions.

With a nod at Trina, she said, "She'll show you where to take it."

I turned to Trina, who aimed a wide smile in my direction and chimed for me to follow her. The glass pitcher she carried was filled with brown liquid that I hoped was extra sweet tea. I smirked at Jermaine as I passed him on the way out of the kitchen. He was pouting! I couldn't believe it. You'd think I had decided to leave instead of simply help set the table that we would be eating at.

"Don't be such a baby," I murmured at him. He frowned even harder, and I had to laugh.

I followed Trina to an area just off of the kitchen, which I discovered was the dining room. There was a long cherry wood table surrounded by eight place settings and dotted with floral centerpieces. I set the breadbasket down on the runner in between to centerpieces and turned to find Trina standing right behind me.

"Where are you going to sit?"

My brows furrowed. "I don't know yet; is there assigned seating or something?"

She giggled and touched my arm briefly before going back into the kitchen. I followed slowly but just before I reached the kitchen, Jermaine appeared in front of me. He grabbed my hand and pulled me back toward the dining room.

"Is that everything," I asked him.

He nodded. "Yeah, they have the rest of it."

Right as the last syllable left his mouth, Sabrina and Sandra entered, carrying the last of the dishes of food into the room. Once Sabrina set down the ceramic bowl in her hands, she waited for Sandra to do the same with the rectangular dish she carried, and they both turned to Jermaine.

"Y'all are all set." She smiled at me. "You enjoy this meal, ya hear."

I smiled back, confused. "Aren't y'all joining us?"

I looked around to see that Trina and Boobie hadn't come back, and Sandra had moved to the entrance of the room. Sabrina hesitated, and I glanced over at Jermaine, once again surprised to see his attention was already on me.

"I'm just saying; it's kind of crazy that they cooked all of this food, and they aren't going to eat it with us. That ain't right."

It sure as hell didn't *feel* right. I don't know how he operated on a regular basis, but I did not feel comfortable with the thought of his family going out to dinner or worse, eating in the kitchen while the two of us sat in the dining room at this big ass table. He didn't say a word, just tugged on his goatee.

Sabrina touched my arm. "I appreciate that baby, but it's fine."

Jermaine spoke up. "Nah, Mama, she's right. We don't even get down like that. You know when I'm home, we eat together."

"If you're sure…"

He nodded. "Yeah, go ahead and call everybody back."

Sabrina looked back at Sandra and nodded, then both women

disappeared down the hallway.

Jermaine pulled out a chair and indicated for me to sit down. "You know she gon' love you now, right?"

I laughed and slid into the seat. "If she loves me because I insisted that she eats the food that she cooked, then I really have to question what kind of selfish ass women you've been fucking with."

Before he could respond, his mother and aunt reappeared with Trina and Boobie behind them. Trina headed right for me and bent, pulling me into another tight hug.

"Thank you! I really wanted some of this parmigiana."

I laughed and tried to lean away from her a little bit. Intentional or not, her titties on the side of my face was too much. She was holding me so tight that if I opened my mouth one of her nipples would fall right in.

"Sis, I'm glad you're happy, but I'm gonna need you to back-back and give me at *least* fifty feet."

"*Trina.*"

"Katrina!"

"Aye, man, chill out with all of that."

She let me go and backed up a few feet. Jermaine, Sandra, and Boobie were all calling out to Trina, and I felt a little bad. I didn't want them to gang up on her. I smiled at her.

"It's all good. Just…personal space, okay, boo?" She winked at me and crossed to the other side of the table where Sandra was waiting to grab her arm and whisper in her ear. My eyebrows shot up, and I looked at Jermaine who laughed and finally dropped down into the seat next to me.

He draped his arm across the back of my chair and leaned in until his lips were near my ear and his goatee tickled my neck.

"It looks like my cousin has a crush on you."

I smirked at him and grabbed the nearest serving spoon, loading my plate with spaghetti then held my hand out for his. That was obvious.

"Of course she does; I'm cute as fuck." He laughed and handed me his plate. "Plus, I'm witty and know how to dress for my shape." I handed him back the plate and shrugged, fingering the utensils at my place setting and waiting for the other dish to make its way over to me. "I'm a catch, to be quite honest."

Boobie passed the dish of breaded eggplant to Jermaine, and he spooned a couple of slices and the marinara sauce they were baked in onto my plate before doing the same to his own before passing the plate to Sabrina. Then he eyed me.

"Are you trying to get caught?"

I'd been watching the movement of the food around the table, waiting for the garlic bread to make its way to me, but my eyes shot up to Jermaine when he asked that question.

Was I?

Honestly, hell no. Being caught up was painful when the shit came to an end and besides...

I shook my head. "I'm still trapped in someone's net."

He nodded, seemingly unsurprised by my answer. "Fair enough."

I bit into the eggplant to keep my mouth from asking a question of my own, and my eyes widened in delight.

"Ooh, this is really tasty!"

Tuning from the idle chatter around me, I dug into my food and didn't come up for air until I heard my name called. By that time, my plate was almost clean. I glanced around until I saw Sabrina staring at me. There was a cloth napkin folded into a fan in front of my plate, I grabbed it and wiped my mouth before addressing Sabrina.

"I'm sorry, what was that?"

"I just asked if you were a vegetarian as well."

I shook my head. "No, ma'am. Why would you ask that?"

"Well, the boys said they saw you at that vegetarian restaurant a while back. And you just cleaned your plate faster than I've ever seen.

"Oh, that's easy. I just enjoy good food." I laughed. "Could you not tell by the size of my thighs? That's ham hocks and collard greens all day."

Sabrina's eyebrows raised then she smiled. "Hawk, gon' put another serving on this baby plate. She say she like good food. Give her what she like."

I laughed then cocked my head. I looked at Jermaine. "Wait a minute, your mama calls you Hawk too?"

A slow smile spread across his face, but instead of answering me, he put more food on my plate. This time, the serving was smaller.

"Of course, I call him Hawk, I gave him that nickname!"

I looked at Sabrina in surprise. "Oh, I thought it was a celebrity thing." At least, that was what Jermaine had said when he insisted that I call him by his first name. But I didn't say all that.

"Oh no. People think we call him Hawk because of his last name, but I've been calling him that since he was a baby because he was always so quiet and observant. He used to watch everyone who came around us, and I started calling him 'my little hawk'. It grew from there."

As I often did, recently, I thought back to the other night at VR. I'd definitely been on the receiving end of his hawk-like observation. The way Jermaine had stared at me that night had been…unnerving. It wasn't just the ogling of a man attracted; it was calculating, invasive, and weirdly possessive. So, yeah. I could see how his nickname came to be.

So, I mumbled a short, "Oh", and forked more of the eggplant into my mouth. My eyes fluttered at the complexity of the flavors in the sauce. There was no way this marinara was anything but homemade. Sabrina started going down memory lane with her sister as I looked back down at my plate. More garlic bread appeared in my peripheral, and I nodded at Jermaine.

"Thanks, *Jermaine*."

His lips twitched, but he said nothing.

I used the bread to sop up the last of the sauce on my plate and sighed. The meal was delicious, but now that it was gone and I could think clearly, I was a little sad. My belly was full from two plates of pasta and four slices of bread and although it wasn't noticeable—due to the smart choice I'd made in attire—I was now bloated.

That meant no fucking.

Tragic.

I pushed away from the table and stood with my plate in hand, but Jermaine grabbed the plate away from me and sat it back on the table.

"I sure as hell ain't letting you do dishes, too."

I snorted. "Too? What else did I do?"

He ticked off his fingers. "Set the table, convinced my family to join in on what was supposed to be a romantic dinner for two," he leaned in until his lips were, once again, near my ear and added, "flirt with Trina—"

I shrieked and slapped his arm. *Damn.* That arm was solid.

"I did not—"

"Y'all gon' head with y'all date. We'll take care of this here."

I looked at Sabrina.

"Are you sure? It's no problem to help."

She made a shooing motion with her hands. "Yes, I'm sure. Now gon'. I won't have Hawk mad at me 'cause I held you up all night."

"But—"

"Thanks, Mama. Goodnight, y'all." Jermaine tossed a wave at his family, grabbed me by the hand, and led me in the opposite direction of the kitchen.

I chewed my bottom lip. This wasn't supposed to be a date. I wasn't supposed to be dating. Hell, I was still married!

Technically.

Legally.

At least until my lawyer called and told me otherwise. Even so, I'd had a really good time with is family. They were cool people and the food was delicious. I could easily tell myself that it wasn't a date because his family was present, but everyone kept saying the word "date". I stared at Jermaine's back as he led me through his house.

No matter what I told myself about what was right and wrong, I couldn't deny being here with Jermaine felt right in a way nothing had in a long time.

CHAPTER ELEVEN
Nedra

We traveled down a hallway that only had two doors, one on either side of the hall. He pushed open the door on the left and stood back so that I could enter before him. Closing the door behind him, he then pressed a few buttons on a panel on the wall. The whole room illuminated, and I heard the unmistakable sounds of bowling pins being lowered. I looked around and my mouth dropped open.

It looked like we were in a real bowling alley. The room was long and narrow and made up of two full-size lanes. Instead of the hard, plastic seats usually found at the bowling alley, each lane had plush leather couches for seating.

I looked up to see Jermaine watching me. That word "unnerving" floated around my head again. I swallowed the thought and smiled. "This is cool."

He nodded. "Thank you. You ready to get swept?"

I laughed at his cockiness. Although, if I had a real-live bowling alley in my house, I'd play enough to be confident as fuck too. I shook my head and followed him to the rack of balls. To my surprise and delight, he had multiple sizes to choose from. "Well, you have an unfair advantage so, nah."

He chose his ball, a big ass fourteen pounder that didn't even look so big once it was in his hands and chuckled. "Is that what you're gon' tell yourself when I win?"

"*Shiiiit. If* you win, that'll be why. It won't have anything to do with skill at all." I was talking mad shit. I hadn't bowled since I was sixteen-years-old, and I couldn't even remember if a strike was a good thing or a bad thing. Regardless, I was determined not to assist in the stroking of his ego. And the easy banter with him turned me on something fierce.

"Oh, okay; well, let's see then!"

We walked over to one of the two lanes and sat our balls on the ball return. He asked for my shoe size before disappearing behind a counter I hadn't noticed, returning quickly with two pairs of classic bowling shoes dangling from his hand. I took the pair he handed me and smiled when I saw that the colorway was in the official Clutch colors. He keyed our names on the small screen in front of the ball return, and I slipped out of my tennis shoes and into the bowling shoes.

I stood up and started bouncing around like a boxer preparing for a fight, but when I glanced up at the screen hanging from the ceiling, I laughed. "Who is 'G'?" Jermaine had input initials instead of our full names but, while the "J" was obviously for him, there was a "G" for me that didn't make sense.

He sat down to change out his shoes. "That's you."

I opened my mouth to ask for a further explanation, but then I remembered how he called me 'goddess' earlier today on the phone. Is that what the 'G' was for? I wanted to ask but also didn't want to know, so I said nothing. I grabbed my ball and walked over to the screen. "Am I first?" I looked back at him as I waited for my answer.

With a silent nod, he leaned back and spread both of his arms along the back of the couch. I bit my lip. Good lord, he was so big and sexy. His simple orange t-shirt stretched across his broad chest, complementing his mahogany skin and showcasing his firm pectorals and washboard abs. That milk dud of his was shiny and smooth and his thick thighs were nearly bursting through the denim of his fitted jeans.

He was fine and he knew it, and damn if I didn't want to climb in his lap and put my pussy on his zipper.

Then, as if it could hear my thoughts, the aforementioned zipper started to rise and my heart tripped up as I watched a sizable lump form along his thigh. *Whew, shit!* Blue jeans don't hide a damn thing. I needed to tear my eyes away from him and throw the ball down the lane, but I couldn't. There was no doubt my lust for him was written all over my face.

"Nedra." His voice was low and rough. My eyes flew from his lap to his face. "Are you going or coming?"

Was I going to roll the ball, or was I coming to get the pussy massage I was overdue for?

"I don't know," I whined. I was thinking too damn much.

He licked those full lips of his and my panties were ruined. I just needed to peel them off and slide them into my purse because they weren't going to do me any good for the rest of the night.

"Why don't you come over here and let me help you figure it out?"

There was something about a man who was down to help a woman in need. I wanted to let him help me. I just knew that he could extinguish the fire inside of me. No doubt about it. But then I imagined lying on my back with a belly full of Italian food and his big frame pressing against me. I could already feel the food moving back up my esophagus and just the thought of it made me sick. I'd be damned if I threw up for some dick, no matter how big and inviting it looked. With that image in mind, I shook my head and turned back to the lane.

I held the ball to my chest and tried to calm my nerves. A few soft inhalations and I felt more in control. I blew out a breath and moved toward the lane, dropping my arm and curling my wrist forward to release the ball. It rolled down the middle of the lane, and I threw my hands in the air in anticipation of a strike when it curved sharply and hit the gutter with a thunk.

"What the hell?!"

A bark of laughter sounded behind me, and I spun around quickly, glaring at Jermaine.

"Are you laughing at me?"

"Hell yeah! You really thought you were doing something, had your hands all in the air like you were calling a damn field goal."

I grinned—unable to refute that—and shrugged, walking back to the ball return. "I just knew I was about to knock something down."

"Luckily, you get a second bowl."

"Mmhm. I'm about to strike out all over this lane." I ignored his unnecessarily loud guffaws and let loose my second bowl. The ball didn't go in the gutter but somehow it managed to only know down one pin at the far end of the setup. I frowned.

"This is some bullshit." With a disgusted huff, I trudged back to the couch and plopped down, leaving an entire seat cushion in between us for some semblance of space, and gave him a side-eye. It was his turn to bowl, and he hadn't made a move to get off the couch.

He'd stopped laughing and—*there it was!*—that nerve-wracking gaze of his landed on me again. There was no way I was going to be able to endure this for too much longer. I twisted in my seat and gave him my full attention.

"*Why* are you always looking at me like that?"

He licked his lips and one corner of his mouth lifted. "My bad. I didn't mean to make you uncomfortable." In one smooth motion, he ran both of his hands over his head and down his face then stood up.

I pursed my lips, unsatisfied with his response. "That definitely wasn't an answer to my question."

He winked at me then scooped up his ball and tossed it down the lane. It was going so fast that it sounded like an explosion when it hit the pins, knocking them all down. When his ball resurfaced, he repeated the phenomenon then returned to his spot on the couch with a smug grin on his face.

"What was the question again?"

I lifted a brow but didn't say a word. He laughed beckoned for me with his hand.

"C'mere."

As if under a spell, I scooted toward him without hesitation. My butt had barely hit the cushion that was once in between us when he beckoned again.

"Come closer."

He wasn't asking me to do anything that I didn't already want to do, but instead of scooting up underneath his arm like he wanted, I took it a step further. I came up on my knees, swung a thigh over his lap and straddled him. My dress rose to my hips as I sat down, *finally* putting my covered pussy on his zipper, and gripped the hem of his shirt with both hands. I didn't lift it up, just held it there, anchoring myself as I felt the length of him grow under the heat of my center.

I dragged my gaze from where we were separated by denim and lace, up the length of his abdomen, and finally locked on to those chestnut colored eyes that were now heavily lidded with desire.

"Is this close enough?"

His hands found their way to the outside of my thighs and squeezed. "Closer," he instructed.

I rolled my hips, grinding down against him, and leaned forward, draping my arms on the back of the couch on either side of his head. My forehead pressed against his and my lips hovered above his own.

I inhaled his scent. *"What about now?"*

"Uh uhn." He bucked his hips, and I gasped at the unexpected action. My arms wrapped around his neck in an attempt to steady myself, and as my eyes leveled with his, I felt this inexplicable pull toward him. Before I knew it, we were kissing. I have no idea who moved first or even if there was a 'first' instead of a simultaneously fluid movement forward by the both of us.

His hands released my thighs and relocated to my waist as his pillow-soft lips devoured my own. He opened his mouth, and I responded in kind, allowing our tongues to meet and dance sensuously. I grabbed his hands and moved them to my ass, moaning when he began to massage my cheeks enthusiastically.

"Hold on," he murmured in between kisses.

I locked my arms around his neck as he shifted on the couch and laid me down on the cushions, settling between my thighs. I heard warning bells go off in my head, but I shook my head to clear them and smiled up at Jermaine. When he bent down to continue kissing me, the pressure on my belly caused my stomach to lurch. I sat up so fast we almost bumped heads.

"What is it? What's wrong?"

My hands cradled my stomach, and I whined petulantly, "I ate too much and now I'm too full for missionary!"

He sighed with relief and smirked at me. "You can always be on top."

Oh, yeah. I grinned. "Lay back."

When he complied, I once again straddled him. I placed my hands on his chest and mimicked riding him, rocking back and forth and hitting his pelvis with my ass. I felt slightly nauseous, and when I stopped moving, we both heard the liquid in my stomach sloshing around. My face fell and I moaned in frustration.

Jermaine laughed and sat up, wrapping his arms around my waist.

"It's all good."

I shook my head. "No, it's not, but there's nothing I can do about it right now."

He chuckled. "Now, I know that next time I need to save dinner for an after-sex treat."

I leaned back. "Why do you think there will be a 'next time'?" I was bullshitting. There would absolutely be a next time. All he had to do was call my ass, and I'd be there like the Jackson 5, but I just wanted to see what he would say. He reached between us and his thumb expertly sought out my clit, swiping across it a couple of times—just enough to pull a moan out of me—before bringing the thick digit up to his mouth and licking off the essence of me that had soaked through my panties.

His gaze burned into me as he husked, "You know why, don't you?"

I nodded, rendered speechless at his audacious move, even though I had just fake fucked him two minutes earlier.

"Do you want to finish the game?" He nodded toward the abandoned lanes, but I shook my head.

"I'm only in the mood for one thing right now, and unfortunately, I can't have it."

How the hell would I be able to concentrate on a damn game when all I wanted to do was ride him like a brand new bicycle on Christmas Day? Nah, it was best if I just moseyed my little self right back across the highway to my temporary home. I climbed out of his lap, pulling my dress back down over my ass and gathered my purse.

"Wait a minute." He grabbed me by the hips and pulled me into the space between his legs. "Lemme see something real quick." Then he shocked the shit out of me by rolling up my dress and tucking it under my bra, effectively exposing me to him. He slid off the couch, onto the floor then reached around me to palm my ass and bring me even closer to him.

With his nose brushing the apex of my thighs, he lifted one of my legs and swung it over his shoulder. I gasped as my center of gravity shifted and brought my hands to his head for leverage. It wasn't hard to guess what he had planned, and I was torn between curiosity and flat-out stopping him. I wasn't a big fan of receiving head since Chris was never successful at it, despite my coaching, but I just wanted to see if Jermaine was about to waste my time.

I didn't have to wait long. Within seconds of me regaining my balance, Jermaine slid the crotch of my panties to the side and spread me open, peppering several lazy licks to my puffy lips. Occasionally, he would stiffen his tongue and dart it inside of me and I would gasp at the sudden intrusion but for the most part, he concentrated all of his attention on my outer stickiness.

He took his time, moaning against me and devouring me unhurriedly as if he had nothing to do and there was nowhere else he'd rather be. I was slowly dissolving into mush right in front of him. Not only did it feel fantastic, but his obvious enthusiasm and expertise heightened my pleasure. He was slowly stoking the fire inside of me and finally decided to pour gasoline on it when his thick tongue brushed my clit. I nearly swallowed my own tongue and tried to jump back, but he held me tight against his face.

"Uh uhn," he murmured. He glanced up at me and held my gaze as he sucked my swollen flesh into his mouth. I cried out and my knees buckled, but once again, he held me firmly. His eyes fluttered closed as if he tasted the sweetest ambrosia, and I shook my head at the sensual image of him feasting between my legs.

This was too much. The raging fire inside of me was building up to an explosion, and I didn't know if I could handle it. I went from pulling his head toward me to trying to push him away. If he didn't stop, I was guaranteed to die right here. He shook my hand away, and I gasped as he continued with the motion while dragging his tongue back and forth against me. My abdomen started convulsing, and I couldn't stop the scream from clawing its way out of my throat as my orgasm hit me like an ocean wave. I collapsed against him and my last thought before I blacked out was that I understood completely what my granny meant by a man being dangerous.

When I came to, I was in the most comfortable bed I'd ever lain in. I stretched and tried to observe my surroundings, but the room was pitch black. I sat up in a panic and hastily recounted my last memories.

Oh yeah.

The best head I'd ever received made me come so hard that I'd passed out. Jermaine deserved an award or a medal or *something* because that was some shit for the history books. My lips curved into a satisfied grin. Wait until I tell my girls about this. I scooted to the edge of the bed and reached out until my fingers brushed what must have been a nightstand. I felt around until I came across the familiar leather of my cross body bag. I snatched it up and searched inside until my fingers brushed my cell phone. A press of my thumb brought the display to life and informed me that it was just after one in the morning.

Damn! I'd been knocked out for almost two hours.

I turned on the flashlight and moved my phone around until I noticed the lamp on the nightstand. I switched it on and turned to get a look at the room I was in. It was a large but sparsely furnished room, with only the bed, two nightstands, and a sofa to break up the empty space. It might have been a guest room since there were no personal touches or mementos. I looked behind me to the other side of the room and swore when I saw a shape on the bed.

I jumped down so fast that I felt a sharp spike of pain shoot up my ankle. The bed was on some sort of platform that raised it about two feet above the floor and the distance caught me by surprise. I limped backward and—putting my hand on the nightstand for balance—rotated my foot a couple of times to see if I'd done some real damage. Satisfied that I'd live, I brought my gaze back to that shape.

Squinting, I realized that the shape was Jermaine, and I released a silent, relieved sigh. He was on his back with one of his arms bent behind his head and the hand of the other resting comfortably on his crotch. My eyebrows rose at that, but I couldn't judge; I'd woken up with my fingers smelling like my precious kitty more times than I could count. Jermaine's face was relaxed, and his breathing was even; he'd been asleep for a while, and I didn't want to wake him.

I dropped my eyes to the floor by my feet. I was barefoot, and I needed to find my shoes. They weren't anywhere around the bottom of the bed, and I started getting frustrated. *What the hell did he do with my damn shoes?* After a couple of minutes, I just said fuck it and switched off the lamp, using the light from my phone to make my way to the door in the center of the wall opposite the bed. Once in the hallway, I was surprised to see that it was illuminated. There were small fairy lights along the baseboards, similar to those I'd seen lighting the stairs in a darkened movie theater. To my left was a dead end, so I turned right and moved as quickly as I could without making any noise.

I came upon a wide set of stairs and descended them without hesitation. At the landing, I realized that I was just outside of the kitchen and a few feet away from the door that led to the garage. The light above the stove was bright and allowed me to see my way around the kitchen. The only problem was, I didn't know where to go. From the outside, Jermaine's home hadn't look terribly large, but he didn't give me a tour, so I had no clue of the layout.

I willed myself to think of a solution and tried not to be distracted by the Bundt cake taunting me from under a glass dome in the center of the island. *Oh!* The garage was located to the side but near the front of the house. If I took the hallway in that general direction, I should hit the front door.

Moving swiftly, for reasons that I didn't understand but felt vital at the moment, I headed toward what I hoped was the front of the house. When I saw the front door by the light of my phone, I could have cried with relief. I disengaged the locks and pulled open the heavy door before stepping outside onto the porch. As soon as I gently pulled the door closed behind me, the gust of wind from the fifty-degree weather reminded me that my jacket was hanging in the mudroom.

I swore and started walking down the drive, grateful that it was paved—since I was still barefoot—and wondering why the lights weren't on. With one hand in my purse, wrapped comfortingly around my .380 and the other tapping furiously at my phone, I fumed as I realized that no rideshare was in service in this part of town at this time of night.

"You gon' have these white folks thinking you're escaping a cult or robbing the place, barefoot and without a jacket."

My heart leapt into my throat as the low voice sounded right behind me and I jumped five feet in the air, turning around with my gun in my hand as I landed.

"Whoa, shit! It's just me!" Jermaine's hands went up in surrender and his eyes widened in surprise.

As soon as I recognized him—and my shoes and jacket dangling from his hands—I gasped, quickly replaced my gun and held a hand over my racing heart.

"Oh my god, I'm so sorry! Are you crazy? Why would you sneak up on me like that? I could have shot you!"

He shoved my stuff at me, and in a voice that was decidedly calmer than I would have expected after having a gun pointed at him, he said, "After watching you try to Mission: Impossible your way out of my house, I figured I'd better hurry up and get your home. Plus you forgot your things in my room. Thought you might want them, even though you left them."

"Thank you." I quickly shrugged on my jacket and used his offered hand as support while I stepped into my tennis shoes. He nodded behind him, and I glanced over at the open garage.

"C'mon, let me run you home." Without waiting for me or ensuring that I was following him, he turned and walked to the garage, climbing into the same car he had picked me up in.

Although outwardly he seemed fine, somehow, I knew that he was upset and I realized that I fucked up again. I'd tried to bounce in an attempt to be on my *fuck niggas, get money* steez, but this hadn't been that type of situation. Jermaine had brought me into his house, introduced me to his family, and trusted me not to exploit his privacy. Not to mention, he literally blew my mind with the best head on this side of the loop. He deserved better than this.

I climbed into the car and waited until he was on the highway before I spoke.

"I apologize. You showed me a really good time tonight, and the way I tried to sneak off was foul."

He didn't say anything for a few miles, and I thought he was going to ignore me.

"I appreciate you saying that."

I frowned. That was dry. "Do you accept my apology?"

He glanced at me quickly. "If you need that, then sure."

"I need you to say it."

"I just said it."

I shook my head. "You said 'Sure'. I need to hear you say the whole thing."

His eyes were trained on the road, but I saw his brows furrow, probably as he tried to figure out what my deal was. I don't know what was wrong with me. I was feeling very needy right then and I couldn't let him get away from me tonight without me making sure that I was good with him.

"I accept your apology."

Turning my head to face the window, I smiled. "Good."

"You sure? Was that good enough?"

Ignoring his sarcasm, I started to nod then hesitated. It was quick but he must have glanced at me at that exact moment because he caught it.

"What else do you want me to say?"

I chewed on my bottom lip for a second and glanced over at him. "I want you to say that you'll invite me over again."

He tugged on his goatee. "I don't know if I can say that. It didn't really end too well the first time."

I sat up in my seat; that wasn't at all what I wanted to hear, and I panicked a little bit. The little information I found on him said that he never went out—not rarely, but *never*—so the chances of me running into him again were nonexistent. The possibility of that was...undesirable.

"Well, I never got my dick so..."

He chuckled lowly. "Well, you had multiple opportunities so...I figured you didn't really want it."

"But that's not true!" I whined.

He pulled into the driveway of Shanice's house and put the car in park. With his head against the seat, he swiveled his neck and blinked at me slowly. I could see the exhaustion in his eyes and gratitude for him bloomed in my chest. He'd gotten out of his bed and driven me across town after I'd disappeared on him without a word, a note, or a text message.

"That's how it looked. I don't make the rules."

I stared at him as he blinked once, twice, and a third time before his eyes stayed closed. *Oh, hell no.* I reached over and pressed the button on the dashboard to turn the car off. Immediately, his eyes snapped open.

"What are you doing?" he slurred.

I got out of the car and rounded to his side, opening his door and tugging him out.

"You're way too tired to be driving back. I can't let you do that."

He blinked at me owlishly, and I thought he was going to argue but he just pushed his door closed and pressed a button on his key fob, causing the car to chirp.

"You're right. Just don't think that this means you're getting some dick. That ship has sailed for you."

I rolled my eyes, and I pulled him up the porch steps and into the house.

"Okay, *Jermaine*. I'm just trying to keep you from falling asleep at the wheel and dying on your way home. We can talk about the dick you owe me tomorrow."

He chuckled and followed me into my room. Neither of us said a word once inside, just stood there staring at each other. Finally, he turned his back to me, and I quickly slipped out of my dress and into the oversized t-shirt I used as a nightgown before crawling into the queen-size bed. When I turned around, Jermaine was standing shirtless at the foot of the bed, wearing a pair of basketball shorts. His eyes closed, and he let out a yawn so loud, I heard his jaw pop. I grabbed his arm and pulled him down to the bed. If he fell out asleep, there was no way I'd be able to pick him up off of the floor. I pulled the duvet over both of us and rolled to my side.

The bed shook as he valiantly tried to make himself comfortable in a bed that was entirely too small for him without touching me "too much".

"Just bend your knees," I admonished quietly, with my back to him.

He did as I said, turning on his side and bending his knees so that his feet only hung off the edge of the bed from his ankles down. His knees were right up underneath my ass, cupping my cheeks like his lap was a seat made just for me. My breath halted in my chest.

"I can sleep on the couch, you know." His words were drowsy, and I knew he would be asleep soon.

"I don't want you to," I whispered. I wanted him near me.

I pressed my hips back slightly and sighed contentedly when his arm snaked around my waist and pulled me flush against him. His chin rested in the middle of my head and his warm, spicy scent enveloped me.

"Good night, *Jermaine*."

"G'night, Misty Knight."

I had no idea who that was, but I chuckled anyway. His whole body relaxed, his arm becoming heavy around me, and I knew he had fallen asleep. I should have done the same, but I couldn't get over how comfortable I was, being wrapped in his arms like this. This was a dangerous place that I was in. Trusting a man so implicitly that I'd just met that I'd be at my most vulnerable around him was crazy.

I didn't even do sleepovers with Chris until he announced to everyone that we were a couple, and by that time, we had been having sex for two months. With Jermaine, I didn't even hesitate to put him in my bed, and I was almost offended when he offered to sleep on the couch.

Crazy.

I was crazy.

He was definitely crazy.

Not only was I trusting him, he was trusting me, a woman he had just met, and he had far more to lose than I did. He didn't know me from Eve. I could be one of those attention-seeking women who would video him asleep in my bed and post it online for the world to see. I could take the loving family interaction that I witnessed earlier and sell the story to the highest bidder. Someone would pay big money for that. I'd done an internet search on him before he picked me up. He was essentially a hermit in the entertainment world. No one knew anything about his life outside of what he did on the court. For a man who valued his privacy the way that he did, he invited me into his life without so much as a conversation about do's and don'ts.

He was crazy as hell.

Had to be.

Maybe even more than me because I was coming out of a relationship I had been in for almost half of my life, and he could only be one other thing if he kept dealing with me.

A rebound.

♥♥♥♥

I woke up before him. Honestly, I don't know how he slept at all because he'd rolled onto his back at some point and his legs hung off the end of the tiny queen-size bed almost up to his knees. There was no way he could be comfortable sleeping like that. He'd adopted what I assumed was his regular sleeping position; one arm was behind his head, but instead of cradling his crotch, the other had stayed wrapped around me, keeping me tucked against his chest. I'd turned over as well, throwing one of my thick thighs across his waist and resting my hand over his heart.

His hard planes and masculine scent coupled with the memory of his tongue between my lower lips had been doing wicked things to my uterus, and I couldn't sleep through the constant clenching transpiring below. I tilted my neck back and observed him quietly. He'd told me last night that the dick ship had sailed and I'd missed the boat, but he wasn't leaving this house until I emptied his balls.

I trailed my fingers lightly down his chest until I reached the waistband of his shorts and came back up. He didn't move. Flicking my eyes back up to his face, I stretched and placed a soft kiss on his jaw.

"Jermaine," I whispered.

Nothing.

I tried again. *"Jermaine."*

He grunted. "Huh?"

I almost laughed. His lips hadn't even moved. The word came straight from his throat. He probably thought he was dreaming.

"Can I have some dick now?" I punctuated my question by reaching down to gently squeeze the flaccid penis in his shorts.

That got his attention. One of his eyes popped open, bearing into me.

"Huh?" he repeated.

I squeezed his now inflating bulge once more. "Can I have some of this, *please*?" I assumed adding a magic word would seal the deal for me.

"You sure that's what you want?"

The early morning gravel in his voice was doing nothing to reduce the heat in my loins. I nodded my consent.

He stretched and pulled his arm from around me to run both of his hands down his face. "I don't know, man; this dick come with strings."

I froze mid-squeeze. "What do you mean? What kind of strings?"

He hit me with the full intensity of his sleepy, chestnut gaze. "The kind you can't run out on in the middle of the night."

Ah, shit. I deserved that shade because I'd definitely committed the crime but also... "I apologized for that."

"You did," he acknowledged.

"But?"

He sighed and raised his gaze to the ceiling. "Do you remember when Fred said I was celibate?"

I gasped, remembering the moment clearly because Ashton followed up with some BS that I threatened to shoot her for. "Are you seriously celibate?" I wasn't going to judge him for it, but if true, it was definitely problematic because just as his dick continued growing in my hand, so was my own arousal.

"Nah, he was fucking around with that shit. *But* it's been a while since I've gone there with someone because I don't do that casual shit."

I considered his revelation. "But you were tryna fuck last night, though."

His gaze dropped and pinned me to the bed. "I brought you to my home and introduced you to my family. That wasn't some casual shit. Not for me. Not by a long shot."

"Oh..." I couldn't even say that I didn't know because I was unsurprised to hear that. Even without doing an internet search on him, the reactions of his family told me that my presence was something out of the ordinary. Everyone had been genuinely nice to me, and I'd dipped out like I was trying to avoid paying my taxes. I felt like shit all over again.

Jermaine shifted from underneath me and I panicked.

"Wait!"

He tried sitting up, and I pushed him back down to the bed and was practically sitting on top of him to prevent him from leaving.

"Look, I'm not trying to force anything on you. You're still getting out of a marriage, and I get it; you're not trying to do anything serious. *I get it.* But I know what I felt when I first laid eyes on you, and that shit was as serious as a heart attack."

My heart did to me, at hearing his words, what I'd just been doing to his dick. It squeezed then froze and restarted, beating doubly fast. I wanted to feel giddy, but I couldn't trust my reaction. Only hours earlier, I was lamenting the fact that we couldn't be anything real *because* I wasn't yet divorced.

"It's not that I'm avoiding getting serious again; it's just...if we went there, it wouldn't be fair to you. I'm basically on the rebound." I expected him to nod and agree; instead, he gave me a disbelieving look.

"Did you know that I led the league in rebounds three years in a row?"

My neck whipped back. Was he being serious? He stared up at me unblinkingly. *He was serious.*

"What?" I didn't even know how to respond to that.

"I catch rebounds for a living," he deadpanned.

I burst out laughing and he sat up fully, moving me off his chest and onto his lap.

"I've made a career out of rescuing something that has hit a backboard, which is often an event there is no coming back from."

I stopped laughing. He actually equated what he did for a living to put our situation into context, and it was working. We were face-to-face and I could clearly see the sincerity in those chestnut orbs of his. His hands framed my face.

"I've spent more than a decade preparing for you."

My eyes burned with tears at his declaration. "I'm being serious."

He nodded. "Do you want to see my stats?"

I sputtered, half-crying and half-laughing, and pressed my lips against his, morning breath be damned. He returned my kiss without hesitation as if he'd been waiting for me to make the first move. His hands dropped from my face to my hips as he lifted me effortlessly and maneuvered me so that I was straddling his lap.

I settled heavily on him, pressing down as if I was trying to melt into him, and the new position brought a different dynamic to our kissing. Suddenly, I needed to feel him everywhere, and the way he rocked my hips back and forth across his hardened erection, it was evident he had the same need. He released my hips and trailed his hands up my sides, bringing my shirt with him. I lifted my arms, allowing him to pull the material over my head and toss it behind me to the floor.

The reverent look in his eyes as he drank in my naked breasts made me gush, flush, and clench. He grabbed both of my breasts in his massive hands and lowered his mouth, sucking both nipples into his mouth at once. I moaned in appreciation as the sensation shot straight to my core, causing me to release even more slickness. I needed him inside of me like yesterday.

Reaching down between us, I grasped the elastic waistband of his shorts and pulled it toward me, shoving my hand inside and gripping his dick. He groaned around the titty in his mouth. I shifted my hips back and pulled the silky steel out of his shorts. There was already a bead of pearlescent fluid emerging from the slit, and I swiped my thumb across it and brought it to my lips, licking the saltiness away. Soon, I would swallow his lengthy thickness down my throat but right now, I needed a pussy massage in the worst way.

I rose to my knees and started to slide the seat of my thong to the side when Jermaine quickly released my breasts and gripped the side of my panties with both hands. Before I realized what he was doing, I heard the sound of seams popping, and he was tossing my ruined panties in the same direction of my shirt. He grabbed my hips and lifted me up so I could position him at my entrance. Moans fell from both of our mouths as I sank onto him.

"Shit."

I dropped my head to his shoulder. This position was a bad idea. I could feel him in my damn lungs. He hadn't even moved but the ridges of his dick were putting pressure on a spot that was making me unhinged. I was afraid to even twist my hips, but the fear dissipated when Jermaine once again gripped my hips and, instead of lifting me, started to rock me back and forth.

I cried out as the motion caused his dick to repeatedly hit that spot. Not even two minutes later, I buried my face in his neck as my orgasm hit me full force and jerked in his lap. While I was still twitching from aftershocks, Jermaine maneuvered us until I was on my back and he was hovering between my thighs, all while still inside of me. He caressed the skin of one thigh as he lifted it and settled it on his waist. Repeating the tender touch on the opposite thigh, he lifted my other leg, this time, resting my ankle on his shoulder.

Then he went to work.

He worked his hips, sliding in and out of me so easily that I would have been embarrassed if I wasn't out of my mind with desire. Without a doubt, he had me well lubricated. I arched my back as he grazed that spot once more. After that first orgasm, my pussy was like a live wire. Every sensation threatened to cause another explosion inside of me.

Jermaine rotated and twisted and snapped his hips, and I was delirious. My second orgasm built in my toes and traveled up my body at breakneck speed, causing me to inhale deeply and my back to fly off the bed as I cried out to the heavens.

"*Baby, shit!*"

Jermaine grimaced as I gripped him like a vise as I came. He leaned down and sucked on the skin of my collarbone briefly before moving my leg from his shoulder to his waist and lowering his chest down to mine. He ran his arms behind me and gripped my shoulders from below, pulling me down with each thrust. His eyes devoured me before his lips descended upon mine and he made love to my mouth. I wrapped my arms around him and cradled his head with both hands. We stared at each other as we kissed, neither willing to miss the expression on the other's face as we both experienced something that was beyond morning sex.

His movements increased and I whimpered with each thrust. The sound of our flesh slapping together filled the small room sensually. Locking my ankles behind him, I gripped his ears and allowed my eyes to flutter closed as he ripped a third orgasm from my hypersensitive pussy. When I clamped down on him, he groaned in my ear and chased my orgasm with one of his own, releasing spurts of liquid warmth into me. He dropped his head to the mattress and we both panted heavily as we came down from our orgasmic high.

I released his ears and rubbed my hands over his bald head before trailing them down his back that was damp with a thin layer of sweat. Including the head from the night before, this man had given me four orgasms in under twelve hours. I don't think I would have been able to give him up just yet, even if I actually wanted to.

He tapped my thigh, and I unlocked my ankles, spreading my legs so that he could pull out of me. I moaned when he did so leisurely before sitting back on his haunches and staring down at my exposed center. With a swift lick of his thumb, he massaged firm, deliberate circles into my moistened clit, causing me to whine and my walls to clench involuntarily. Just as I felt the flow of our combined come begin to trickle out of me, he stopped moving.

"Bear with me, I'm about to ask a stupid question."

"Mmhm." Even though I had three in the game this morning, my hips moved against him, shamelessly chasing a fourth.

"Are you on birth control?"

My previously closed eyes flew open and met his in a panic. I expected an accusing glare, but he only looked contemplative...and a smidgen hopeful. That second one made my blood rush through my veins, and my eyes widened in realization as I instantly remembered that I hadn't been on birth control since Chris told me that he'd filed for divorce almost three months ago.

I swallowed heavily. Would he think that I was trying to trap him? I had been the one to initiate sex. Hell, I'd basically begged for it.

"Why is that a stupid question?" I hedged.

He quirked an eyebrow. "Well, since I'm watching some of my soldiers march out of you right now, I figure it's a little too late to ask that. But I'm doing it anyway, just to satisfy my curiosity. I have an idea, but I want to hear it from you first."

I reached down and felt the come still oozing out of me. I sucked in a breath and released it audibly. "No, I'm not on birth control. Haven't been for about three months now."

An indecipherable look passed over Jermaine's face before he grabbed his—surprisingly—still hard dick and slid it effortlessly into my dripping opening. The squelch of air being pushed into a hole filled with liquid enveloped the room, and I closed my eyes from the embarrassment even as I moaned in ecstasy, unable to believe what was happening. *Was he mad?*

He hovered over me until we were face-to-face and I opened my eyes when I felt the heat of his stare. "You know what this means, right?"

I shook my head, biting my lip to keep from crying out as he moved inside of my sensitive canal at an agonizingly steady pace.

"It means you're mine now." He grunted and thrust inside of me deeply, hitting the back wall of my pussy, and causing me to hiss. He waited for my eyes to stop blinking and refocus on him before he continued speaking. "I was already prepared to convince you that we're meant to be together. I knew it as soon as I saw you, but if you get pregnant..." Another slow stroke followed a rigid thrust. "I'm never letting you out of my sight again." He thrust once more, and tears sprang to my eyes, both from how deep he was drilling inside of me, and the words coming out of his mouth. "Do you understand me?"

I nodded, unable to say a word for the threat of my tears spilling down my cheeks.

"Do you have any problems with what I said?"

I shook my head.

"Say it."

I shook my head once more.

He pulled my hips down on his upthrust, and I screamed from the fusion of pleasure and pain. "I said," he growled, "say it."

The dam broke on both my tears and my fourth orgasm. "I'm yours!" I screamed at him, dragging the *yours* out until I broke off on a sob.

His lips crashed down on mine, and I clung to him desperately, wishing I could pull him wholly inside of me because that's how close I felt to him at that moment. We were connected, both body and soul. He pummeled me with several shallow pumps followed by a thrust so deep, I was sure he had rearranged my organs. Then, while our tongues were still entwined, he snapped his hips back and forth until heat bloomed in my belly and stars burst beneath my eyelids. I begged him—for what, I didn't know—and he responded by murmuring my name just as he crashed into the wave of his own orgasm, once again filling me with all of him.

Exhausted, I fell asleep before Jermaine hit the mattress.

CHAPTER TWELVE
Nedra

"Any day now" turned into a month and a half before I received the call I had been waiting for. At seven a.m. on a warm Thursday morning in April, Danielle—my lawyer—was giddy as she told me that my divorce had been finalized and all of my terms had been approved. For the first time in seven years, I was a "legally" single woman. She reminded me that once our house sold, I would never have to speak to Chris again, and she ended the conversation by requesting that I refer her to my friends.

As luck would have it, the one lesson I had scheduled for that day was canceled and with Jermaine in California for an away game, I didn't even bother getting out of bed. I needed some time to quietly mourn the loss of my marriage without being bothered, so I put my phone on 'do not disturb' and burrowed under the covers.

I didn't realize I had fallen back asleep until the constant ringing of the doorbell jolted me awake. I shuffled out of the bed and to the front door, groaning when I looked through the peephole. I took a calming breath and opened the door to let my mama inside.

She stepped into the living room, her shrewd gaze quickly observing surroundings and falling on me, no doubt, immediately deducing my melancholy state. She hugged me tightly and kissed my cheek before passing me by and having a seat on the sofa. Instead of sitting next to her or even taking the chair, I sat on the floor. My back had recently started hurting and the floor was the only thing that gave me relief.

"What brings you by, Mama?"

Her amber eyes curiously roved over my frame. "Why are you sitting on the floor?"

I explained my recent pain to her and her eyebrows met knowingly.

"Hmm, have you taken something for it?"

I shook my head. "Not yet; I thought it would eventually go away, but it hasn't. I'll probably visit the chiropractor soon. It's more than likely the bed I'm sleeping in, though."

"*Hmm.* If you say so. Well, I just came to check on you."

"Oh?" That was surprising. "How did you get here?"

"My friend dropped me off."

I pursed my lips. By "friend", she surely meant the man she had been living with for the past three years. He was essentially her boyfriend, but she never gave the men in her life titles, referring to them as her "friend" for as long as I could remember. Most of the time, she never even said their names. It used to me annoy me as a teenager, but now that I was in my mid-thirties, I didn't give a damn.

"That was nice of him."

"Tish called me."

Whoop there it is. Tish was Chris and Ashton's mother. If Tish called my mama, it could only be for one reason. The next words out of my mama's mouth confirmed it.

"She said your divorce is final."

I expelled a soft breath. "Yep. I got the call this morning."

Shocking the shit out of me, she got down on her knees and pulled me into a hug. I was so overcome with emotion at her unexpected gesture that I burst into tears. I cried hot, salty tears into my mama's cap-sleeved peasant blouse, but she didn't seem to care. She rocked me back and forth, murmuring words I didn't understand but soothed me anyway, and rubbed my back in wide, circular patterns.

Finally, the spring behind my eyes dried up, and my mama leaned back to observe me with all-seeing eyes.

"You alright, baby?"

I nodded. "Yes, ma'am."

"You go' stay on the floor?"

I nodded again. It just felt better down here.

"Okay, well I'm gonna stay down here with you. He'll be back to pick me up in about an hour so I wanna talk to you before he get here."

I cocked my head. Now that sounded ominous.

"Nedra, baby, I hate that you're hurting, and I know you gon' be mad when I say this, but this would never have happened if you had listen to me in the first place."

She was damn right. I couldn't believe my ears. Was she really hitting me with an 'I told you so' on the day of my divorce? I mean, I wasn't hurting as much as she might think I was, after all of that crying—and I couldn't deny that it was partly due to Jermaine's presence in my life—but she didn't know that.

My mama continued on as if she heard my thoughts instead of correctly reading the disbelief on my face. "Yeah, I said it. I told you from the get-go that you were too young to be so serious."

"I was twenty-seven when I married Chris! How is that too young?"

"You might have been twenty-seven when you got married, but you were eighteen when you decided that fool was the love of your life. You committed yourself to him when you were way too young to even understand what that meant."

My lips snapped shut. She was right about that. As soon as Chris kissed me my freshmen year of college, I stopped considering other guys as anything other than a study partner. I looked away from her as I sat without a rebuttal to give. Unfortunately for me, my mama came with intentions of getting shit off her chest this morning.

"I told you being exclusive at eighteen years old was a bad idea. I told you to date, to keep your options open, but did you listen? No! You didn't want to hear anything I had to say because I wasn't married like your grandparents had been or like Chris' parents were. You didn't respect me or my opinions because I wasn't in a 'traditional relationship'."

She was in full-blown fuss mode, and even though I was grown and now divorced, I had to sit through it because everything she was saying was the God's honest truth, even though I hated to admit it. As a teenager, I hated how my mama cycled through men. She wouldn't keep a man around for longer than six months and back then, it embarrassed me. As a frequent visitor to the homes of friends who had what I considered "real families" with both parents in the home, I became a self-righteous know-it-all, and I'd felt like my mama couldn't tell me anything about something she didn't know. And to my knowledge, she definitely *did not* know anything about love or marriage.

Hearing her repeat the arguments she gave me all those years ago only served to piss me off and make me want to fight something or someone. Not her, though. I got my scrappiness from my mama, and I didn't want her to put those hands on me.

"Mama..."

She held her hand up. "Don't *Mama* me! I tried to save you from the heartache you're experiencing now, and you would still rather listen to my misguided mama than to your own!"

My eyes widened at her allusion. I had never heard her speak ill of my granny, but mentioning her had me recalling the conversation I'd had with Granny a couple of months ago.

"What do you mean by 'misguided'?"

My mama fixed me with a knowing look. "Didn't she try to convince you to hold on to Chris?"

I nodded without hesitation. I remember that part vividly.

"Of course, she did," she muttered, sarcastically. "Let me tell you why I never married and just know it wasn't for a lack of prospects, that's for damn sure. Shoot, even your daddy proposed to me before *and* after I had you, but I turned him down. I didn't want to be married. For years, I watched how miserable my mama was, being married to my daddy, and when I was old enough to understand why I knew that I didn't want to live that life."

I sat forward. "Wait, wait, wait. Granny said that you begged her, along with Granddaddy, not to leave and break up the family. If you knew she was miserable, why would you do that?"

"Nedra, I was ten when my mama tried to leave my daddy. Up until that point, she had kept me in the dark about a lot of things that went on between them. All I knew was that she was trying to tear up the only home I had known. When I was a teenager, I learned different. Daddy might have loved me, but the only thing he felt for Mama was possession. He treated her like a piece of property that he owned instead of like the loving, stupidly loyal woman that she was."

"Oh wow," I breathed. My family had more secrets than I could have imagined. "So the misguided comment…?"

"Oh, Mama encouraging you to fight for your marriage even though she knows first-hand that marriage ain't shit? Please, please, listen to me this time. Stop trying to conform to what you think is tradition. All of that stuff is made up by controlling men, and all it serves to do is make you lose yourself. *Only* do what feels right in your gut—not your heart, because hearts can be swayed—and screw anyone who says that it's the wrong thing."

The earnest look in her eyes brought another round of tears to mine. Why did I have to experience some bullshit like divorce in my thirties for my mama to start making sense to me? I tried to think of a way to articulate how I was feeling but I kept coming up blank. This advice was even more valuable to me than my mama could know.

I had been struggling with the depth of my feelings for Jermaine for the past six weeks. Every day that passed, I fell deeper and deeper into something I was hesitant to name, but for the life of me, I couldn't ignore. How was it possible for my soul to connect with someone so soon after I ended a marriage to a man I had known since I was a teenager? It felt insane and unbelievable, so I told myself it wasn't. Now, hearing my mama basically call me out for something she couldn't possibly know anything about was even more astonishing. My gut had been telling me that Jermaine was *the one* ever since he called me back after I literally hung up in his face, but I didn't want to trust it. Then, there was that small kernel of fear I had of being judged harshly for moving on from Chris *so quickly,* into something new that was undoubtedly *so intense.*

I pulled her back in for a hug and squeezed her as tight as I could in an attempt to communicate what I didn't know how to say. My mama and I never could positively communicate with one another—mostly.because we were both hotheads—but I loved her like no other.

The chuckle I basically squeezed out of her voiced the surprise I know she felt at my affection. "I take it you ain't too mad at me, then?"

I huffed a laugh and shook my head, releasing her. "Nah, Mama. You only said what I needed to hear, and I can't be mad about that."

"Hmph, that sounds like music to my ears."

I laughed loudly. "I just bet it does."

"Oh!" She scooted across the floor and grabbed the blood-red duffel bag she called a purse. The thing was so big, when she dug into it, she sank down to her shoulder. After rifling around in the enormous monstrosity, she pulled out a white paper bag with the familiar red and brown logo of my favorite donut shop.

"I brought you some kolaches. He insisted we stop and get you some breakfast since it was so early, and I agreed since you tend to eat your feelings." She handed me the bag nonchalantly and I had to stop myself from snatching it out of her hand.

I did eat my feelings, so, once again—even though her little barb was fucked up—I held my tongue. Whenever I got too comfortable and sappy with my mama, Rose always knew how to bring me right back down to earth. I sucked my teeth instead of saying anything—forgoing my thanks since she wanted to take shots—and pulled out a still warm kolache. I took a hefty bite and immediately spit it back out as I gagged.

Confused, I poked at the doughy breakfast treat, thinking that it might have been old or spoiled. The bread felt too soft to be anything other than fresh, so I squeezed the sausage to see if it was what my mouth had instantly rejected, but as soon as I saw a few clear beads of juice appear on the broken piece of meat, I felt bile rise in my throat. I scrambled off the floor and ran into the kitchen, barely making it to the trash can before everything I ate the night before came out of me as I heaved violently.

When I had nothing more but bitter, orange spit to give to the trash can, I felt a cool cloth on my forehead. I tried to look at her but a dry heave kept my head over the can.

"Thank you."

She pressed a glass of water into my hand, and I quickly rinsed my mouth of all traces of vomit, spitting the water out when it got warm.

"Ned?"

"Huh?" Finally feeling like it was safe to do so, I stood upright and look at my mama.

"When was your last period?"

My eyes fluttered closed as I realized immediately what she was asking me. "I haven't had an actual period in years because I had the IUD, but I had some light spotting last month."

She gave me a knowing look. "Have you taken a test?"

I shook my head. "No," I whispered. I'd been afraid to. This wasn't the first time I had succumbed to nausea this month, but I didn't want to jump to conclusions and get my hopes up before I felt sure. I had been wanting a baby for so long that if I rushed to take a test and found out that my nausea was just food poisoning, I would be devastated. I'd been puking regularly for two weeks but hadn't said anything to anyone.

"Does Chris know?"

My face morphed into confusion so fast that my mama frowned at me. That was when I realized that I hadn't told her about Jermaine. I guess there was no time like the present.

"Mama, I haven't slept with Chris since December. I'm...seeing someone, though, but he doesn't know. Hell, I don't really know."

To my mama's credit, she didn't even blink an eye. She whipped out her phone and called her "friend", instructing him to head our way after making a stop at the pharmacy to pick up two tests.

"Why two tests, Mama?"

She winked at me. "The first one don't count."

Forty minutes later, I sat on the floor in front of the bathroom, nervously chewing on the skin of my nail bed while my mama checked both tests.

When she emerged from the bathroom, I saw the results all over her face. I burst out crying, and she dropped to her knees to envelop me in a hug tighter than the one she'd given me earlier. I guess she could tell I was about to float up to ceiling, and I needed an anchor.

"You're making me a grandmama," she whispered in my ear, and I sobbed my joy into her shoulder.

"I'm proud of you," she declared.

"You can do this," she affirmed.

"You're not alone," she reminded.

"Mama!" I cried, "I'm having a baby!"

She rocked me back and forth. "I know, baby. I know. I checked the pissy test, remember?"

I laughed through my tears. On a day that I just knew was going to be one of the most depressing of my life, I was blessed with the best news I could have possibly received. Nothing could top or deflate the elation I felt. I knew that the next steps I made had to put me in position to be the best mama to this baby that I could be. As soon as I finished crying, I got up off the floor and went to get my phone.

I shot a text to Shanice, requesting the assistance of her and—if possible—her PYT in officially moving out of the house Chris and I shared. It was beyond late notice, but I wanted to sever all connections with him, like yesterday. When she hit me back with an affirmative, I immediately started to call Jermaine then I stopped. I couldn't tell him something this important over the phone. I needed him in front of me, so I could see his face when I informed him that he would be a father. It would also be a good time to see if he meant what he said about his actions if I were to ever become pregnant.

After another half an hour that was mostly filled with her reiterating the need for me to take it easy tomorrow, my mama finally left. My veins were pumping with the adrenaline I received from my news, and all I wanted was to bounce around and announce it to everyone, but Jermaine had to hear it first. Now, I was suddenly exhausted. It was still early, not even noon, but I bounced my behind into my bedroom, under the covers, and into a nap.

I didn't wake up until the next morning and when I did, I was starving. With the first week of puking, I discovered that the only thing I could keep down—and my number one craving—was fried eggs with cheese. I cooked, ate, and promptly cooked a second serving. Sated, I called Shanice to confirm her help that morning and then got myself ready to completely remove myself from my house.

When I pulled up to the two-story home I hadn't lived in or visited for almost three months, I was surprised that I didn't feel anything but disappointment. No overwhelming sense of sadness, no joy, not even relief. I was simply disappointed. It supposed to be a one-and-done situation; married one time, to the one man I would grow old with, and never have to worry about learning someone new ever again. My mission this morning was vastly different from the last mission I'd had concerning Chris, and I felt nothing but disappointment.

Sliding my bag over my head, I rubbed my belly, took a deep breath, and headed up the path to the front door. I'd parked on the street, leaving the driveway empty for the moving truck that the storage company would be delivering in about an hour. It would be a small, fourteen-foot truck that could back into the space easily. I'd decided not to take any furniture with me, intent on starting fresh with pieces that wouldn't resurrect years of memories at a glance.

Chris hadn't cared either way, so he was keeping a few pieces and would sell what wouldn't fit in his new place. I wasn't surprised to hear that he had already signed a lease on a condo in a nearby neighborhood, even though the house hadn't sold yet. It appeared that he was as eager to escape our marital home as I had been.

As soon as I stepped over the threshold, the scent of cinnamon and sugar bombarded me. I held my phone in one hand as I dropped my purse and keys on the side table and followed the smell into the kitchen. My usually pristine kitchen was a mess; there were bags and canisters of ingredients, mixing bowls, and more all over the counter. I was genuinely shocked at what I saw. What the fuck did Chris call himself doing? The entire time we were married, he had never stepped foot in this kitchen except to grab a plate, but now he wanted to "make" something that required him to leave shit everywhere like this? If his intent was to piss me off, then he'd succeeded.

The kitchen was one of the few rooms I was emptying. Aside from leaving a single pot and pan each for Chris, the entire contents of the kitchen were coming with me. I loved to cook and bake and had purchased almost everything myself. Chris had not objected, so I assumed everything was cool. The scene before me told a different story, however. I walked to the counter nearest me and picked up a melamine mixing bowl. The lumpy brown substance inside smelled like cinnamon but was questionable to the eye.

I heard a door slam, and my clumsy ass dropped the bowl which, thankfully, didn't break. All of its contents spilled out onto the tile floor and splattered the bottom of the cabinets. I groaned loudly. Of. Fucking. Course.

I stomped across the kitchen, muttering to myself while also feeling genuinely surprised that the sight didn't make me nauseous, and grabbed a couple of rags and a bottle of cleanser from the laundry so I could rid the kitchen of my and Chris' mess. As I was bent over on the floor on my hands and knees, Chris' ringtone started playing on my phone. Months ago, I had changed it from Love Of My Life by Common and Erykah Badu to Resentment by Beyonce. It occurred to me right then, that this was the first time I had heard this song since I'd made the change. Not once had Chris called me after he announced he wanted a divorce; instead, he sent all correspondence through our lawyers. Instead of getting up to answer my phone, I put some extra elbow grease into my cleaning as I sang along with the chorus.

I have no idea how many rings sounded on Chris's end but I was going hoarse from the emphasis I put in as I repeated "You lied!" over and over when a pair of feet appeared next to my elbow. Startled, I sucked in a breath and fell backward, one hand clutching at my heart and the other clutching my lower belly as I took in the body attached to those feet. Chris frowned down at me for a second, his eyes flicking to the hand on my abdomen, before bending down and pulling me up into a standing position.

"My bad, Ned. I called your phone when I came in, but you were really into the song so I guess you didn't hear it ring."

I patted my chest a couple of times then rubbed my belly and shook my head. He must not have realized that the song *was* the ringtone.

"I heard it, but I was jamming."

He pointed to my phone on the counter which was now silent.

"*That* was your jam?"

I nodded and bent to pick up the rag I had dropped. "You know I love Queen Bey, and that song speaks to me on a spiritual level."

He frowned again. "Since when?"

I shrugged slowly as I realized what he was getting at.

"Since I had to learn the hard way what she was talking about."

He scratched his head, and I noted that he needed a haircut. His usually low cut was starting to kink up, and he always used to hate when I would try to comb it out into a neat afro. His shoulders lifted then fell.

"I didn't cheat on you, Ned, and I never lied about anything."

Now, it was my turn to frown. I held up a hand and started to tick off fingers as I proved him wrong.

"You said you would "have me" forever. *Lie.* You said you would "love me" forever. *Lie.* You said "until death, do us part", and unless you are hiding a terminal illness from me, *that* was a muthafuckin' lie." I stood there, staring at the man I was convinced was my soul mate since I was eighteen years old. He stared right back at me, the pain in my eyes reflecting in his own.

"Nedra, I still love you; I keep telling you that it's not about that—"

I tossed the rag back to the floor and threw my hands up to stop him from saying the complete and utter bullshit I definitely didn't want to hear.

"Save it, Chris." I backed away from him. "The damage is done. We're divorced now, and there is no going back from that. Just stop trying to act like you didn't fuck up." I turned to leave him standing there, but he caught my arm. I stared at his hand like it was a parasite, but he didn't remove it.

"You're right; I fucked up. I'm not denying that. What I'm saying is stop looking at our situation like it's the same as everyone else who has ever had to divorce."

I tried to yank my arm from his grasp, but his grip was firm.

"We didn't *have* to divorce Chris. *You* made that decision because you were too cowardly to admit you weren't happy."

His eyes blazed at me. "Or maybe I made the decision because one of us had to stop pretending that everything was okay."

I gasped and tried to pull away even more.

"Let me go; I don't have to listen to this! You aren't my husband anymore, so I'm not obligated to hear anything you have to say!" I pushed against him, but instead of releasing me, he grabbed my other arm and pulled me toward him.

"You love to keep throwing our vows in my face, but you never list them all. You forgot how we said we'd be a friend to one another and that we'd push each other to be the best we could be. Are you going to stand here and say that you were at your best with me? That I was?"

I stared up at him, speechless at what he was saying.

"I filed for divorce because we'd reached our peak about ten years ago, and if I had to continue to go through the motions on this plateau—feeling stagnated—then I would have been no good to anyone, including myself. *I love you, Nedra*, just not romantically anymore. As your friend, I want you to achieve everything you ever wanted in life, but realistically, I understand that it won't happen with me by your side. This isn't about betrayal or infidelity; this is about realizing what we said seven years ago so that we can do what ya girl Oprah be saying and live our best lives. Don't you want that?"

He stared at me openly, allowing me to see the hope and earnestness he felt in his amber eyes. I hated to admit it, but what he said made sense. Just as I had acknowledged months ago that even though he knew my passion, Chris wouldn't invest in it. I knew that what he was saying was true. It wasn't that he didn't care about it, he just didn't understand its importance to me. The same could be said for how I felt about him and his coaching football. All I saw was him spending ungodly amounts of time at the high school, but maybe he saw something bigger that I couldn't fathom because I wasn't meant to take that journey with him. *Damn*, I hated it when Chris was right!

I released the tension in my shoulders and dropped my chin to my chest. Being a divorcee still hurt, but it was now the reality that I was a divorcee and not that I felt like I was losing. I nodded and Chris crushed me to his chest in a hug. When he released me, I stepped back and looked down at the mess still on the floor. Chris's gaze followed my own.

"I got this. I'm going to clean this whole kitchen." He chuckled at the sight before us. "I know you about had a damn heart attack when you walked in here."

I nodded. "Hell yeah; I thought I was going to have to pistol-whip your ass."

He laughed hard at that. "Damn; pistol-whipped because of some bowls on the counter? That's harsh."

I giggled, glad for the lighthearted teasing between the two of us. Chris waved me off.

"Go ahead and do what you came here to do, I'm going to take care of this and listen out for Niecy and Byron to get here."

With a nod, I spun on my heel and grabbed my phone from the counter.

"Okay, I'll be upstairs."

As I walked back through the home I had built picture-by-picture, trinket-by-trinket, I wondered if it was as crazy as it sounded that I was no longer upset about my divorce and even anticipating the things to come. Instinctively, my hand came up to cradle my belly, softly rubbing over my tank top. I smiled to myself as I climbed the stairs to the second floor.

CHAPTER THIRTEEN
Jermaine

My phone buzzed just as the cryo-sleeve sounded the completion of its final cycle. It was just after eight in the morning, and I was indulging in some light physical therapy after returning home from an away game. I'd planned to do a round of cryo on each knee before heading over to see Nedra. It had been two days since I'd laid eyes on my goddess, and I wasn't ashamed to admit that I missed her.

Besides the days when I had away games, I'd gotten used to seeing her every day. It took some convincing, but I finally got her to spend nights at my house. That little ass bed at her spot had me cramped up every time, but luckily, I only had to suffer in it two times after that first night. I unzipped the cryo-sleeve and stretched my left leg as I picked up my phone to see that I'd received a text from Fred.

Fred: Did you know your girl was moving today?

My brows met in confusion. I quickly typed out a response.

Me: What do you mean?

To Buy A Vow

Fred: Nedra is moving out of her ex-husband's house today.
Fred: Supposedly a last minute thing. I take it you ain't know.

Hell naw, I ain't know that shit. I didn't have to say that because Fred already knew, or he wouldn't have reached out to me. I also didn't have to ask how he knew. Two months later, and there was still more going on between Fred and Ashton than a simple one night stand, that was for damn sure. The morning after that night at VR, I couldn't help but notice how comfortable they were with each other. That shit was obvious to anyone paying attention, but I had yet to question Fred about it.

I wasn't mad that Nedra hadn't told me she was moving today. I could believe that it was last minute. When I left for California two days ago, Nedra had still been married. If she was moving out of the house today, then she must have finally gotten that call. Not only that, she never called me when I had away games, claiming that she didn't want to be a distraction. I low-key thought that was some fuckboy shit that her ex had pulled on her, but I was working on her with that as well. She just didn't understand that I would be there for her in situations like this—no matter what—because she hadn't wrapped her mind around the fact that she was really mine. It was all good. Actions spoke louder than words. Today she was moving in with me.

Me: Good looking out, bruh. I'll get at you later.
Fred: Already, bruh. Stay up.

I disconnected the cryo-sleeve and hopped out of the reclining chair, already dialing out on my phone. An hour later, Boobie and I were pulling up to a two-story home in a neighborhood filled with newer model homes. There was a car and a moving truck in the driveway, and the garage door was open. We parked on the street behind a silver Toyota truck and climbed out of the SUV. I rung the doorbell and shoved my hands in the pockets of my sweatpants.

A short, brown-skinned dude with a fade answered the door, and I watched as the question in his eyes was replaced instantly with recognition. His face stretched into a star-struck smile. If I hadn't been sure this was Nedra's ex old man, I would have offered him a handshake. He rubbed his hands over his head.

"*Oh, shit!* Hawk? Yooo, I'm a huge fan!"

I nodded. "Thanks, man." I expected him to ask me what I was doing there, and I was ready to drop the bomb on his ass and watch that starry expression morph into something else. *Would it be surprise? Anger? Jealousy?* But instead of asking why a professional basketball player was standing at his door early on a random Friday morning, he continued talking.

"Man, I've followed your career since you were at UAPB. I went to an HBCU too. I still think you should have gone higher in the draft, but I'm just glad they brought you here. *Man!* No one is going to believe this shit. Can I get a picture with you man? I mean—"

"Jermaine?"

Ole dude turned around, and I looked behind him to see my future standing on the stairs holding a shoebox in her arms. Surprise was written all over her face as her eyes flickered from me to her, now ex-husband. He whipped his head back to me, eyes clouded in confusion. I didn't say a word, just waited for Nedra to make a move.

As if she knew my intention, she finished coming down the stairs, dropping the box on the floor as she hit the bottom step and slid smoothly in front of her ex. She looked up at me.

"What are you doing here? When did you get back?"

I looked down at her, greedily taking in every detail of the face I hadn't seen in a week. Her ever-present lipstick was dark gray today and matched the loose tank top and leggings she wore. Briefly, I wondered if this was a stain-free formula like the last one I'd had the pleasure of testing out. Her skin was clear and shiny like she'd had a facial this morning, but what caught and held my attention were her eyes; they were slightly red and puffy. Since I knew she didn't smoke, that only meant one thing. That she had been crying for whatever reason caused me to be concerned; the thought that she cried behind this dude had me hot.

She didn't need my anger right now, though, even though it wasn't directed at her. This day was hard enough for her without me adding my unnecessary emotions to the mix. So, instead of mushing her little ass ex, who couldn't be more than 5'10", I smiled at her.

"I got in around two, and I brought some muscle to help with your boxes."

The way her face lit up when I said that made my chest puff out. I'd never tire of seeing her glow like the goddess she was, man, I swear. Not only did her chocolate-brown eyes shine with gratitude, but I saw that thing that she had been trying to deny and *shit*; I felt like the big fucking man on campus.

Nedra surprised the hell out of me when she stepped forward, pushing up on her tiptoes, and wrapped her arms around my neck. My arms instantly wrapped around her waist, and I lifted her up as she pulled my head down, pressing her lips against mine in a sweet, albeit brief, kiss. While I never had a problem publicly showing affection to her, I didn't think she would have done that in front of ole dude. That she did brought a smug smile to my face. She didn't have to say a word; everything she felt in that moment transferred through that short connection we shared.

She released me, and I set her back down, glancing behind her to see ole dude barely keeping the anger off his face. I noticed his hands clenched into fists at his side but when he saw that I saw him, he forcibly relaxed his hands and his face. It happened within seconds and when Nedra turned around, he looked like a man trying not to observe a tender moment between lovers. *Fake ass*.

Nedra grabbed my hand. "Hawk, this is Chris. Chris, this is Hawk, and that's Boobie."

Chris looked behind me and nodded at Boobie. His ass was fangirling so hard, he probably ain't even see nobody but me when he opened the door. It also didn't escape my notice that she had introduced me to him as Hawk instead of Jermaine.

"Come on." Nedra pulled me into the house, and Chris stepped to the side, almost tripping over the box she had abandoned when she saw me. Instead of going up the stairs, she kept straight. Chris closed the door behind Boobie, and I glanced back to see my cousin walk past him slowly.

"Aye, bruh. You still want that picture?" Boobie's ass laughed heartily after he asked the question, but he didn't stop to wait for the answer. I chuckled lowly. I didn't want to rub it in his face; I'm sure it was embarrassing enough.

Nedra turned her head and eyed me. "What are you laughing at?"

I shook my head. "Don't worry about it."

She pursed her lips but then nodded. We stopped in the kitchen, and I looked around at the space. There were boxes everywhere.

"These are the heaviest boxes, not including the ones in the living room that hold the contents of my bookshelves. This is the perfect place to put those muscles to use. You can load all of the ones that have my name on them into the moving truck."

Boobie bent to grab the box closest to him and left the kitchen. I looked at Nedra.

"Are these supposed to be going to Niecy's house?" I didn't plan on letting that happen.

She shook her head. "All of these boxes, except the ones containing food, are going to a storage unit."

It was on the tip of my tongue to tell her that she would be bringing all of this to my house. I wanted to speak those words so badly, but I had to bite my tongue and mentally chastise myself. Timing was everything.

"Got it."

Boobie and I worked to clear the kitchen and then moved to the living room for those boxes of books. Nedra had gone back upstairs but resurfaced every now and then to check on us. Old dude—Chris—didn't show his face again, and that may have been for the best. I hadn't forgotten about Nedra's puffy eyes. *What the fuck had he said to her to have her crying?* I was trying not to stew on it but that anger fueled me. Between me and Boobie, the whole downstairs was packed into the truck in less than forty-five minutes.

I knew there were things upstairs that needed to be moved to the truck, but I hesitated on going up there for a minute. Nedra hadn't come down in at least twenty minutes, and I needed to brace myself to see her with her ex. He might have been the one to divorce her, but I knew niggas. Seeing her move on with someone who was—without a doubt—an upgrade could bring out the bitch in a nigga. I needed to make sure I didn't put my hands on this dude.

"Aye, bruh."

I turned to see Boobie standing to my right with his arms folded across his chest. I raised a brow at him.

"The longer you stand here contemplating your next move, the more time he spends in her face."

Shit. He was right. I was bullshitting. I took the steps three at a time, my long legs bringing me to the landing in no time. The sound of voices brought me down the hall to the first door. Just as I thought, ol' dude was in her fucking face. Nedra was on the floor in front of a chest of drawers, legs folded underneath her while she filled a box beside her with items from a bottom drawer. Ol' dude was standing behind her, no doubt getting his fill of the sight of her ass that was poking out deliciously behind her.

"I'm just saying; I can't believe you went out and found a ballplayer, Nedra. I didn't think that was your style."

What did this bum ass nigga mean by *"not her style"*?

"I didn't 'go out and find' anybody, Chris. Not that it's any of your business, but I met him the same way that I met you."

He folded his arms across his chest. "Okay, Ned," he spat sarcastically, "you're telling me that my sister introduced you to the greatest basketball player of this decade? The man who has broken the records for scores, rebounds, and triple-doubles, all before the age of thirty; Ashton pulled him over to you and made introductions?"

To Buy A Vow

I turned and met Boobies amused gaze with a nod. Shit, I was impressed. I guess dude really was a fan. And *greatest basketball player of the decade*? I was flattered as well. Ah, shit, I didn't want to like this dude. Not caring if I was caught blatantly eavesdropping, I leaned against the doorjamb and settled in for the rest of their conversation.

Nedra folded the top of the box and looked up at her ex. "Yes, Chris. It was more like, Ashton pulled me over to him, but yes. She asked his friend, Fred, if he was cool then basically shoved me at him."

I almost laughed at the comical way that ol' dude's jaw dropped. His hand clutched at his chest.

"Fred. As in, Fred Pierce, starting forward for the Clutch?"

Nedra shrugged as if she wasn't sure of those details. "I don't know; maybe?"

"My sister knows Fred Pierce *and* Hawk Hawkins?"

Nedra sighed, her voice stale as she drolled, "I guess."

Ol' dude sputtered. "But...why didn't she ever introduce me? She knows I'm a huge Clutch fan!" His face was the picture of disbelief as he whined at the unfairness of it all.

Nedra stood up and brushed nonexistent lint off the back of her luscious ass before propping her fists on her hips. "When is she supposed to introduce you, Chris? You never call to check on her, and she's your only sister! Seriously, though, you sound like a lil' ass boy whining about not getting to meet Elmo at Sesame Street Live."

Boobie elbowed me, and I snickered at that one. They both turned toward me and I straightened. My focus on Nedra, I asked, "You ready for us up here?"

She looked down at the box at her feet then pointed to the three boxes lined against the wall to the left of the door. "All of those are ready, plus the ones in the hallway."

I felt movement behind me and glanced over my shoulder to see Boobie starting on the boxes that were stacked on one side of the narrow hallway.

I held Nedra's gaze. "You good?"

She bucked her eyes at me. "I'm straight."

One corner of my mouth lifted. "Of that, I'm absolutely sure."

Despite her attempt, she couldn't stop herself from grinning and shaking her head. I pushed off the door and picked up one of the boxes.

"Imma run these down to the truck."

"I'll help you!" Chris skirted around Nedra and damn near sprinted across the room to where I stood.

"*Chris*," Nedra warned.

I stopped her. "He good."

I got the feeling that he had something he wanted to get off his chest, and since I was a mature individual, I would give him the opportunity. Besides, if he was outside with me, he wasn't in Nedra's face, and that was best for everyone. I carried the box downstairs and came face-to-face with Boobie as I tried to enter the garage. When he saw who was behind me, he gave me a questioning look. I shrugged and he stepped aside to let us out of the house before following us to the truck.

Once we loaded the boxes into the back of the truck, I turned and folded my arms across my chest, waiting. Chris' were going every which way but at me. I sighed. I guess I would have to initiate this thing.

I lifted my chin. "What's up?"

He rubbed the back of his neck but finally met my eyes confidently. "I've known Nedra since we were kids and—"

I held up a hand, palm facing him. "Hold up; are you trying to *warn* me about her or something? Cause I can tell you right now that—"

"No, no, no! That's not it at all, I swear. I just want to tell you that I've never seen her glowing like she's been this past couple of months. I can see clearly that you're the cause of her happiness, and I want to thank you for it."

Well, damn. Dude had me all kinds of confused. I was ready for a fight and instead, I was being thanked.

"You don't have to say anything; I just needed to say that." He looked up at the window in the front of the house and smiled wryly. "As long as I've known Nedra, she's never been good at accepting love and affection from people. I mean, besides my sister and Niecy, and her grandmother, of course. She'll play it off with a joke or change the subject, but she never really believes it's real. I don't know why because—and I'm ashamed to say this but—I never asked. I just got used to her rejecting it, and I never tried to force the issue.

I know this is unconventional, but I'm telling you this because that woman in there, you can't let her get away. I told her that, as soon as I moved out of the way, she'd find the right one for her and now, here you are. Now, you have to make sure that you don't let her run you off."

I licked my lips, contemplating all of the information he'd just unpacked for me. The woman he'd described wasn't at all the same woman that I spent most of my free time imagining my future with. "Is that what happened with you? She ran you off?"

He laughed. "Oh no, that's not it. She was my college sweetheart from a relationship that I should have left in college. I let my family pressure me into making a decision that I knew I shouldn't have made. She's not my soulmate, and I'm not hers and for a long time, we were just going through the motions. We both deserved better than that, so I did what she didn't have the courage to do. I pulled the plug."

I nodded. I had to respect that. It took a real man to admit that he wasn't the best candidate for a position. Especially when it came to a woman. And especially a woman as bad as Nedra. I stuck my hand out and shook his twice when he eagerly slapped it with his own.

"You alright, man."

His eyes lit up. "Yo, thanks, man! I really appreciate that."

Hooking my thumb toward the house, I said, "Let's finish up these boxes."

He agreed and thirty minutes later, the three of us—me, Boobie, and Chris—had emptied the house of all things Nedra. I don't know what the house looked like before she had started removing her things, but I couldn't tell anything was missing once we finished loading up the truck. Without many personal touches, I thought the house looked staged or more like a model home than a house people actually lived in. I guess that was what my goddess brought, "homey-ness". She had asked for a few moments alone in the house, so the three of us stood outside on the sidewalk. I observed the moving truck that was backed into the driveway.

"Aye, Boobie."

My cousin looked my way then over at the truck. He already knew what I was thinking. "Do you even have to ask?"

I smirked. "Common courtesy, my dude." We slapped hands and then snapped. My gaze slid over to Chris, who was watching us with wide eyes and a goofy grin on his face. Dude was a fan for real.

"You good, man?"

He blinked and rubbed the back of his neck. "Oh, yeah. I'm good. Super good. Man, I know imma probably sound like a simp, but I'm just glad Nedra found somebody to be here for her like this."

He was definitely simping, but that reminded me of the question I'd had since I'd first arrived.

"Where is everyone else? Her family and friends and 'nem. Why are we," I pointed between Boobie and me, "the only ones here?"

"Oh, Niecy and Byron were here for about an hour, but they got a call from Jada's daycare and had to leave. I guess it was an emergency. And Rose never liked coming over here, so I'm assuming she's going to help Ned unpack...wherever she's going." He shrugged and raised his eyebrows at me. I hope he didn't think I was going to give him any information with that lame ass bait he tried to lay out there.

"Oh, okay." I knew of Niecy, that was one of Nedra's best

friends. I'd met her and her boyfriend, Byron, a young but cool dude. I had no idea who Rose was, though. But he didn't have to know that.

"She's really lucky to have you."

What? My head jerked back like something burned me. Did he really just say what it sounded like he said? This nigga was tripping.

"Nah, you got it backwards, bruh; I'm lucky that she even gave me the time of day after the way you ended things with her."

A panicked look overtook him. "No, no, no! I'm just saying; you're this multi-millionaire, celebrity athlete and she's—"

"She's a fucking celestial ass being who decided to grace the both of us with her wonders!" I huffed in an even tone, annoyed that this fool had gotten to see and know parts of the Nedra that I'd loved most. And I'm not just talking physically. "Fortunately for me, it looks like I'm the only one who can recognize a goddess when I see one. *I'm* the chosen one, bruh. You're a clown." I was 31-hot and I needed to get away from this dude before I was called to lay hands on him.

I motioned to Boobie, who had moved closer to me when I started going off, probably so he'd be ready to pull me back if I heeded that call. We rounded the truck and stopped short. Nedra stood there with her hand on the handle and parted lips and an indecipherable look on her face.

"You ready to bounce?"

She nodded silently.

"Aight; Boobie is going to drive the truck, so gon' head and slide him those keys. You'll be riding with me."

She gaped at me for a moment longer before holding her hand out to Boobie. He plucked the keys from her grasp and put his hands on her shoulders, gently pushing her toward me. Seconds later, he was in the truck and cranking the engine.

Grabbing her hand, I forced myself to walk calmly and not drag Nedra to the truck and throw her inside. I needed to get away from her ex in the worst way. After helping her step up into the

SUV, I rounded the hood and climbed in. I glanced back at the house and saw this. Damn. Dude. Standing on the sidewalk, staring at the truck. I cursed under my breath, causing Nedra to look over. She rolled down her window.

"Chris, what are you doing?"

"Oh, I was just...um...wondering if I could still get a picture with Hawk? Ya know...before he heads off. 'Cause I don't know when I'll see him again..." Then he rubbed the back of his neck. Again. I swear I saw fucking red.

If this *muthafucka* rubbed the back of his neck *one more time*, I was going to set something on fire. What is he rubbing for? Is he trying to stimulate his brain cells so he can give a halfway decent answer? *Damn!*

Leaning across Nedra's lap, I pasted the fake smile I gave the interviewers who asked me dumb ass questions after we lost a game.

"Hey man, I want to get Nedra settled and get her things out of the truck, and I need to do it before I head to practice so I can't today. I got you next time I see you though, aight?"

He nodded and started walking backward, to his house. "Yeah, okay. That's makes sense. I got you. It was good to see you, man. I'm a huge fan."

I nodded and sat back, squeezing Nedra's thigh. "Roll up the window."

I threw the truck into gear and sped down the street, not even waiting to see if Boobie was behind me. He knew where to go and didn't have to follow me to get there. Once I'd cleared the neighborhood, Nedra looked over and smirked.

"So, y'all taking selfies the next time you see each other?"

"If I can help it, I won't be seeing him again. Ever."

She giggled. "That was...interesting to witness. Chris' whole face changed when you were around. He probably don't even care that I've moved on because it's with you."

I glanced at her quickly. She probably didn't even realize what she'd just revealed. Hearing her say that she'd "moved on" with me made my chest swell. I had been steadily becoming addicted to her, but I was trying to give her the space she needed to completely get over her ex. Now, she was saying that she was over him, and I wondered if it wasn't too soon to claim her as my own.

"What do you have planned for the rest of the day?" It was just after two p.m. and even though she'd just spent the morning officially closing one chapter of her life, all I wanted to do was make sure I was a main character in the rest of her book.

She shook her head. "Nothing at all. I rescheduled my lessons for today so that I could take care of this."

I nodded, understanding completely. "I want you to come to the house with me."

She eyed me. "To 'The House' or to the house you live in?"

I laughed. "Right now, just the house I live in. I would like to take you to *The House* one day, though."

She bit her lip. "Okay."

"Okay? To which one?"

Her lips curved up into a small grin. "Both."

I know my smile was big and cheesy as shit, but I didn't give a fuck.

My goddess.

I glanced at her one more time. "You ready?"

She giggled. "I think so. I've been to one multiple times, and I've met just about everyone who is important to you from the other one."

My cheeks stretched even further at her answer. "I meant, are you ready to move in with me?"

Her mouth dropped into a perfect 'o', and her eyes glazed as she stared at me unblinkingly. Then, as if a switch was flipped, she burst into tears. Alarmed, I pulled onto the side of the road and put the truck in park. I lifted the center console and pulled her into my lap.

"Baby. Why the tears? Is that a yes?"

She gasped in a shaky breath and nodded. "I'm pregnant."

It was my turn to drop my jaw. I knew it was only a matter of time since I'd been shooting up in her club on a regular basis. We never really discussed *that*, but it was understood that we both wanted children. Nedra even admitted to researching sperm banks before we met. My heart swelled with joy. I was getting my woman and my child. My family was in my arms.

Still crying in my lap, Nedra wrapped her arms around my neck. "I found out yesterday."

I pressed my lips to her temple. "Thank you, baby. This is the ultimate gift." I held her until she stopped crying then handed her some napkins to dry her face. Once she was settled back in her seat with her seatbelt secured, I maneuvered the truck back onto the road. I reached a hand across the console and grasped her hand, squeezing lightly.

"You know what this means, right?"

She tilted her head at me to indicate she was listening. I brought her hand up to my lips and kissed the center of her palm.

"I'm never letting you out of my sight again."

Those luscious lips curved into a beatific smile.

"You promise?"

EPILOGUE
Nedra

As soon as the blue gel plopped onto my rounded belly, I swore, jerking on the narrow table. I glared at my doctor.

"You could have a warned a bitch or *something*, Ashley!"

That damn gel was as cold as ice, and no matter how many times I was tortured with it, the temperature always caught me off guard. *Why was it so cold anyway?* Did it only work if it was near arctic levels? Inquiring minds demanded to know!

Jermaine chuckled and I aimed my glare up at him. He grabbed my hand from where he stood on my right and placed a kiss in the center of my palm. The tender, loving gesture melted some of my ire, and I pursed my lips in a request for a kiss, smiling pleasantly when he gave me what I asked for.

Dr. Vail didn't pay us any mind; she just grinned as she positioned the handheld wand in the freezing goop and drove it across my belly. I held my breath as she stared at the black and white screen next to the bed.

ze of an avocado,
e." She glanced
ne. "But that's
months in, and
need." Her

burst out

for three or

his eyes at me in

hand that he wasn't
playfully.
for the range. You know
e telling her this yourself."
Ashley, as she had instructed us
consult, didn't need to know how
chocolate shakes I could consume in a
sitting. As long as I continued taking the gummy
natal vitamins she had prescribed me, I was good.

"No worries," she said, interrupting our stare-off. "I'll just make a note to monitor that in the next couple of months. If baby doesn't start to put on the weight they need, I might have to change up your diet a bit."

I nodded and Jermaine squeezed my hand.

Smiling, Ashley tapped a couple of keys on the keyboard below the screen. "Do you two want to know the sex of the baby?"

I glanced up at Jermaine again. We'd gone back and forth over whether we wanted to wait to find out but finally, I decided that I need to know. He nodded at me, and I looked at the doctor and dipped my chin once. She moved the wand across my belly and a few minutes went by before she said anything. I assumed she was trying to catch the baby before he or she flipped around inside of me but suddenly, her movements stuttered.

"Oh, wow!"

My eyes widened and I craned my neck to see the screen as Jermaine grabbed my hand quickly. "What is it? What's wrong?"

"Just a moment," she murmured distractedly as she alternated between moving the wand around and typing keys. Finally, after three tense minutes, she turned to us with excitement in her eyes. "Okay, are you ready?"

I nodded haltingly. I was ready to find out what she saw on that screen. She turned around and pointed to the screen.

"That is your baby boy. You can see his penis sticking out just there."

She pointed to a glob on the screen, but I couldn't see anything through the tears in my eyes. *I was having a boy.* A baby boy, who would be so handsome, just like his daddy. I looked up at Jermaine, and my heart swelled to see him glassy-eyed as well. He was getting the son that he wanted; his legacy.

"*A boy,*" I whispered. When Jermaine looked down at me, he smiled and kissed me sweetly on the lips.

"I love you. Thank you for carrying my son."

Ashley cleared her throat. "If I can, regretfully, interrupt and get you to turn your attention back to the screen."

I whipped my neck around, fear clutching at me, once again. She winked at me and moved the wand to the other side of my belly, closer to her and pointed to the screen.

"Now if you look here, you'll see your baby girl. She's curled up behind her brother."

It was like a record scratched. The room went still. "What?!"

"*Twins,*" Jermaine whispered in awe.

I shook my head at him. "Nah, that's not what she said." I looked at the doctor and she smiled at me. "Right?"

"Actually, Nedra, that is exactly what I'm saying. You're having a set of fraternal twins. A girl and a boy."

I nodded absently, tears falling silently down my cheeks as I glanced down at my exposed belly. There were two babies in there. *Two.* Two people were growing inside of me. It was unreal.

I'd spent so much time wishing for just *one* child and now, I was getting two in one go.

"Baby?"

I looked up just as Jermaine brought his thumbs to my face and brushed the salty droplets away from my cheeks. The question in his eyes was clear. *How did I feel about this revelation?*

I smiled up at him. "We're getting a twofer."

When he unleashed the bright, ecstatic smile—he'd apparently been trying to mute—on me, my breath caught. This beautiful man—in body and soul—had given me my hearts' greatest desire. Because of him, I was going to be a mother of not one but two precious babies. I was a little overwhelmed at the prospect of having two times the diapers to change at once, but more than anything, I was over the moon.

I reached up and Jermaine bent down, meeting me halfway. He kissed me gently, nibbling on my lower lip and pulling away before I could deepen it. His forehead pressed to mine as he stared into my eyes, allowing me to see all of him in those chestnut orbs.

"You know what this means, right?"

I nodded, my eyes fluttering closed as tears once again attempted to escape. He kissed each of my eyelids and I sighed contentedly.

"I'm yours."

The End

I hope you enjoyed reading Jermaine and Nedra's story!

To be informed about future releases,
join my mailing list and connect with me online!

www.therealchencia.com
Facebook: Author Chencia C. Higgins
Twitter: @therealchencia
Instagram: @ohchencia
Join my Facebook readers group: Reading With Chencia
Mailing list: http://eepurl.com/dhCDsz

Other titles by Chencia C. Higgins

JustOneNight.com Novella Series:
No Strings Allowed - Book 1
No Love Allowed - Book 2
The Week Before Forever - A JustOneNight.com Short Story
No Games Allowed - Book 3

The Vow Series:
To Buy a Vow
To Build a Vow – *Coming Summer 2018*

Standalones:
Her & Them
Remember Our Love

Made in the USA
Middletown, DE
22 April 2018